NEWGATE CALENDAR.

NEWGATE CALENDAR;

CONTAINING

THE LIVES OF THE MOST NOTORIOUS CHARACTERS

WHO HAVE VIOLATED THE

LAWS OF THEIR COUNTRY.

BY G. THOMPSON.

LONDON:

PUBLISHED BY J. S. PRATT.

—

MDCCCXLV.

NEWGATE CALENDAR,
ETC.

JONATHAN WILD,

(THE PRINCE OF ROBBERS,)

Executed at Tyburn, May 24th, 1725.

JONATHAN WILD was born at Wolverhampton, in Staffordshire, about the year 1682. He was the eldest son of his parents, who at a proper age put him to a day school, which he continued to attend till he had gained a sufficient knowledge in reading, writing, and accounts to qualify him for business. His father intended to bring him up to his own trade; but changed that design, and at about the age of fifteen, apprenticed him for seven years to a buckle-maker in Birmingham. Upon the expiration of his apprenticeship, he returned to Wolverhampton, where he married a young woman of good character, and gained a tolerable livelihood by following his business as a journeyman.

He had been married about two years, in which time his wife had a son, when he formed the resolution of visiting London, and very soon after deserted his wife and child, and set out for the metropolis, where he got into an employment and maintained himself by his trade; being of an extravagant disposition, many months had not elapsed since his arrival in London, when he was arrested and thrown into Wood-street Compter, where he remained a prisoner for upwards of four years. In a pamphlet which he published, and which we shall more particularly mention hereafter, he says, that during his imprisonment it was impossible but he must, in some measure, be let into the secrets of the criminals there under confinement; and particularly Mr. Hitchin's management.

During his residence in the Compter, Wild assiduously cultivated the acquaintance of the criminals who were his fellow prisoners, and attended to the exploits in which they had been engaged, with singular satisfaction. In this prison was a woman named Mary Milliner, who had long been considered as one of the most notorious pick pockets, and abandoned prostitutes, in the town. After having escaped the punishments due to the variety of felonies of which she had been guilty, she was put under confinement for debt. An intimacy subsisted between them while they remained in the Compter. They had no sooner obtained their freedom than they lived under the denomination of man and wife. By their iniquitous practices, they soon obtained a sum of money, which enabled them to open a little public house in Cock-alley, facing Cripple-gate Church.

Milliner being personally acquainted with most of the notorious characters by whom London and its environs was infested, and perfectly conversant as to the manner of their proceedings, she as considered by Wild as a most useful companion; and indeed she very materially contributed towards rendering him one of the most accomplished characters in the arts of villany.

Wild industriously penetrated into the secrets of felons of every denomination, who resorted in great numbers to his house, in order to dispose of their booty; and they looked upon him with a kind of awe; for being acquainted with their proceedings, they were conscious that their lives were continually in his power.

Wild was at little difficulty to dispose of the articles brought to him by thieves, at something less than the real value; for at this period no law existed for the punishment of the receivers of stolen goods; but the evil increasing to so enormous a degree, it was deemed expedient by the legislature to frame a law for its suppression. An act therefore was passed, consigning such as should be convicted of receiving goods, knowing them to have been stolen, to transportation for the space of fourteen years.

Wild's practices were considerably interrupted by the above-mentioned law; to obviate the intention of which, however, he suggested the following plan: he called a meeting of all the thieves whom he knew, and observed to them, that if they carried their booties to such of the pawn-brokers who were known to be not much troubled with the scruples of conscience, they would scarce advance on the property one-fourth of its real value; and that if they were offered to strangers, either for sale, or by way of deposit, it was a chance of ten to one but the parties were rendered amenable to the laws. He observed that the most industrious thieves were now scarcely able to obtain a livelihood; and that they must either submit to be half starved, or to be in great and continual danger of Tyburn. He informed them that he had devised a plan for removing the inconveniences under which they laboured, recommending them to follow his advice, and to behave towards him with honour. He then proposed that when they had gained any booty they should deliver it to him, instead of carrying it to the pawn broker, and he would restore the goods to the owners, by which means greater sums would be raised than by depositing them with the pawn-brokers, while the thieves would be perfectly secure from detection.

This proposal was received with general approbation, and it was resolved to carry it into immediate execution. All the stolen effects were to be given into the possession of Wild, who soon appointed convenient places wherein they were to be deposited, judging that it would not be prudent to have them left at his own house.

The infamous plan being thus concerted, it was the business of Wild to apply to persons who had been robbed, pretending to be greatly concerned at their misfortunes, saying that some suspected property had been stopped by a very honest man, a broker, with whom he was acquainted, and that if their goods happened to be in the hands of his friend, restitution should be made. But he failed not to plead that the broker might be rewarded for his trouble and disinterestedness, and to use every argument in his power or exacting a promise that no disagreeable consequences should ensue to his friend, who had imprudently neglected to apprehend the supposed thieves.

Happy in the prospect of regaining their property, without the trouble and expense necessarily attending prosecutions, people generally approved the conduct of Wild, and sometimes rewarded him even with one half of the real value of the goods restored. Persons who had been robbed, however, were not always satisfied with Wild's declaration: and sometimes they questioned him particularly as to the manner of their goods being discovered. On those occasions he pretended to be offended that his honour should be disputed, saying, that his motive was to afford all the service in his power to the injured party, whose goods he imagined might possibly be those stopped by his friend; but since his good intentions were received in so ungracious a manner, and himself interrogated respecting the robbers, he had nothing further to say on the subject, but must take his leave; adding, that his name was Jonathan Wild, and that he was every day to be found at his house in Cock-alley, Cripplegate. This affection of resentment seldom failed to possess the people who had been robbed, with a more favourable opinion of his principles; and the suspicion of his character being removed, he had an opportunity of advancing his demands.

Wild received no gratuity from the owners of stolen goods, but deducted his profits from the money which was to be paid to the broker;

thus did he amass considerable sums without
danger of prosecution, for his offences came under
the description of no law then existing. For se·
veral years he preserved a tolerably fair charac·
ter, so consummate was the art he employed in the
management of all his schemes.

Wild's business greatly increasing, and his
name becoming exceedingly popular, he altered
his mode of proceeding. Instead of applying to
persons who had been robbed, he opened an
office to which great numbers resorted, in hopes
of recovering their effects. He made a great
parade in his business, and assumed a conse·
quence that enabled him more effectually to im·
pose on the public. When persons came to this
office, they were informed that they must each
pay a crown in consideration of receiving his
advice. This ceremony being dispatched, he en·
tered in his book the names and places of abode
of the parties, with all the particulars which they
could communicate respecting the robberies, and
the rewards that would be given, provided the
goods were recovered ; and they were then de·
sired to call again in a few days, when he hoped
he should be able to give them some agreeable
intelligence.

Upon calling to know the success of his enqui·
ries, he informed them that he had received some
information concerning their goods, but that the
agent he had employed to trace them had in·
formed him that the robbers pretended they
could get more money by pawning the property,
than by returning it for the proposed reward
saying, however, if he could by any means pro·

cure an interview with the villains, he doubted not of being able to settle matters agreeably to the terms already proposed ; but at the same time, artfully insinuating that the most safe, expeditious and prudent method would be to make an addition to the reward.

Wild, at length, became eminent in his profession, which proved highly lucrative. When he had discovered the utmost sum that it was likely the people would give for the recovery of their property, he requested them to call again, and in the mean time he caused the goods to be ready for delivery.

He derived considerable advantages from examining persons who had been robbed! for he thence became acquainted with the particulars which the thieves had omitted to communicate to him, and was enabled to detect them, if they concealed any part of their booties. Being in possession of the secrets of all the notorious robbers, they were under the necessity of complying with whatever terms he thought proper to exact ; for they were conscious, that by opposing his inclination they should involve themselves in the most imminent danger of being sacrificed to the laws of their country.

Through the infamous practice of this man, articles, which had been before considered as of no use but to the owners, now became matters claiming a particular attention from the thieves by whom the metropolis and its environs were infested. Pocket-books, books of accounts, watches, rings, trinkets, and a variety of articles of but small intrinsic worth, were now esteemed very profitable

booty. Books of account, and other writin
being of great importance to the owners, produ
ed very handsome rewards; and the same may
said of pocket-books, but they contained memora
dums, and sometimes bank notes, and other articl
on which money could readily be procured.

Wild accumulated money so fast, that he co
sidered himself as a man of consequence, and
support his imaginary dignity, he dressed hims
in laced clothes, and wore a sword. He first e
ercised his martial instrument on the person
his accomplice and reputed wife, Mary Milline
who having on some occasion provoked him, h
instantly struck at her with it, and cut off h
ears. This event was the cause of a separation
but in acknowledgement of the great services sh
had rendered him, by introducing him to so lucr
tive a profession, he allowed her a weekly stipen
till her decease.

Before Wild had brought the plan of his offic
to perfection, he for some time acted as an a
sistant to Charles Hitchin, the city marshal,
man as wicked as himself. These celebrated co
partners in villainy, under the pretext of reformin
the manners of the dissolute part of the public
paraded the streets from Temple bar to th
Minories, searching houses of ill fame, and ap
prehending disorderly and suspected persons; bu
such as complimented these public reformers wit
private douceurs, were allowed to practise ever
species of wickedness with impunity. Hitche
and Wild, however, became jealous of each other
and an open rupture taking place, they parted

ch pursuing the business of thief-taking on his
wn account.

In the year 1715, Wild removed, from his house
Cock alley, to a Mrs. Sergoe's in the Old Bailey,
here he pursued his business with the usual suc-
ss, notwithstanding the efforts of Hitchin, his
val in iniquity, to suppress his proceedings.

In 1718, the marshal attacked Wild in a pam-
let, called The Regulator: or, a Discovery of
hieves, Thief takers, &c. which was answered by
s antagonist.

Hitchin having so greatly debased the respect-
le post of city marshal, the Lord Mayor suspend-
him from his office. In order to repair this
ss, he determined upon the affectation of burying
s resentment, and confederating with Wild.

Wild readily accepted the ex-marshal's pro-
osal; towards dark they proceeded to Temple-
ar, and called in at several brandy shops and ale-
ouses, between that and Fleet-ditch; some of
e masters of these houses complimented the
arshal with punch, others with brandy, and some
esented him with fine ale, offering their services
their worthy protector.

The marshal made them little answer; but gave
em to understand, all the service he expected
om them was, to give information of the pocket-
ooks, or any goods stolen, as a pay back: For
u women of the town, (addressing himself to the
males in one of the shops,) make it a common
ractise to resign things of this nature to the bul-
ies and rogues of your retinue: but this shall no
nger be borne with, I'll give you my word both
y and you shall be detected, unless you deliver

all the pocket-books you meet with to me. Wh
do you think I bought my place for, but to ma
the most of it? and you are to understand t
this is my man (pointing to the buckle maker,)
assist me. And if you at any time for the futu
refuse to yield up the watches and books you ta
either to me or my servant, you may be assur
of being all sent to Bridewell, and not one of y
shall be permitted to walk the streets. For n
withstanding I am under suspension, (the ch
reason of which is, for not suppressing the practi
of such vermin as you,) I have still a power
punishing, and you shall dearly pay for not payi
your respects to me. Then asking them to wh
part of the town they were rambling, and wheth
they did not see him? to which they answer
that they saw him at a distance, but he caug
hold of them so hastily, that they had no time
address him. We have been strolling, continu
the pickpockets, over Moorfields, and from the
to Blue Boar, in pursuit of you: but not findi
you as usual, we were under some fears that y
were indisposed! The marshal replied, he sho
have given them a meeting there, but had be
employed the whole day with his new man. Y
are to be very careful, said he, not to oblige a
person but myself or servant, with pocket-boo
if you presume to do otherwise, you shall sw
for it, and we are out in the city every night
observe your motions. These instructions giv
the pick-pockets left, making their masters a l
congee, and promising obedience. This was t
progress of the first night with the buckle-mak

whom he told that his staff of authority terrified the ignorant to the extent of his wishes.

Some nights afterwards, walking towards the back part of St. Paul's, the marshal thus addressed the buckle-maker, I'll now show you a brandy shop that entertains no company but whores and thieves. This is a house for our purpose, and I am informed that a woman of the town, who frequents it, has lately robbed a gentleman of his watch and pocket-book; this advice I received from her companion, with whom I have a good understanding. We will go into the house, and, if we can find the woman, I will assume a more stern countenance, (though at best I look like an infernal,) and by continued threats extort a confession, and by that means get possession of the watch and pocket-book; in order to do which, do you slily accost her companion.— Here he described her. Call to her, and inform her, that your master is in a d——d ill humour, and swears, if she does not instantly make a discovery where the pocket-book may be found, at farthest by to-morrow, he will certainly send her to the Compter, and thence to the work house.

The means being thus concerted to gain the valuable goods, both master and man entered the shop in pursuit of the game, and according to expectation, they found the person wanted, with several others; whereupon the marshal, shewing an enraged countenance, becoming the design, and Wild being obliged to follow his example, the company said that the master and man looked as sour as two devils. Devils, said the marshal, I'll make some of you devils, if you do not im-

mediately discover the watch and the pocket-book
I am employed to procure. We do not know
your meaning, sir, answered some.—Who do
you discourse to? said others, we know nothing
of it. The marshal replied, in a more soft tone,
You are ungrateful in the last degree, to deny me
so small a request, when I never was let into the
secret of any thing being taken from a gentleman, but I communicated it to you, describing
the person so exactly, that you could not mistake
the man; and there is so very little got at this
rate, that the devil may trade with you for me.

This speech being over. the marshal gave a nod
to the man, who called one of the women to
the door, and telling the story above directed, the
female answered, Unconscionable devil, when he
gets five or ten guineas, not to bestow above five
or ten shillings upon us unfortunate wretches,
but however, let us go to the Compter—I'll try
what is to be done.

The woman, returning to the marshal, asked
him what he would give for the delivery of the
watch, being seven pounds in value, and the
pocket-book, having in it several notes and gold-
smiths' bills; to whom the marshal answered, a
guinea: and told her it was much better to comply than to go to Newgate, which she must certainly expect upon her refusal.

The woman replied, that the watch was in pawn
for forty shillings, and if he did not advance the
sum, she should be obliged to strip herself for the
redemption, though, when her furbelowed scarf
was laid aside, she had nothing underneath but
furniture for a paper mill. After abundance of

words, he allowed her 30s. for the watch
pocket-book, which she accepted, and the wa
was never returned to the owner.

The infamous coadjutor of Wild, the most de-
testable villain of the two, having been fined
twenty pounds, and pilloried for a crime too de-
testable to be named in these pages, left the latter
once more alone to execute his plans of depredations on the public. When the thieves with
whom he was in league faithfully related to him
the particulars of the robberies they had committed, and entrusted to him the disposal of their
booties, he assured them that they might safely
rely upon him for protection against the ven-
geance of the law ; and, indeed, it must be acknowledged, that in cases of this nature he would
persevere in his endeavours to surmount very
great difficulties, rather than falsify his word.

Wild's artful behaviour, and the punctuality
with which he fulfilled his former engagements,
obtained him a great share of confidence
in thieves of every description ; insomuch, that
if he caused it to be intimated to them that
he was desirous of seeing them, and that they
would not be molested, they would attend with
the utmost willingness, without entertaining
the most distant apprehension of danger, although conscious that he had information
against them, and that their lives were absolutely
in his power ; but if they presumed to reject his
proposals, or proved otherwise refractory, he addressed them to the following effect: I have
given you my word that you shall come and go
in safety ; and so you shall : hut take care of

yourself, for if ever you see me again, you see an enemy.

The great influence that Wild obtained over the thieves, will not be thought very extraordinary, if it is considered that when he promised to use his endeavours to rescue them from an impending fate, he was always desirous, and generally able, to succeed. Such as complied with his measures he would never interrupt, but on the contrary, afford them every encouragement for prosecuting their iniquitous practices: and if apprehended by any other person, he seldom failed of procuring their discharge. His most usual method (in desperate cases, and when matters could not be managed with more ease and expedition) was to procure them to be admitted evidence, under the pretext that it was in their power to make discoveries of higher importance to the public. When they were in prison he frequently attended them, and communicated to them from his own memorandums such particulars as he judged it would be prudent for them to relate to the court. When his accomplices were apprehended, and he was not able to prevent their being brought to trial, he contrived stratagems (in which his invention was amazingly fertile,) for keeping the principal witnesses out of court, so that the delinquents were generally dismissed for want of evidence.

Jonathan was ever a most implacable enemy to those thieves who were hardy enough to reject his terms, and dispose of their stolen effects for their own separate advantage. He was industrious to extremes in his endeavours to surrender them into the hand of justice, and being acquainted with their usual places of resort, it was scarcely possible for them to escape his vigilance.

By subjecting those who incurred his displeasure to the punishment of the law, he obtained the rewards offered for prosecuting them to conviction, greatly extended his ascendancy over the other thieves, who considered him with a kind of awe; and at the same time established his character as being a man of great public utility.

It was the practice of Wild to give instructions to the thieves whom he employed, as to the manner in which they should conduct themselves: and if they followed his directions, it was seldom that they failed of success. - But if they neglected the strict observance of his rules, or were through inadvertency or ignorance, guilty of any kind of mismanagement or error in the prosecution of the schemes he had suggested, it was to be understood almost to an absolute certainty that he would procure them to be convicted at the next sessions, deeming them to be unqualified for the profession of roguery.

He was frequently asked how it was possible he could carry on the business of restoring stolen effects, and not be in league with the robbers; and his replies were always to this purpose :—My acquaintance among thieves is very extensive, and when I obtain information of a robbery, I make inquiry after the suspected parties, and leave word at proper places; and the goods are to be left where I appoint, the reward shall be paid, and no questions asked. Surely, no imputation of guilt can fall upon me; for I hold no interviews with the robbers, nor are the goods given into my possession.

We shall now proceed to a relation of the most remarkable exploits of the hero of these pages; and our account must necessarily include many particulars relating to notorious characters.

A lady of fortune being on a visit in Piccadilly, her servants leaving her sedan at the door, went to refresh themselves at a neighbouring public house. Upon their return the vehicle was not to be found: in consequence of which the men went immediately to Wild, and informed him of their loss, and complimented him with the usual fee: they were desired to call in a few days. Upon their second application, Wild extorted from them a considerable reward, and then directed them to attend the chapel in Lincoln's-Inn Fields on the following morning during the time of prayers. The men went according to appointment, and under the piazzas of the chapel perceived the chair, which upon examination they found to contain the velvet seat, curtains, and other furniture, and had received no kind of damage.

A young gentleman named Knap, accompanied his mother to Sadler's Wells, on Saturday, March 21st, 1716. On their return they were attacked, about ten at night, near the wall of Gray's Inn Gardens, by five villains. The young gentleman was immediately knocked down, and his mother, being exceedingly alarmed, called for assistance, upon which a pistol was discharged at her, and she instantly fell down dead. A considerable reward was offered by proclamation in the Gazette, for the discovery of the perpetrators of this horrid crime ; and Wild was remarkably assiduous in his endeavours to apprehend the offenders. Wild immediately adjudged the gang to be composed of William White, Thomas Thurland, John Chapman, alias Edward Darvel, Timothy Dun, and Isaac Rag.

In the evening of Sunday, April 8th, Wild received intelligence that some of the above-named men were drinking with their prostitutes at a house kept by John Weatherley, in Newtoner's-lane. He went to Weatherley's, accompanied by his man Abraham, and seized White, whom he brought away about midnight in a hackney coach, and lodged him in the Round-house.

White being secured, information was given to Wild, that a man named James Aires, was then at the Bell Inn, Smithfield, in company with a woman of the town. Having an information against Aires, Wild, accompanied by his assistants, repaired to the inn, under the gateway of which they met Thurland, whose person had been mistaken for that of Aires. Thurland was provided with two brace of pistols, but being suddenly seized, he was deprived of all opportunity of making use of those weapons and taken into custody.

They went on the following night to a house in White-Horse-alley, Drury lane, where they apprehended Chapman, alias Darvel. Soon after the murder of Mrs. Knap, Chapman and others stopped the coach of Thomas Middlethwate, but that gentleman escaped being robbed by discharging a blunderbuss, and wounding Chapman in the arm, on which the villains retired.

In a short time after this, Wild apprehended Isaac Ragg at a house he frequented in St. Giles's, in consequence of an information charging him with a burglary. Being taken before a magistrate, in the course of his examination, Ragg impeached twenty two accomplices, charging them with being house-breakers, foot-pads, and receivers of stolen effects: and, in consequence thereof, he was admitted as evidence for the crown.

Ragg was convicted for a misdemeanor in January, 1714-15, and sentenced to stand three times in the pillory. He had concealed himself in the dust hole belonging to the house of Thomas Powell, where, being discovered, he was searched and a pistol, some matches and a number of pick lock keys, were found in his possession. His intention was evidently to commit burglary, but as he did not enter the house, he was indicted for a misdemeanor in entering the yard with intent to steal, He was indicted in October 1715, for a burglary, in the house of Elizabeth Stanwell, on the 24th of August: but he was acquitted of this charge.

White, Thurland, and Chapman, were arraigned on the 18th of May 1716, at the sessions house in the old Bailey, on an indictment for assaulting John Knap, gent, putting him in fear and taking from him a hat and a wig, on the 31st of March, 1716. They were also indicted for the murder of Mary Knap, widow: White by discharging a pistol loaded with powder and bullets, and thereby giving her a wound, of which she immediately died, March 31st, 1716. They were a second time indicted for assaulting and robbing John Gough. White was a fourth time indicted by James Russel for a burglary, in the house of George Barklay: and Chapman was a fourth time indicted for a burglary, in the house of Henry Cross. These three offenders were executed at Tyburn, on the 8th of June, 1716.

Wild was indefatigable in his endeavours to apprehend Timothy Dun, who had hitherto escaped the hands of justice by removing to a new lodging, where he concealed himself in the most cautious manner. Wild, however, did not despair of discovering this offender, whom he supposed must either perish through want of the necessaries of life, or obtain the means of subsistence by returning to his felonious practices; and so confident was he of success that he made a wager of ten guineas that he would have him in custody before the expiration of an appointed time.

Dun's confinement, at length, became exceedingly irksome to him, he sent his wife to make enquiries respecting him, of Wild, in order to discover whether he was still in danger of being apprehended. Upon her departure from Wild's, he ordered one of his people to follow her home. She took water at Black-friars, and landed at the Falcon, but suspecting the man was employed to trace her, she again took water and crossed to White-friars; observing that she was still followed, she ordered the waterman to proceed to Lambeth, and having landed there, it being nearly dark, she imagined she had escaped the observation of Wild's man, and therefore walked immediately home. The man traced her to Maiden-lane, near the Bank side, Southwark, and perceiving her to enter a house, he marked the wall with chalk, and then returned to his employer with an account of the discovery he had made.

Wild, accompanied by a fellow named Abraham, a Jew, who acted the part he had done to the worthless marshal, one Riddlesden, and another man, went on the following morning, to the house where the woman had been seen to enter. Dun hearing a noise, and thence suspecting that he was discovered, got through a back window on the second floor upon the roof of the pantry, the bottom of which was about eight feet from the ground. Abraham discharged a pistol, and wounded Dun in the arm: in consequence of which he fell from the pantry into the yard; after his fall Riddlesden discharged a pistol, and wounded him in the face with small shot. Dun was secured, and carried to Newgate, and being tried at the ensuing sessions, he was soon after executed at Tyburn.

At this time Wild had quitted his apartments at Mrs Seagoe's and hired a house adjoining to the Cooper's Arms, on the opposite side of the Old Bailey. The unexampled villainies of this man were now become an object of so much consequence, as to excite the particular attention of the legislature. In the year 1718, an act was passed deeming every person guilty of a capital offence who should accept a reward in conse-

uence of restoring stolen effects without prosecuting the chief.

It was the general opinion that the above law
would effectually suppress the iniquitous practices
of Wild : but after some interruptions to his proceedings he devised means for evading the law,
which were for several years attended with success.

He now declined the custom of receiving money
from the persons who applied to him ; but upon
the second or third time of calling, informed
them, that all he had been able to learn respecting their business was, that if a sum of money
was left at an appointed place, their property
would be restored the same day.

Sometimes, as the person robbed was returning
from Wild's house, he was accosted in the street
by a man who delivered the stolen effects, at the
same time producing a note expressing the sum
that was to be paid for them.

In cases wherein he supposed danger was to be
apprehended, he advised people to advertise, that
whoever would bring the stolen goods to Jonathan
Wild should be rewarded, and no questions asked
them.

In the two first instances it could not be proved that he either saw the thief, received the
goods, or accepted of a reward, and in the latter
case he acted agreeable to the directions of the
injured party, and there appeared no reason to
criminate him as being in confederacy with the
felons.

When he was asked what would satisfy him for
his trouble, he told the persons who had recover-

ed their property, that what he had done
without any interested view, but merely from
principle of doing good; that therefore he m
no claim; but if he expected a present, he sho
not consider it as being his due, but as an
stance of generosity, which he should acknowled
accordingly.

Our adventurer's business increased exceedin
ly, and he opened an office in Newtoner's lane,
the management of which he appointed his m
Abraham. This Israelite proved a remarkable
dustrious and faithful servant to Jonathan, w
intrusted him with matters of the greatest i
portance.

By too strict an application to business, Wi
much impaired his health, so that he judged
prudent to retire into the country for a sho
time. He hired a lodging at Dulwich, leavi
both his offices under the direction of Abraham.

A lady had her pocket picked of bank notes
the amount of seven thousand pounds. She
lated the particulars of her robbery to Abraha
who in a few days apprehended three pickpocke
and conducted them to Jonathan's lodgings
Dulwich. Upon their delivering up all the note
Wild dismissed them. When the lady applied
Abraham, he restored the property, and she ge
erously made him a present of four hundr
pounds, which he delivered to his employer.

Wild's business would not permit him to
main long at Dulwich; and being under gre
inconvenience for want of Abraham's assistanc
he did not keep open his office in Newtoner'
lane more than three months.

About a week after the return of Wild from
Dulwich, a mercer in Lombard-street ordered a
porter to carry to a particular inn a box containing goods to the amount of two hundred pounds.
On his way the porter was observed by three
thieves, one of whom being more genteelly dressed
than his companions, accosted the man in the following manner: If you are willing to earn sixpence, my friend, step to the tavern at the end of
the street, and ask for the roquelaur I left at the
bar; but, lest the waiter should scruple giving it
to you, take my gold watch as a token. Pitch
your burthen upon this bulk, and I will take care
of it till you return; but be sure you make haste.
The man went to the tavern, and having directed
his message, was informed that the thing he inquired for had not been left there; upon which
the porter said, Since you scruple to trust
me, look at this gold watch the gentleman gave
me to produce as a token.—what was called a gold
watch being examined, proved to be only pewter
lacquered. In consequence of this discovery, the
porter hastened back to where he had left the
box, but neither that nor the sharpers were to be
found.

The porter was, with reason, apprehensive that
he should incur his master's displeasure if he related what had happened; and in order to excuse
his folly, he determined upon the following
stratagem: he rolled himself in the mud, and
then went home, saying, he had been knocked
down, and robbed of his goods.

The proprietor of the goods applied to Wild,
and related to him the story he had been told by

his servant. Wild told him he had been deceiv
as to the manner in which the trunk was lost, a
that he should be convinced of it, if he would se
for his servant. A messenger was despatched f
the porter, and, upon his arrival, Abraham co
ducted him into a room separated from th
office only by a slight partition. Your mast
(said Abraham,) has just been here concernin
the box you lost ; and he desired that you mig
be sent for, in order to communicate the partic
lars of the robbery. What kind of people we
the thieves, and in what manner did they ta
the box away ? In reply, the man said, Why tw
or three fellows knocking me down, carried o
the box. Hereupon Abraham told him, that i
they knocked him down, there was but littl
chance of the property being recovered, sinc
that offence rendered them liable to be hanged.
But (continued he,) let me prevail on you t
speak the truth ; for, if you persist in a refus
be assured we shall discover it by some othe
means. Pray, do you recollect nothing about
token ? Were you not to fetch a roquelaur fro
a tavern, and did you not produce a gold watch
a token to induce the waiter to deliver it ? A
tonished at Abraham's words, the porter declare
he believed he was a witch, and immediately a
knowledged in what manner he had lost the box

One of the villains concerned in the above tran
action, lived in the house formerly inhabited b
Wild, in Cock-Alley, near Cripplegate. To thi
place Jonathan and Abraham repaired, and whe
they were at the door, they overheard a disput
between the man and his wife, during which th

rmer declared that he would set out for Holnd the next day. Upon this they forced open
e day, and Wild saying he was under the nessity of preventing his intended voyage, took
m into custody, and conducted him to the
ompter.

On the following day, the goods being returned
the owner, Wild received a handsome reward;
nd he contrived to procure the discharge of the
hief.

On the 23rd or 24th of January, 1718—19,
Margaret Dodwell and Alice Wright went to Wild's
ouse, and desired to have a private interview
ith him. Observing one of the women to be
ith child, he imagined she might want a father
her expected issue; for it was part of his
usiness to procure persons to stand in the place
f the real fathers of children born in consequence
f illicit commerce. Being shewn into another
oom, Dodwell spoke in the following manner:—
do not come, Mr. Wild, to inform you that I
ave met with any loss, but that I wish to find
omething. If you will follow my advice, you may
cquire a thousand pounds, or perhaps many
housands. Jonathan here expressed the utmost
villingness to engage in an enterprise so highly
ucrative, and the woman proceeded thus: My
lan is this: you must procure two or three stout
esolute fellows who will undertake to rob a house
n Wormwood-street, near Bishopsgate. This
ouse is kept by a cane chair maker, named John
Cooke, who has a lodger, an ancient maiden lady,
mmensely rich; and she keeps her money in a
ox in her apartment: she is now gone into the

country to fetch more.   One of the men m
find an opportunity of getting into the shop
the evening, and conceal himself in a saw
there: he may let his companions in when
family are retired to rest.   But it will be partic
larly necessary to secure two stout apprentic
and a boy, who lay in a garret.   I wish, howev
that no murder may be committed.   Upon t
Wright said, pho! pho! when people engage
matters of this sort, they must manage as well
they can, and do so as to provide for their ow
safety.   Dodwell now resumed her discourse
Jonathan: The boys now secured, no ki
of difficulty will attend getting possession
the old lady's money, she being from hom
and her room under that where the bo
sleep.   In the room facing that of the old lad
Cooke and his wife lay: he is a man of gre
courage; great caution, therefore, must be o
served respecting him: and, indeed, I think
would be as well to knock him on the head;   f
then his drawers may be rifled, and he is nev
without money.   A woman and a child lay und
the room belonging to the old lady, but I hop
no violence will be offered to them.

Having heard the above proposal, Wild too
the women into custody, and lodged them
Newgate.   It is not to be supposed that his con
duct in this affair proceeded from a principle
virtue or justice, but that he declined engaging
the iniquitous scheme, from the apprehension th
their design was to draw him into a snare.

Dodwell had lived five months in Mr. Cooke
house, and though she paid no rent, he was t

enerous to turn her out, or in any manner op-
ress her. Wild prosecuted Dodwell and Wright
r a misdemeanor, and being found guilty, they
ere sentenced each to suffer six months impri-
onment. Wild had inserted in his book a gold
atch, a quantity of fine lace, and other property
f considerable value, which John Butler had
tolen from a house at Newington-Green: but
utler, instead of coming to account as usual, had
eclined his felonious practices, and lived on the
roduce of his booty. Wild, highly enraged at
eing excluded his share, determined to pursue
very possible means to subject him to the power
f justice.

Being informed that he lodged at a public house
n Bishopgate-street. Wild went to the house
arly one morning, when Butler, hearing him as-
ending the stairs, jumped out of the window of
is room, and climbing over the wall of the yard,
ot into the street. Wild broke open the door of
he room; but was exceedingly disappointed and
nortified to find that the man of whom he was in
ursuit had escaped. In the mean time Butler
an into a house, the door of which stood open,
nd descending to the kitchen, where some wo-
nen were washing, he told them he was pursued
y a bailiff, and they advised him to conceal him-
elf in the coal hole.

Jonathan coming out of the ale house and see-
ng a shop on the opposite side of the way open,
e enquired of the master, who was a dyer, whether
man had not taken refuge in his house. The
yer answered in the negative, saying he had not

left his shop more than a minute since it had been opened. Wild requested to search the house, the dyer readily complied. Wild asked the women, if they knew whether a man had taken shelter in the house, which they denied; but informing them that the man was a thief, they they said he would find him in the coal hole.

Having procured a candle, Wild and his attendants searched the place without effect, and they examined every part of the house with no better success. He observed that the villian must have escaped into the street: on which the dyer said, that it could not be the case: that if he had entered, he must still be in the house, for he had not quitted the shop, and it was impossible that a man could pass to the street without his knowledge; and he advised Wild to search the cellar again. They now all went into the cellar, and after some time spent in searching, the dyer turned up a large vessel, used in his business, and Butler appeared. Wild asked him in what manner he had disposed of the goods he had stole from Newington-Green, upbraiding him as being guilty of ingratitude, and declared that he should certainly be hanged.

Butler, however, knowing the means by which an accommodation might be effected, directed Wild to go to his lodging, and look behind the head of his bed, where he would find what would recompense him for his time and trouble   Wild went to the place, and found what perfectly satisfied him; but as Butler had been apprehended in a public manner, the other was under the necessity of taking him before a magistrate, who committed him for trial. He was tried the ensuing sessions at the Old Bailey; but by the artful management of Wild, instead of being condemned to die, he was only sentenced to transportation.

Being at an inn in Smithfield, Wild observed a large trunk in the yard, and imagining that it contained property of value, he hastened home, and instructed one of the thieves he employed, to carry it off. The man he employed in this matter was named Jeremiah Rann, and he was reckoned one of the most dexterous thieves in London. Having dressed himself so as exactly to resemble a porter, he succeeded in carrying away the trunk without being observed.

Mr. Jarvis a whip-maker by trade, and the proprietor of the trunk, had no sooner discovered his loss, than he applied to Wild, who returned him the goods, in consideration of receiving ten guineas. Some time after, a disagreement took place between Jonathan and Rann, and the former apprehended the latter, who was tried and condemned to die. The day preceeding that on which Rann was executed, he sent for Mr. Jervis, and related to him the affair of the trunk. Mr. Jarvis threatened Wild with a prosecution, but all apprehensions on that score were soon dissipated by the decease of Mr. Jarvis.

Wild being much embarrassed in endeavouring to find out some method by which he might safely dispose of the property that was not claimed by the respective proprietors, revolved in his mind a variety of schemes; but at length he adopted that which follows; he purchased a sloop, in order to transport the goods to Holland and

Flanders, and gave the command of the vessel to a notorious thief named Rodger Johnson.

Ostend was the port where this vessel principally traded; but when the goods were not disposed of there, Johnson navigated her to Bruges, Ghent, Brussels, and other places. He brought home lace, wine, brandy, &c. and these commodities were landed in the night, without adding any increase in the business of the revenue officers. This trade was continued about two years, when five pieces of lace being lost, Johnson deducted the value of them from the mate's pay. Violently irritated by this conduct, the mate lodged an information against Johnson for running a great quantity of various kinds of goods.

In consequence of this the vessel was exchequered, Johnson cast in damages to the amount of £700, and the commercial proceedings were entirely ruined.

A disagreement had for some time subsisted between Johnson and Thomas Edwards, who kept a house for thieves in Long lane, concerning the division of some booty. Meeting one day in the Strand, they charged each other with felony, and were both taken into custody. Wild bailed Johnson, and Edwards was not prosecuted. The latter had no sooner recovered his liberty, than he gave information against Wild, whose private warehouses being searched, a great quantity of stolen goods was there found. Wild arrested Edwards in the name of Johnson, to whom he pretended the goods belonged, and he was taken to the Marshalsea, but the next day he procured bail. Edwards determined to wreak his revenge upon Johnson, and for some time industriously sought for him in vain; but meeting him accidentally in Whitechapel-road, he gave him into the custody of a peace officer, who conducted him to an adjacent ale-house. Johnson sent for Wild, who immediately attended, accompanied by his man Quilt Arnold. Wild promoted a riot, during which Johnson availed himself of an opportunity of effecting an escape.

Information being made against Wild for the rescue of Johnson, he judged it prudent to abscond, and he remained concealed for three weeks; at the end of which time, supposing all danger to be over, he returned to his house. Learning that Wild had returned, Mr. Jones, high constable of Holborn division, went to his house in the Old Bailey, on the 15th of February, 1725, and apprehended him and Quilt Arnold; and took them before Sir John Fryer, who committed them to Newgate, on a charge of having assisted in the escape of Johnson.

On Wednesday the 24th of the same month, Wild moved to be either admitted to bail, or discharged, or brought to trial that sessions. On the following Friday a warrant of detainer was produced against him in the court.

The information of Mr. Jones was also read in court, setting forth that two persons would be produced to accuse the prisoner of capital offences. The men alluded to in the above affidavit were John Follard and Thomas Butler, who had been convicted: but it being deemed expedient to grant them a pardon on condition of their appearing in support of a prosecution against Wild, they pleaded the same, and were remanded to Newgate till the next sessions.

Saturday, May the 25th, 9725, Jonathan Wild was indicted for privately stealing in the house of Catharine Stretham, in the parish of St. Andrew, Holborn, fifty yards of lace, the property of the said Catharine, on the 22nd of January, 1724—5. He was a second time indicted for feloniously receiving of the said Catharine, on the 10th of March, ten guineas on account, and under pretence of restoring the said lace, without apprehending and prosecuting the felon who stole the property.

Previous to his trial, Wild distributed among the jurymen, and other persons who were walking on the leads before the court, a great number of printed papers, under the title of A List of Persons discovered, apprehended and convicted of several Robberies on the High Way; and also of Burglary and House-breaking ; and also for returning from Transportation; by Jonathan Wild. This list contained the names of thirty-five for robbing on the highway, twenty-two for house breaking: and ten for returning from transportation. To the list was annexed the following *Nota Bene*.

Several others have been also convicted for the like crimes, but remembering not the person's names who had been robbed, I omit the criminal's names.

Please to observe, that several have been also convicted for shop lifting, picking of pockets, &c. by the female sex, which are capital crimes, and which are too tedious to be inserted here, and the prosecutors not willing of being exposed.

In regard therefore to the numbers above convicted, some, that have yet escaped justice, are endeavouring to take away the life of the said

JONATHAN WILD.

The prisoner being put to the bar, he requested that the witnesses might be examined apart, which was complied with. Henry Kelley deposed that by the prisoner's directions he went, in company with Margaret Murphy, to the prosecutor's shop under pretence of buying some lace : that he stole a tin box, and gave to Murphy in order to deliver to Wild, who waited in the street for the purpose of receiving their booty, and rescuing them if they should be taken into custody : that they returned together to Wild's house, where the box being opened was found to contain eleven pieces of lace ; that Wild said he could afford no more than five guineas, as he should not be able to get more than ten guineas for returning the goods to the owner ; that he received, as his share, three guineas and a crown, and that Murphy had what remained of the three guineas.

Lord Raymond presided when Wild was tried, and summing up the evidence his Lordship observed, that the guilt of the prisoner was a point beyond all dispute ; but that as a similar case was not to be found in the law books, it became his duty to act with great caution ; he was not perfectly satisfied that the construction urged by the counsel for the crown could be put upon the indictment ; and as the life of a fellow-creature was at stake, recommended the prisoner to the mercy of the jury, who brought in their verdict *Not Guilty.*

Wild was indicted a second time for an offence committed during his confinement in Newgate. The jury pronounced him guilty, and he was executed at Tyburn, on Monday the 24th of May, 1725, along with Robert Harpman.

Wild, when he was under sentence of death, frequently declared that he thought the service he had rendered the public in returning the stolen goods to the owners, and apprehending felons, was so great, as justly to entitle him to the royal mercy. He said, that had he considered his case as being desperate, he should have taken timely measures for inducing some powerful friends, at Wolverhampton to intercede in his favour; and that he thought it not unreasonable to entertain hopes of obtaining a pardon through the interest of some of the dukes, earls, and other persons of high distinction, who had recovered their property through his means. It was observed to him, that he had trained up a great number of thieves, and must be conscious, that he had not enforced the execution of the law from any principle of virtue, but had sacrificed the lives of a great number of his accomplices, in order to provide for his own safety, and to gratify his desire of revenge against those who had incurred his displeasure.

He was observed to be in an unsettled state of mind, and being asked whether he knew the cause thereof, he said, he attributed his disorder so the wounds he had received in apprehending felons, and particularly mentioned two fractures of his skull, and his throat being cut by Blueskin.

He declined attending divine service in the chapel, excusing himself on account of his infirmiies, and saying, that there were many people highly exasperated against him, and therefore he could not expect but that his devotions would be interrupted by their insulting behaviour. He said he had fasted four days, which had greatly increased his weakness. He asked the ordinary the meaning of the words, Cursed is every one that hangeth on a tree, and what was the state of the soul immediately after its departure from the body? He was advised to direct his attention to other matters of more importance, and sincerely repent of the crimes he had committed.

By his desire the ordinary administered the sacrament to him, and during the céremony he appeared to be somewhat attentive and devout. The evening preceding the day on which he suffered, he enquired of the ordinary whether self murder could be deemed a crime, since many of the Greeks and Romans, who had put a period to their own lives, were so honourably mentioned by historians. He was informed, that the most wise and learned heathens accounted those guilty of the greatest cowardice, who had not fortitude sufficient to maintain themselves in the station to which they had been appointed by the providence of Heaven: and that the Christian doctrine condemned the practice of suicide in the most express terms.

He pretended to be convinced that self-murder was a most impious crime; but about two in the morning he endeavoured to put an end to his life by drinking laudanum: however, on account of the largeness of the dose, and his having fasted for a considerable time, no other effect was produced than drowsiness, or a kind of stupefaction. The

situation of Wild being observed by two of
fellow-prisoners, they advised him to rouse
spirits, that he might be able to attend to
devotional exercises, and taking him by the ar
they obliged him to walk, which he could not h
done alone, being much afflicted with the go
The exercise revived him a little, but he present
became exceedingly pale, then grew very fain
a profuse sweating ensued, and soon afterwar
his stomach discharged a great part of the lau
anum. Though he was somewhat recovered,
was nearly in a state of insensibility, and in t
situation he was put into the cart and convey
to Tyburn.

In his way to the place of execution, the pop
lace treated this offender with remarkable seve
ty, incessantly pelting him with stones, dirt, &
and execrating him as the most consummate v
lain that ever disgraced human nature.

Upon his arrival at Tyburn, he appeared to
much recovered from the effects of laudanu
and the executioner informed him that a reason
ble time would be allowed him for preparing hi
self for the important change that he must so
experience. He continued sitting some time
the cart; but the populace were at length so e
raged at the indulgence shown him, that they ou
rageously called to the executioner to perform t
duties of his office, violently threatening hi
with instant death if he presumed any longer
delay. He judged it prudent to comply with the
demands, and when he began to prepare for the
execution, the popular tumult ceased.

About two o'clock the following morning, t

emains of Wild were interred in St. Pancras church yard; but a few nights afterwards the body was taken up, for the use of the surgeons it was supposed. At midnight a hearse and six was waiting at the end of Fig-lane, where the coffin was found the next day.

Wild had, by the woman he married at Wolverhampton, a son about nineteen years old, who came to London a short time before the execution of his father. He was a youth of so ungovernable a disposition, that it was judged prudent to confine him while his father was conveyed to Tyburn, lest he should create a tumult, and prove the cause of mischief among the populace. Soon after the death of his father, he accepted a sum of money to become a servant in one of our plantations.

Besides the woman to whom he was married at Wolverhampton, five others lived with him under the pretended sanction of matrimony; the first was Mary Milliner; the second Judith Nun, by whom he had a daughter; the third Sarah Grigson, alias Perrin; the fourth Elizabeth Man, who cohabited with him above five years; the fifth, whose real name is uncertain, married some time after the death of Wild.

History cannot furnish an instance of such complicated villany as was shewn in the character of Jonathan Wild, who possessed abilities which, if they had been properly cultivated, and directed to a right course, would have rendered him a respectable and useful member of society: but it is to be lamented that the profligate turn of mind which distinguished him in the early part of his

life, disposed him to adopt the maxims of
abandoned people with whom he became
quainted.

During his apprenticeship, Wild was obser
to be fond of reading, but as his finances wo
not admit of his buying books, his studies w
confined to such as casually fell in his w
and they unfortunately happened to cont
abominable doctrines those to which thousa
have owed the ruin both of their bodies a
and souls. In short, at an early period of life
imbibed the principles of Deism and Athei
and the sentiments he thus early contracted,
strictly adhered to till nearly the period of his
solution.

Wild trained up and instructed his depende
in the practice of villany, and when they beca
the objects of his displeasure, he laboured w
unremitting assiduity to procure their deaths
Thus his temporal and private interest sought g
tification at the expense of every moral and r
gious obligation. We might conceive it to be
possible for a man acknowledging the existe
of an Almighty being, to employ his attention
on the means of corrupting his fellow creatur
and cutting them off, ' even in the blossom of th
sins !' But the Atheist having nothing after
world either to hope or fear, is only careful to
to secure himself from detection, and the suc
of one iniquitous scheme naturally induces
to engage in others, and the latter actions are
nerally attended with circumstances of more
gravated guilt than the former.

RICHARD FERGUSON.

(GALLOPPING DICK.)

*nvicted at the Lent Assizes. 1800, at Aylesbury,
and executed for a Highway Robbery.*

T few desperadoes on the road gained so much
oriety as this daring highwayman, who, for his
d riding when pursued, obtained the name
Gallopping Dick.

This extraordinary character was born at a
age in Herefordshire. His father was a gen-
man's servant, and being frequently in London,
th, and other places, with his master, he could
t consequently bestow that strict attention to
e education and the morals of his son, which
own conduct gave every proof he would
erwise have done.

Young Dick was sent to school at a very early
e, but made indifferent progress, and gave early
oofs of a daring and wicked disposition. While
ong his companions, if any mischievous project
s set on foot, young Dick was sure to be their
der, and promoted it as far as in his power.

At about fifteen years of age, Dick's father,
ding him to make so small a progress in learn-
g, and given so much to mischievous pranks, re-
lved to employ him under his own eye. The
achman being at this time in want of a stable-
y, young Dick was taken to fill up the vacancy
e took great delight in his new employment

and being a smart and active youth, was ve
much noticed in the family. As he paid particul
attention to the horses, he made astonishing pr
gress in the management of them.

About a year afterwards young Dick came
London with the family. During their stay
town the postillion was taken ill, and Dick w
appointed to supply his place until he recovere
which was not very long. Dick was now stripp
of his fine livery, and sent to fill his situation
stable boy. This his haughty spirit could n
brook. Fond of dress, and being thought a ma
of consequence, he resolved to look out for ano
ther place. Accordingly he told his father of h
resolutions and asked his advice. His fathe
knowing he was well qualified, in respect to th
management of horses, told him he would loo
out one for him.

A circumstance happened that very afternoon
highly gratifying to our hero's pride. A lady wh
frequently visited the family, being in want of
postillion, asked Dick's master what had becom
of his late postillion? Being informed he was i
his place, and was very fit for her employ, he wa
sent for and hired.

Dick was now completely his own master, and
for some time behaved to the satisfaction of hi
mistress. He was a great favourite with the fa
mily, particularly among the female part. He
was now in his twentieth year, and though not
handsome, there was something very agreeable,
if not captivating. in his person. For some time
he lived happily, until his mistress discharged him

an improper connection with one of the fe-
e servants.

He soon afterwards got another place, in which
did not long remain. He had at this time be-
e connected with some other servants of a
e character, and as their idle and dissipated
nners suited his disposition, he soon became
mate with them. After losing several good
es by negligence, he applied at a livery stable
Piccadilly, and succeeded in obtaining employ-
nt.

Dick's father now died, and left him the sum
£57, which he had saved during the time that
lived in the family. With this sum he com-
nced gentleman. He left his place, bought
urning, frequented the theatres, &c. One
ning, at Drury-lane, he got seated by a female
o particularly engaged his attention. He took
r to be a modest lady, and was very much cha-
ned at finding her readily grant his request to
nduct her home. He resolved to leave her, but
nd his resolution fail him, and at the end of
e play he conducted her to her residence in St.
orge's Fields, and stopped with her the whole
ght.

Next morning, after making her a handsome
esent, he took his leave, with a promise of soon
eating his visit. He went home, but this artful
rtezan had so completely enamoured him, that
could not rest many hours without paying her
other visit; and only for the accidental visit of
me companions, he would have returned imme-
ately. With them he reluctantly spent the day,

and in the evening flew again, on the impatient
wings of desire, to his dear Nancy.

She, suspecting him to be a person of considerable property, from the specimen she had of his
generosity, received him with every mark of en-
dearment in her power. At the time Richard
Ferguson became acquainted with her, she was
the first favourite of several noted highwaymen
and housebreakers, who, in turn, had all their fa-
voured hours. While they could supply cash to
indulge her in every species of luxury and extravagance, she would artfully declare that no other
man on earth shared her affections with them;
but their money once expended, cold treatment
or perhaps worse, compelled them to hazard their
lives for the purpose of again enjoying those favours, which any thinking, reasonable man would
have spurned at.

Unfortunately for himself, Ferguson became as
complete a dupe as ever she had ensnared. What
money he possessed, what he could obtain by bor-
rowing or otherwise, was all lavished on this insa-
tiable female, and he was, after all, in danger of
being discarded. He was a total stranger to her
connection with the gentlemen of the road, though
he knew that she bestowed her favours on others.

Not able to bear the thoughts of parting with
his dear Nancy, he went to an inn in Piccadilly,
offered himself as a postillion, and was accepted.
Whenever he could obtain a little money, he flew
with impatience to his fair Dulcinea, and squandered it away in the same thoughtless manner.

As he drove post chaises on the different roads
round the metropolis, he frequently saw his rival

on the road gaily mounted and dressed. One day driving a gentleman on the north road, the chaise was stopped by the noted Abershaw and another, with crapes over their faces. Abershaw stood by the driver, till the other went up to the chaise and robbed the gentleman. The wind being high, blew the crape off his face, and gave Ferguson a full view of his face, They stared at each other; but before a word could pass, some company coming up, the two highwaymen gallopped off.

At this period Ferguson was under the frowns of his mistress, for want of money. They perfectly knew each other, from having often met together at Nancy's. Abershaw was very uneasy at the discovery, which he communiccated to his companion. A consultation was immediately held, and it was resolved to wait at an inn on the road the return of Ferguson, and bribe him, to prevent discovery. They accordingly went to the inn, and when Ferguson came back, and stopped to water his horses, the waiter was ordered to send him in. After some conversation, Dick accepted of the present offered him, and agreed to meet them at night to partake of a good supper.

With this fresh recruit of cash he fled to his Nancy. But she, being otherwise engaged, and not expecting him so soon to possess sufficient for her notice (being now acquainted with his situation in life,) she absolutely refused to admit him, and shut the door in his face. Mad with the reception he had met with, he quitted the house, and resolved never to visit her more, which he strictly adhered to.

D

Ferguson, nettled to the soul, was proceeding homewards, when he met the highwayman who accompanied Abershaw, and went with him to the place of rendezvous in the Borough, where he was received by those assembled with every mark of attention. They supped sumptuously, drank wine, and spent the time in noisy mirth; and, when sufficiently elevated, eagerly closed with a proposition to become one of their number. He was, according to their forms, immediately initiated.

When the plan of their next depredations on the public was settled, Ferguson was not immediately called into action, as it was suggested by one of the members, that he could be better employed in giving information at their rendezvous, of the departure of gentlemen from the inn where he lived, &c., whereby those who were most likely to afford a proper booty might be waylaid and robbed. This diabolical plan he followed too successfully for some time, taking care to learn from the drivers the time the post chaises were ordered from other inns, &c. He shared very often considerable sums, which he quickly squandered away in gambling, drunkenness, and debauchery.

At length he lost his place. and consequently his knowledge respecting travellers became confined, and he was obliged himself to go on the road.—As a highwaymen he was remarkably successful. Of a daring disposition, he defied danger, and from his skill in horses, took care to provide himself with a good one, whereby he could effect his escape. Of this we shall mention one remarkable instance. Two others and himself stopped two gentlemen on the Edgeware-road, and robbed them; soon after, two or three other gentlemen coming up, they pursued, and Ferguson s two companions were taken, tried, and executed.— When his associates complimented him on his escape, he triumphantly asserted that he would gallop a horse with any man in the kingdom.

He now indulged himself in every excess: his amours were very numerous, particularly among those married women he could, by presents or otherwise, induce to listen to his brutal desires. He prevailed on the wives of two publicans in the Borough to elope with him, and carried on several private intrigues with others.

At one of the last places in which he lived, he was frequently employed to drive post chaises between Hounslow and London; and notwithstanding he drove close by his old companion, Abershaw, where he hung in irons, it had no effect in altering his conduct.

We have now given a faithful detail of the early part of the life of this noted highwayman, and the manner of his first taking to the road. To follow him through the various wicked exploits in which he was afterwards engaged, would require volumes to enumerate. We shall only briefly state, that he was concerned in a number of robberies, committed round the metropolis.

At the time that he lived at different inns, as a post chaise driver, he went on the road, and kept up a connection with almost every infamous character of the day. He was concerned, as appeared by the evidence of an accomplice, with Mid-

dleton, Harper, &c., in the robbery at Buxton
Causeway, in 1799, and most other robberies committed on that road.

He latterly became very infamous. He was
repeatedly in custody at Bow-street; suspected of
committing different highway robberies; he had
been tried at the Old Bailey; but nothing could
be properly brought home till the crime for which
he suffered. He was apprehended by some pa-
troles belonging to Bow-street, and taken there;
thence conveyed to Aylesbury, Bucks; and there
tried and convicted of a highway robbery in that
county.

When he found himself left for execution, he
seriously prepared for his approaching end; and
when he came to the fatal tree, met his awful
fate with becoming resignation.

DANIEL AND ROBERT PERREAU.

(THE UNFORTUNATE TWIN BROTHERS.)

*Executed at Tyburn, much lamented, January 17,
1776, for Forgery.*

NEVER had the public mind been more interested
in the case of individuals, convicted of a crime
short of treason, than that of the Perreaus, and
never had such efforts been made in similar cases,
for pardon.

Though their offence was forgery, striking at
the very root of trade, yet such was the mercan-

tile opinion on the peculiar hardship of the fate of Robert, that seventy-eight of the most eminent merchants and bankers in London signed a petition for mercy, and presented it to the King, only two days previous to his execution.

His miserable wife, accompanied by her three children, dressed in deep mourning, on their knees, presented a petition to the Queen, imploring her to save the husband and the father.

Such a picture of distress was seldom seen.—— The queen was greatly affected, and her interest would have succeeded in a case less heinous in the eyes of the law; perhaps, indeed, in any save that of forgery.

To follow the reporter in the parti ulars of the trial, would occupy a great part of our work; we shall therefore confine ourselves to the outlines.

They appear to have been the dupes of an artful woman, Margaret Catherine Rudd, who cohabited with Daniel. Robert Perreau, at any rate, was thought to have been by her art implicated in the crime for which they both suffered, while she escaped the hands of justice for want of sufficient evidence.

When apprehended, Daniel kept an elegant house in Harley-street, Cavendish-square, London, wherein Mrs. Rudd passed as his wife; and Robert was a surgeon of eminence in Golden-square.

From the evidence given upon trial, there is every reason to believe that Mrs. Rudd forged a bond for £7500 in the name of William Adair, Esq., then a well known agent, which was given by Daniel to Robert, in order to raise money upon.

This fatal instrument the latter presented for that purpose, to Messrs. Drummonds, the bankers, who, suspecting its validity, the brothers and Mrs. Rudd were apprehended for forgery.

Robert made a long and ingenious defence ; and though many were of opinion that he was ignorant of the instrument being a forgery, yet the jury convicted him of uttering it, knowing it to be such.

Daniel solemnly declared that he received the bond from Mrs. Rudd, as a true bond, and both urged the truth of their assertions, from the proof that she had pretended some acquaintance with Mr. Adair. They called many witnesses of the first respectability, who testified to their unblemished character ; among whom was Lady Lyttleton, who being asked if she believed that Robert, on whose behalf she appeared, could be capable of such a crime ? She answered that ' She supposed she could have done it herself as soon.'

The unhappy brothers lay in prison, after conviction, seven months before the warrant was signed for their execution. This delay of executing the sentence of the law arose from giving time far the trial of Mrs. Rudd, in order thereby to ascertain whether any thing material to the case of the Perreaus might be brought to light: but, as we have already observed, no evidence could reach the part she took in the transaction, and she was accordingly acquitted.

The day fixed for their execution was Wednesday, the 17th of January, 1776, at which the multitude of spectators outnumbered any within the memory of man on such an occasion ; being computed at 30,000, a much greater number than witnessed that of Lord Ferrars.

They went to Tyburn in a mourning coach; and at the same time five others were carried, in carts, to the same fatal tree, and also executed.

George Lee, for a highway robbery.

Saunders Alexander and Lyon Abrahams, for house-breaking.

Richard Barker and John Ratcliffe, for coining.

When the Perreaus quitted the coach, they ascended the cart from which they were to be launched into eternity with manly fortitude, and bowed respectfully to the sheriffs, who in return waved their hands, as a final adieu! They were dressed exactly alike, in deep mourning.

After the customary devotions, they crossed their hands, joining the four together, and in this manner were launched into eternity. They had not hung more than half a minute when their hands dropped asunder, and they appeared to die without pain.

Each of them delivered a paper to the ordinary of Newgate, which declared their innocence, and ascribed the blame of the whole transaction to the artifices of Mrs. Rudd: and, indeed, thousands of people gave credit to their assertions, and a great majority of the public thought Robert wholly innocent.

On the Sunday following, the bodies were carried from the house of Robert in Golden-square, and, after the usual solemnities, deposited in the vault of of St. Martin's church. The coffins were covered with black cloth and nails, and a black plate on each, inscribing their names, the day of their death, and their ages (42). They were carried in separate hearses; their friends attending in mourning-coaches. The crowd was so great, that the company could with difficulty get into the church; but at length the ceremony was decently performed, and the mob dispersed.

MARIA THERESA PHIPOE.

Executed before Newgate, December 11, 1797, for Murder.

THIS abandoned woman was remarkable for her masculine behaviour, and a daring disposition; as will be fully shewn in detailing the particulars of her very interesting trial.

Two years only, previous to her committing the horrid murder for which she suffered, she was convicted of forcibly taking from Mr. John Cortois, a promissory note of hand for £2000.

The manner in which she extorted this property is highly characteristic of the ferocity of her nature. She then kept a house and a servant, for the purpose of receiving visits from the other sex.

Among other dupes to her artifice, was Mr. John Cortois, whom she seized soon after he sat down in her house, and knowing that he possessed considerable property, bound him, with the assistance of the other desperate female, acting as her servant, to his chair with a cord, and with horrid imprecations, threatening, and even attempting to cut his throat, unless he gave her his note for £2000. In a state of terror he signed

he written instrument. This done, the ferocious
male thought she might negociate the note with
more safety, if he was killed, calling to mind
Satan's proverb, that 'dead men tell no tales.'
For this diabolical purpose, she again attempted
to murder him, and ordered him instantly to prepare for death, either by swallowing arsenic, a
pistol, or stabbing with a knife, which she bran-
ished over his head. At length the terrified
gentleman became desperate in his turn, and attempted to escape. Mrs. Phipoe seized him, from
whose masculine gripe, with the utmost exertion,
he extricated himself, but not without having
several of his fingers badly cut in the struggle.

For this most atrocious offence, she was indicted and tried.

The infamous accomplice, acting the character
of her servant, was admitted evidence for the
prosecution, and she, as well as Mr. Cortois,
swore to the facts above mentioned.

She was found guilty; her counsel moved in
arrest of judgment, an argument upon a point of
law, and it was determined, that great as were
the aggravations in committing the crime, it did
not come within the statute of felony.

She was therefore indicted for the assault, found
guilty, and sentenced on the 23rd of May, 1795,
to twelve months imprisonment in Newgate, and
was discharged at the expiration of that term.

So great was her propensity to vice, that a very
few months elapsed before she committed the
murder for which she executed. The following
are the shocking particulars of the horrid transaction :—

She was indicted by the different names alrea given, for that she, the said prisoner, not havi the fear of God before her eyes, but being mov by the instigation of the devil, did in Garde Street, in the parish of St. George's in the Ea with malice aforethought, on the body of Ma Cox, commit the foul crime of murder.

It appeared in evidence that the deceased v acquainted with the prisoner, and that she h called at her lodgings that morning.

Soon after the mistress of the house heard scuffle and a groaning; she called two neig bours, and, going to the prisoner's door, whi was locked, asked what was the matter? S replied, the woman was only in a fit, and that was getting better. She then opened the door little, when the witness saw she was bloody; t persons went for a doctor, and a third push open the door, saw the deceased bleeding up the ground; she ran down stairs, crying murd and to her great terror, was followed by wounded woman, who had laid hold of her; M Benson came down after the deceased was into the kitchen, where she was when the s geon and beadles came; she was unable to spe but yet made herself understood by one of beadles, that she had been thus wounded by woman up stairs.

He went up to the prisoner who was sitting the bed, and said to her, For God Almigh sake, what have you done to the woman belo She answered, I don't know; I believe the d and passion bewitched me. There was part o finger and a case knife lying upon the tables,

d, Is this the knife you did the woman's busi-
ss with?—Yes;—Is this your finger?—Yes—
d the woman below cut it off?—Yes; but this
e deceased denied, upon his afterwards ques-
ning her with it.

The surgeon described the deceased to have
ceived five stabs upon the throat and neck, be-
des several wounds in different parts of the body,
d agreed with the surgeon, who afterwards at-
nded her in the hospital, that those wounds
ere undoubtedly the cause of her death. The
y after the deceased made a declaration before
magistrate, wherein she stated, that she had
rchased of the prisoner a gold watch and other
ticles, for which she paid eleven pounds, and
en asked for a china coffee cup, which stood
on the chimney piece, into the bargain; the
isoner bid her take one; but in doing so, she
abbed her in the neck, and afterwards had her
der her hands more than an hour; she called
urder all the time, till at last she got her upon
e bed, when she said she would kill her out-
ght, that she might not tell her own story.
he prisoner, in her defence, said, that the de-
ased wanted to purchase only part of the things
hich she wanted to dispose of, and, upon her
fusing to divide them, she became angry. and
id that she only wanted the money to go to
ondon to be Cortois's mistress again: the pris-
ner replied, that it was a lie, for she never had
en Cortois's mistress; the deceased retorted,
at it had been proved so at the Old Bailey.
he said that was a ——— lie; and from this

they both proceeded to very abusive langu
and much violence.

There were two knives lying on the table;
deceased took up one, and making a violent
at the prisoner cut off one of her fingers. I
heat of her passion, full of pain, and strea
with blood, she stabbed her; but solemnly
clared that she had no recollection of what pı
afterwards, until she found herself in her
room, covered with blood. This, she said
the truth; the deceased, if alive, must confen
had been most in fault, and that which affe
her the most was, that she had done her
injury.

The landlady where the deceased lived,
another person to whom she was well kn
proved that she had great respect for the priz
and had often heard her declare she believed
prisoner had the same for her.

Mr. Baron Perryn, who tried the prisoner,
addressed the jury, as follows :—

Gentleman,

This is a charge against the prisoner at the
Maria Theresa Phipoe, otherwise Mary Ben
for the wilful murder of Mary Cox, by stab
her in different parts of the body, and giving
several mortal wounds, of which she died;
have heard the evidence on both sides, both
the side of the prosecution, and on the part of
prisoner, at considerable length; and all that
be necessary for me, in the discharge of my
will be to recapitulate that evidence, and
mistake in any point, I request the counse
both sides will correct me. [Here the lea

e summed up the evidence on both sides, and
added,] Gentlemen, this is the evidence; it
very suspicious circumstance against the pris-
, that she should send her out her landlady,
at particular time to buy brandy and bread,
when she returned, to prevent her bringing
stairs, saying that it would not be wanted
some time; that is a presumption that she
occupied about something which interested
at that time: with respect to the understand-
of the prisoner, the witnesses have all sworn,
speak to that point, that she was in her pro-
senses; you have heard the defence which she
made; now, to be sure, if she had given the
e account to the beadles, which she has done
ur court to-day, it would have operated very
ch in her favour; if this latter account was
, what could be the meaning of concealing
knife in her bosom, and giving it up with so
ch reluctance.

t was stated by the deceased and by several
nesses, that she had locked the door, and for
e time denied admission to her neighbours.
he had been attacked, as she alledged, and was
remarkably subject to passion, why did she ob-
ct the means of preventing her passion from
ducing any mischief Her threatening to kill
deceased outright, that she might not be able
tell her own story, was a very unfavourable cir-
nstance to her. There does not appear to be
colour for her barbarous treatment of the de-
sed, who had always regarded her with affec-
; and all the evidence which the prisoner has
duced in her behalf, does not appear to me to

diminish the enormity of the charge against
But it is for you to pronounce, in the case,
appears to your judgments and consciences;
from all the circumstances, you are of opinion t
she has intentionally and maliciously commit
the crime charged against her, you must find
guilty; but if it appears to you that the decea
was the aggressor, and drew her fate upon her
you will of course pronounce a verdict of
quittal.

The jury retired for twenty minutes, and retun
ed with a verdict of 'Guilty.'

Proclamation being made in the usual for
Mr. Baron Perryn immediately proceeded to p
sentence, that she should be executed on
Monday following, and her body afterwards d
sected and anatomised, according to the statu
When the judge came to this part of the senten
the prisoner said, You may speak out, I am
afraid : and when he had finished with the us
words, the Lord have mercy on your soul, she sai
I do not place very great dependence on yo
mercy.

The prisoner appeared, both before and af
the examination of the witnesses, much concern
about her property, and said, she had not recei
back all the money that lay about the room wh
the officers entered it; and on the two notes b
ing produced in court, she said they were not he
for the property she required was all in gold.

However improper her conduct was before, s
now behaved with due decorum, being attended
a Roman Catholic priest.

She left a guinea for the most deserving deb

he jail, and gave the same sum to the execu-
er.

fter hanging an hour in the view of a great
ber of spectators, one third of whom were fe-
es, the body was cut down, and delivered to
surgeons for dissection.

n her last moments she confessed the justness
her sentence, but denied having cut off her
finger, saying it was done in the scuffle with
woman she murdered. She also denied to the
having poisoned a young woman some years
re, who had left her a legacy of one thousand
nds. She owed to have been guilty of many
rmities, and attributed her frequent gusts of
sion to the use of laudanum.

Her body was publicly exhibited in a place
t for the purpose in the Old Bailey.

DR. WILLIAM DODD,

(HAPLAIN IN ORDINARY TO HIS MAJESTY,)

ecuted at *Tyburn, June 27, 1777, for Forgery*

"But I have now seen death? Is this the way
I must return to native dust? O sight
Of terror foul, and ugly to behold,
Horrid to think, how horrible to feel."
          PARADISE LOST.

E apprehending of such a man as Doctor Dodd,
a charge of forgery, was a matter of surprise
conjecture, among all ranks of people. He

stood high in estimation as a divine, a popu
preacher, and an elegant scholar. He was (
promoter of many public charities, and of so
others he may be said to have been the institu
The Magdalen for reclaiming young woman w
have swerved from the path of virtue; the Soci
for the relief of Poor Debtors; and that of
Humane Society, for the recovery of persons ap
rently drowned, owe their institution to Dr. Do
He was patronised by the King, and more imm
diately by Lord Chesterfield, and his church p
ferments were lucrative. It, however, appean
that his expenses out-ran his income, and for
supply of cash, he committed a forgery on his
pupil the Earl of Chesterfield.

Another singular circumstance in the life of I
Dodd was, his publication, a few years previou
his execution, of a sermon, entitled 'The frequen
of capital punishment inconsistent with justi
sound policy, and religion.' This, he says, was i
tended to have been preached at the Chapel-roy
at St. James's; but omitted on account of the
sence of the court, during the author's month
waiting.

The following extract will shew the unfortun
man's opinion on this subject, while perhaps, co
templating the very crime for which he suffer
He says,

It would be easy to show the injustice of the
laws which demand blood for the slightest offenc
the superior justice and property of inflicting p
petual and laborious servitude; the greater uti
hereof to the sufferer, as well as to the state, es
cially wherein we have a variety of necessary oc

ations, peculiarly noxious and prejudicial to the ves of the honest and industrious, and in which ey might be employed, who had forfeited their ves and their liberties to society.

The method adopted in this forgery is also re-arkable. He pretended that the noble lord had rgent occasion to borrow 4000l. but did not hoose to be his own agent, and begged that the atter might be secretly and expeditiously con-ucted.

The doctor employed one Lewis Robertson, a roker, to whom he presented a bond, not filled p or signed, that he might find a person who ould advance the requisite sum to a young no-leman who had lately come of age.—after apply-g to several persons who refused the business, ecause they were not to be present when the ond was executed, Mr. Robertson absolutely con-ding in the doctor's honour, applied to Messrs. letcher and Peach, who agreed to lend the oney. Mr. Robertson returned the bond to the octor, in order to its being executed and witness-d by himself. Mr. Robertson, knowing Mr. letcher to be a particular man, and who would onsequently object to one subscribing witness nly, put his name under the doctor's. He then ent and received the money, which he paid into he hands of Dr. Dodd, 4000l. and produced the ond.

Lord Chesterfield was surprised, and immediate-y disowned it. Upon this Mr. Manly went di-ectly to Mr. Fletcher to consult what steps to ake. Mr. Fletcher, Mr. Innis, and Mr. Manly, went to the Guildhall, to prefer an information respecting the forgery against the broker and Dr. Dodd. Mr. Robertson was taken into custody, with Fletcher, Innis, and Manly, and two of the lord Mayor's officers went to the house of doctor in Argyle-street.

They opened the business—the doctor was very much struck and affected. Manly told him, if he would return the money, it would be the only means of saving him. He instantly returned six notes ot 500l. each, making 3000l. he drew on his banker for 500l. the banker returned 100l. and the doctor gave a second draft on his banker for 200l. and a judgement on his goods for the remaining 400l. which judgement was immediately carried into execution. All this was done by the doctor in full reliance on the honour of the parties, that the bond should be returned to him cancelled; but, notwithstanding this restitution, he was taken before the lord mayor, and charged as above-mentioned. The doctor declared he had no intention to defraud lord Chesterfield, or the gentleman who advanced the money. He hoped that the satisfaction he had made in returning the money would atone for his offence. He was pressed, he said exceedingly for 300l. to pay some bills due to a tradesman. He took this step as a temporary resource, and would have repaid it in half a year. My Lord Chesterfield, added he, cannot but have some tenderness for me, as my pupil. I love him, and he knows it. There is nobody wishes to prosecute. I am sure my lord Chesterfield don't want my life—I hope he will shew clemency to me. Mercy should triumph over justice. Clemency, however, was denied; and the doctor was committed to the Compter, in preparation for his trial. On the 19th of February, Dr. Dodd being put to the bar at the Old Bailey, addressed the court in the following words:—

" My Lords,

"I am informed that the bill of indictment against me has been found on the evidence of Mr. Robertson, who was taken out of Newgate, without any authority or leave from your lordships, for the purpose of procuring the bill to be found. Mr. Robertson is a subscribing witness to the bond, and as I conceive, would be swearing to exculpate himself, if he should be admitted as a witness against me; and as the bill has been found upon his evidence, which was surreptitiously obtained, I submit to your lordships that I ought not to be compelled to plead on this indictment; and upon this question, I beg to be heard by my counsel.

"My lord, I beg leave also further to observe to your lordships, that the gentlemen on the other side of the question are bound over to prosecute Mr. Robertson."

Previous to the arguments of the counsel, an order, which had been surreptitiously obtained from an officer of the court, dated Wednesday, February 19th, and directed to the keeper of Newgate, commanding him to carry Lewis Robertson to Hick's-Hall, in order to his giving evidence before the grand inquest on the present bill of indictment; likewise a resolution of the court, reprobating the said order; and also the

recognizance, entered into by Mr. Manly, Mr.
Peach, Mr. Innis, and the right honourable the
Earl of Chesterfield, to prosecute and give evidence against Dr. Dodd and Lewis Robertson, for
the said forgery, were ordered to be read ; and
the clerk of the arraigns was directed to inform
the court whether the name of Lewis Robertson
was indorsed as a witness on the back of the
indictment, which was answered in the affirmative.

The counsel now proceeded in their arguments
for and against the prisoner. Mr. Howarth, one
of Dr. Dodd's advocates, contended, that not any
person ought to plead or answer to an indictment,
if it appears upon the face of that indictment
that the evidence upon which the bill was found
was not legal, or competent to have been adduced
before the grand jury.

Mr. Cooper, counsel on the same side, followed
this idea, and hoped that Dr. Dodd might not be
called on to plead to the bill of indictment, and
that the bill might be quashed.

The other counsel employed for the prosecution, replied to these arguments with equal inge-
nuity and professional knowledge. It was now
agreed that the trial should proceed, and the
question respecting the competency of Robertson's
evidence, be reserved for the opinion of the twelve
Judges. Hereupon, Dr. Dodd was indicted for
forging a bond for the payment of 4000l. with intent to defraud, &c., and the facts already stated
were sworn to by the respective witnesses. When
the evidence was gone through, the court called

upon the doctor for his defence. which was as follows :—

" My Lords and Gentlemen of the Jury,

" Upon the evidence which has been this day produced against me, I find it very difficult to address your lordships ; there is no man in the world who has a deeper sense of the heinous nature of the crime for which I stand indicted than myself. I view it, my lords, in all its extent of malignancy towards a commercial state like our's, but, my lords, I humbly apprehend, though no lawyer, that the moral turpitude and malignancy of the crime always, both in the eye of the law, and of religion, consists in the intention. I am informed. my lords, that the act of parliament on this head, runs perpetually in this style, ' with an intention to defraud.' Such an intention, my lords and gentlemen of the jury, I believe, has not been attempted to be proved upon me, and the consequences that have happened, and which have appeared before you, sufficiently prove that a perfect and handsome restitution has been made. I leave it, my lords, to you, and the gentlemen of the jury, to consider, that if an unhappy man ever deviates from the law of right, yet in the first single moment of recollection, he does all he can to make a full and perfect amends, what, my lords and gentlemen of the jury, can God and man desire further ?

" My lords, there are a variety of little circumstances, too tedious to trouble you with, with respect to this matter. Were I to give vent to my feelings, I have many things to say which I am

sure you would feel with respect to me; but my
lords, as it appears on all hands; as it appears,
gentlemen of the jury, in every view, that no injury, intentional, or real, has been done to any
man living, I hope, therefore, you will consider
the case in its true state of clemency. I must
observe to your lordships, that though I have met
with all candour in this court, yet I have been
pursued with excessive cruelty; I have been prosecuted after the most express engagements, after
the most solemn assurances of Mr. Manly; I have
been prosecuted with a cruelty scarcely to be pa-
ralleled. A person avowedly criminal in the
same indictment with myself, has been brought
forth as a capital witness against me; a fact, I believe, totally unexampled. My lords, oppressed
as I am with infamy, loaded as I am with distress,
sunk under this cruel prosecution, your lordships
and the gentlemen of the jury cannot think life a
matter of any value to me. No, my lords, I so-
lemly protest, that death, of all blessings would
be the most pleasant to me after this pain. I
have yet, my lords, ties which call upon me—ties
which render me desirous even to continue this
miserable existence. I have a wife, my lords,
who for twenty-seven years has lived an unparal-
leled example of conjugal attachment and fidelity,
and whose behaviour during this trying scene
would draw tears of approbation, I am sure, even
from the most inhuman. My lords, I have creditors, honest men, who will lose much by my
death. I hope, for the sake of justice towards
them, some mercy will be shown to me. If, upon
the whole, these considerations at all avail with

you, my lords, and you, gentlemen of the jury,—
if, upon the most impartial survey of matters, not
the slightest intention of injury can appear to any
one—and I solemnly declare it was in my power
to replace it within three months—of this I assured Mr. Robertson frequently, and had his solemn assurances that no man should be privy to it
but Mr. Fletcher and himself—and if no injury
was done to any man upon earth, I then hope, I
trust, I fully confide myself in the tenderness, humanity, and protection of my country."

The jury retired for about ten minutes, and
then returned with a verdict, that " the prisoner
was guilty ;" but at the same time they presented
a petition, humbly recommending the doctor to
the royal mercy.

The opinion of the judges, was, that he had
been legally convicted.

On the last day of the sessions, Dr. Dodd was
again put to the bar, when the clerk of the arraigns said,—

" Dr. William Dodd,
" You stand convicted of forgery—what have
you to say why this court should not give you
judgement to die according to law ?

Hereupon, Dr. Dodd addressed the court as
follows :

" My Lord,
"I now stand before you a dreadful example of
human infirmity. I entered upon public life with

the expectations common to young men whose
education has been liberal, and whose abilities
have been flattered; and when I became a clergyman, I considered myself as not impairing the
dignity of the order. I was not an idle, nor I
hope, an useless minister; I taught the truths of
Christianity with the zeal of conviction, and the
authority of innocence.

My labours were approved—my pulpit became
popular: and I have reason to believe, that of
those who heard me, some have been preserved
from sin, and some have been reclaimed—Conde-
scend, my lord, to think, if these considerations
aggravate my crime, how much they must embitter
my punishment! Being distinguished and elevated by the confidence of mankind, I had too much
confidence in myself, and thinking my integrity,
what others thought it, established in sincerity,
and fortified by religion, I did not consider the
danger of vanity, nor suspect the deceitfulness of
my own heart. The day of conflict came, in which
temptation seized and overwhelmed me! I committed the crime which I entreat your lordships
to believe that my conscience hourly represents to
me in its full bulk of mischief and malignity.
Many have been overpowered by temptation, who
are now among the penitent in heaven!

To an act now waiting the decision of vindic-
tive justice, I will now presume to oppose the
counter balance of almost thirty years (a great
part of the life of man) passed in exciting and
exercising, charity in relieving such distresses as
I now feel—in administering those consolations
which I now want. I would not otherwise ex-

nuate my offence, than by declaring, what I
ope will appear to many, and what many cir-
umstances make probable, that I did not intend
nally to defraud; nor will it become me to ap-
ortion my own punishment by alleging that
y sufferings have not been much less than
y guilt. I have fallen from reputation which
ught to have made me cautious, and from for-
ne, which ought to have given me content. I
m sunk at once into poverty and scorn; my
ame and my crime fill the ballads in the streets;
e sport of the thoughtless, and the triumph of
e wicked! It may seem strange my lord, that,
emembering what I have lately been, I should
ill wish to continue what I am! but contempt
f death, how speciously soever it may mingle to-
ther with heathen virtues, has nothing in it
itable to Christian penitence. Many motives
pel me to beg earnestly for life. I feel the
atural horrors of a violent death, the universal
ead of untimely dissolution. I am desirous to
compense the injury I have done to the clergy,
the world, and to religion, and to efface the
andal of my crime, by the example of my repent-
ce; but, above all, I wish to die with thoughts
ore composed and calmer preparation. The
oom and confusion of a prison. the anxiety of a
ial. the horrors of suspense. and inevitable vi-
ssitudes of passion, leave not the mind in a due
sposition for the holy exercises of prayer and
lf-examination Let not a little life be denied
e, in which I may, by meditation and contrition,
epare myself to stand at the tribunal of Omni-
otence, and support the presence of that Judge

who shall distribute to all according to th
Works—who will receive and pardon the repe
ing sinner, and from whom the merciful shall o
tain mercy!   For these reasons, my lords, ami
shame and misery I yet wish to live; and m
humbly implore, that I may be recommended
your lordships to the clemency of his majesty.

Here he sunk down overcome with ment
agony; and some time elapsed before he was su
ciently recovered to hear the dreadful sentence
the law, which the Recorder pronounced upon hi
in the following words.

Dr. William Dodd,
You have been convicted of the offence of pu
lishing a forged and counterfeit bond, knowing
to be forged and counterfeited; and you have h
the advantage which the laws of this country affo
to every man in that situation, a fair, an imparti
and an attentive trial.   The jury to whose justi
you appealed, have found you guilty; their verdi
has undergone the consideration of the learn
judges, and they have found no ground to impea
the justice of that verdict; you yourself have a
mitted the justice of it; and now the very painf
duty that the necessity of the law imposes up
the court, to pronounce the sentence of that la
against you, remains only to be performed.   Y
appear to entertain a very proper sense of th
enormity of the offence you have committed; y
appear to be in a state of contrition of mind, a
I doubt not have duly reflected how far th
dangerous tendency of the offence you have bee
guilty of, is increased in the influence of exampl

eing committed by a person of your character,
of the sacred functions of which you are a
mber. These sentiments seems to be yours; I
ld wish to cultivate such sentiments; but I
ld not wish to add to the anguish of a person
our situation by dwelling upon it. Your ap-
ation for mercy must be made else-where—
ould be cruel in the court to flatter you; there
power of dispensing mercy where you may
ly. Your own good sense, and the contrition
express will induce you to lessen the influence
he example, by publishing, your hearty and
ere detestation of the offence of which you are
victed: and that you will not attempt to palliate
extenuate, which would indeed add to the
ree of the influence of a crime of this kind
g committed by a person of your character
known abilities; I would therefore warn you
nst any thing of that kind. Now, having said
, I am obliged to pronounce the sentence of
law, which is—That you Dr. Wm. Dodd, be
ied from hence to the place from whence you
e; that from thence you are to be carried to
place of execution, when you are to be hanged
he neck until you are dead. To this Dr. Dodd
ied, Lord Jesus receive my soul.

reat exertions were now made to save Dr.
d. The newspapers were filled with letters
paragraphs in his favour. Individuals of all
ks exerted themselves in his behalf: parish
ers went, in mourning, from house to house,
rocure subscriptions to a petition to the king:
this petition, which, with the names, filled
nty-three sheets of parchment, was actually

presented. Even the lord mayor and com
council went in a body to St. James's to so
mercy for the convict.

As clemency, however, had been denied to
unfortunate Perreaus, it was deemed unadvi
to extend it to Dr. Dodd. This unhappy cle
man was attended to the place of execution,
mourning coach, by the Rev Mr. Tillette, ordi
of Newgate, and the Rev. Mr. Dobey. Ano
criminal named John Harris, was execute
the same time. It is impossible to give an
of the immense crowds of people that thro
the streets from Newgate to Tyburn. When
prisoners arrived at the fatal tree and were p
in the cart, Dr. Dodd exhorted his fellow-suff
in so generous a manner as testified that he
not forgotten the duty of a clergyman, and
very fervent in the exercise of his own devot
Just before the parties were turned off, the
tor whispered to the executioner. What he
is not ascertained ; but it was observed that
man had no sooner driven away the cart, tha
ran immediately under the gibbet, and took
of the Doctor's legs, as if to steady the body,
the unhappy man appeared to die without pa

JOHN SHEPPARD,

*cuted at Tyburn, November 23rd, 1724, for
Highway Robbery.*

public robber ever obtained more notoriety
the man whose life and adventures are now
ented. No violator of the law had more hair-
dth escapes than Jack Sheppard. He found
loyment for the bar, the pulpit, and the stage.
arts, too, were busied in handing to posterity
emoranda for us never to follow the example
ohn Sheppard.

ohn Sheppard was born in Spital-fields in the
1702. His father, who was a carpenter,
the character of an honest man ; yet he had
ther son named Thomas, who, as well as Jack,
ned out a thief.

he father dying while the boys were very
ng, they were left to the care of the mother,
placed Jack at school in Bishopsgate street,
ere he remained two years, and was then put
rentice to a carpenter. He behaved with
ency in this place for about four years, when
quenting the Black Lion ale house in Drury-
e, he became acquainted with some abandoned
men, among whom the principal was Elizabeth
on, otherwise called Edgworth Bess, from the
n of Edgworth, where she was born.

While he continued to work as a carpenter, he
en committed robberies in the houses where he
s employed, stealing tankards, spoons, and

other articles, which he carried to Edg[...]
Bess: but not being suspected of having com[...]
ted these robberies, he at length resolved to [...]
mence house breaker.

Exclusive of Edgworth Bess, he was acquain[...]
with a woman named Maggot, who persu[...]
him to rob the house of Mr. Bains, a piece bro[...]
in White Horse Yard: and Jack having bro[...]
away a piece of fustian from thence, (which [...]
deposited in his trunk) went afterwards at [...]
night, and taking the bars out of the cellar [...]
dow, entered, and stole goods and money to [...]
amount of £22. which he carried to Maggot.

As Sheppard did not go home that night, [...]
the following day, his master suspected that [...]
had made bad connections, and searching [...]
trunk, he found the piece of fustian that had be[...]
stolen; but Sheppard, hearing of this, broke [...]
his master's house in the night, and carried [...]
the fustian, lest it should be brought in evide[...]
against him.

Sheppard's master sending intelligence to [...]
Bains of what had happened, the latter loo[...]
over his goods, and missing such a piece of f[...]
tian as had been described to him, suspected t[...]
Sheppard must have been the robber, and det[...]
mined to have him taken into custody; but Ja[...]
hearing of the affair, went to him. and threaten[...]
a prosecution for scandal, alledging that he h[...]
received the piece of fustian from his moth[...]
who bought it for him in Spitalfields.   The [...]
ther, with a view to screen her son, declared th[...]
what he had asserted was true, though she cou[...]
not point out the place where she had made [...]

chase. Though this story was not credited, Bains did not take any farther steps in the ir.

heppard's master seemed willing to think well im, and he remained some time longer in the ily; but after associating himself with the st of company, and frequently staying out the le night, his master and he quarrelled, and head strong youth totally absconded in the year of his apprenticeship. and became con-ted with a set of villains of Jonathan Wild's g.

ack now worked as a journeyman carpenter, a view to the easier commission of robbery; being employed to assist in repairing the se of a gentleman in May Fair, he took an ortunity of carrying off a sum of money, a ntity of plate, some gold rings, and four suits lothes.

ot long after this, Edgworth Bess was appre-ded, and lodged in the round house of the pa- of St. Giles's, where Sheppard went to visit , and the beadle refusing to admit him, he cked him down, broke open the door, and car- her off in triumph; an exploit which acquir-him a high degree of credit with the women abandoned character.

n the month of August, 1723, Thomas Shep-d, the brother of Jack. was indicted at the Bailey, for two petty offences, and being con-ted, was burnt in the hand. Soon after his harge, he prevailed on Jack to lend him forty llings, and take him as a partner in his robberies. first act they committed in concert was the

robbing of a public-house in Southwark, when
they carried off some money, and wearing appa
rel: but Jack permitted his brother to reap the
whole advantage of this booty.

Not long after this, the brothers in conjunction
with Edgworth Bess, broke open the shop of
Mrs. Cook, a linen-draper in Clare Market, and
carried off goods to the value of several pounds
and in less than a fortnight afterwards they stole
some articles from the house of Mr. Phillips in
Drury lane.

Tom Sheppard going to sell some of the goods
stolen at Mrs. Cook's, was apprehended and com
mitted to Newgate. when, in the hope of being
admitted an evidence, he impeached his brother
and Edgworth Bess; but they were sought for in
vain.

At length James Sykes, otherwise called Hell
and Fury, one of Sheppard's companions. meeting
with him in St. Giles's enticed him into a public
house, in the hope of receiving a reward for ap
prehending him: and while they were drinking
Sykes sent for a constable, who took Jack into
custody, and carried him before a magistrate
who, after a short examination, sent him to St
Giles' round house: but he broke through the
roof of that place and made his escape in the
night.

Within a short time after this, as Sheppard
and an associate, named Benson, were crossing
Leicester fields, the latter endeavoured to pick
gentleman's pocket of his watch, but failing in
the attempt. the gentleman called out a pickpoc
et, on which Sheppard was taken and lodged in

St. Anne's round-house, where he was visited by Edgworth Bess, who was detained on suspicion of being one of his accomplices.

On the following day they were carried before a magistrate, and some persons appearing who charged them with felonies, they were committed to Newgate; and as they passed for husband and wife, they were permitted to lodge together in a room well known by the name of Newgate ward.

Sheppard being visited by several of his acquaintance, some of them furnished him with implements to make his escape, and early in the morning, a few days after his commitment he filed off his fetters, and having made a hole in the wall, he took an iron bar and a wooden one out of the window; but as the height from which he was to descend was twenty five feet, he tied a blanket and sheet together, and making them fast to a bar in the window, Edgworth Bess first descended, and Jack followed her.

Having reached the yard, they had still a wall of twenty-two feet high to scale; but climbing up by the locks and bolts of the great gate, they got quite out of the prison, and effected a perfect escape.

Sheppard's fame was greatly celebrated among the lower order of people by this exploit; and the thieves of St. Giles's courted his company. Among the rest, one Charles Grace, a cooper, begged that he would take him as an associate in his robberies, alledging as a reason for this request that the girl he kept was so extravagant, that he could not support her on the profits of his

F

own thefts. Sheppard did not hesitate to make this new connection; but at the same time said that he did not admit of the partnership with a view to any advantage to himself, but that Grace might reap the profits of their depredations.

Sheppard and Grace making an acquaintance with Anthony Lamb, an apprentice to a mathematical instrument maker, near St. Clement's church, it was agreed to rob a gentleman who lodged with Lamb's master, and at two o'clock in the morning Lamb let in the other villains who stole money and effects to a large amount. They put the door open, and Lamb went to bed, to prevent suspicion; but notwithstanding this, his master did suspect him, and having him taken into custody, he confessed the whole affair before a magistrate, and being committed to Newgate, he was tried, convicted, and received sentence to be transported.

On the same day Thomas Sheppard (the brother of Jack) was indicted for breaking open the dwelling house of Mary Cook, and stealing her goods, and being convicted, was sentenced to transportation.

Jack Sheppard not being in custody, he and Blueskin committed a number of daring robberies, and sometimes disposed of the stolen goods to William Field. Jack used to say that Field wanted courage to commit a robbery though he was as great a villain as ever existed.

Sheppard seems to have thought that courage consisted in villany; and if this were the case Field had an undoubted claim to a man of courage: for in October, 1721, he was tried on four indictments for felony and burglary, and he was an accomplice to a variety of robberies. He was likewise an evidence against one of his associates on another occasion.

Sheppard and Blueskin hired a stable near the Horse-Ferry, Westminster, in which they deposited their stolen goods till they could dispose of them to the best advantage; and in this place they put the woollen cloth which was stolen from Mr. Kneebone; for Sheppard was concerned in his robbery, and at the sessions held at the Old Bailey, in August, 1724, he was indicted for several offences, and among the rest for breaking and entering the house of William Kneebone, and stealing 108 yards of woollen cloth, and other articles, and being capitally convicted, received sentence of death.

We must now go back to observe, that Sheppard and Blueskin having applied to Field to look at these goods, and procure a customer for them he promised to do so; nor was he worse than his word; for in the night he broke open their warehouse, and stole the ill gotten property, and then gave information against them to Jonathan Wild in consequence of which they were apprehended.

On Monday the 30th of August, 1724, a warrant was sent to Newgate for the execution of Sheppard, with other convicts under sentence of death.

It is proper to observe that in the old goal at Newgate there was within the lodge, a hatch, with large iron spikes, which hatch opened into a large dark passage. whence there were a few steps into the condemned hold. The prisoners being permitted to come down to the hatch to speak with their friends, Sheppard, having been supplied with instruments, took an opportunity of cutting one of the spikes in such a manner that it might be easily broken off.

On the evening of the above mentioned 30th of August, two women of Sheppard's acquaintance going to visit him, he broke off the spike, and thrusting his head and shoulders through the space the women pulled him down, and he effected his escape, notwithstanding some of the keepers were at that time drinking at the other end of the lodge.

On the day after his escape he went to a public house in Spitalfields, whence he sent for an old acquaintance, one Page, a butcher in Clare-market, and advised with him how to render his escape effectual for his future preservation. After deliberating on the matter, they agreed to go to Warnden in Northamptonshire, where Page had some relations; and they had no sooner resolved than they made the journey; but Page's relations treating him with indifference, they returned to London, after being absent only about a week.

On the night after their return, as they were walking up Fleet street together, they saw a watch maker's shop open, and only a boy attending; having passed the shop, they turned back, and Sheppard driving his hand through the window, seized three watches, with which they effected their escape.

Some of Sheppard's old acquaintance informing him that very strict search was making after him, he and Page retired to Finchley, in hope of laying there concealed, till the diligence of the gaol-keepers should relax : but the keepers of New-gate having gained intelligence of their retreat, took Sheppard into custody, and conveyed him back to his old lodgings.

Such steps were taken as were thought would be effectual to prevent his future escape. He was put into a strong room called the castle, hand-cuffed, loaded with a heavy pair of irons, and chained to a staple fixed in the floor.

The curiosity of the public being greatly excit-ed by his former escape, he was visited by great numbers of people of all ranks, and scarce any one left him without making him a present in money ; though he would have more gladly re-ceived a file, a hammer, or a chisel : but the ut-most care was taken that none of his visitors should furnish him with such implements.

Notwithstanding his disadvantageous situation, Sheppard was continually employing his thoughts on the means of another escape. On the 14th of October, the sessions began at the Old Bailey, and the keepers being engaged to attend the court, he thought they would have very little time to visit him ; and therefore the present juncture would be most favourable to carry his scheme into execution.

About two o'clock in the afternoon of the fol-lowing day, one of the keepers carried him his dinner, and having carefully examined his irons, and finding them fast, he left him for the day.

Some days before this Jack had found a small nail in the room, with which he could at pleasure

unlock the padlock that went from the chain to
the staple in the floor ; and in his own account of
this transaction, he says, that he was frequently
about the room, and had several times slept on
the barracks, when the keepers imagined he had
not been out of his chair.

The keeper had not left him more than an hour
before he began his operations.   He first took off
his hand cuffs, and then opened the padlock that
fastened the chain to the staple.   He next, by
mere strength, twisted asunder a small link of
the chain between his legs, and then drawing his
fetters as high as he possibly could, he made them
fast with his garters.

He then attempted to get up the chimney ; but
had not advanced far before he was stopped by an
iron bar that went across it ; upon which he descended, and with a piece of broken chain picked
out the mortar, and moving a small stone or two
about six feet from the floor, he got out the iron
bar, which was three feet long, and an inch
square, and proved very serviceable to him in his
future proceedings.

He in a short time made such a breach as enabled him to get into the red room over the
castle ; and here he found a large nail, which he
made use of in his further operations.   It was
seven years since the door of the red-room had
been opened : but Sheppard wrenched off the
lock in less than seven minutes, and got into the
passage leading to the chapel.   In this place he
found a door which was bolted on the opposite
side ; but making a hole through the wall, he
pushed the bolt back, and opened the door.

Arriving at the door of the chapel, he broke off one of the iron spikes, which keeping for his further use, he got into an entry between the chapel and the lower leads. The door of this entry was remarkably strong, and fastened with a large lock; and night now coming on, Sheppard was obliged to work in the dark. Notwithstanding this disadvantage, he, in half an hour, forced open the box of the lock, and opened the door; but this led him to another room, still more difficult, for it was barred and bolted as well as locked; however, he wrenched the fillet from the main post of the door, and the box and staples came off with it.

It was now eight o'clock, and Sheppard found no farther obstruction to his proceedings; for he had only another door to open, which being bolted on the inside, was opened with difficulty, and he got over a wall to the upper leads.

His next consideration was, how he should descend with the greatest safety; accordingly he found that the most convenient place for him to alight on, would be the turner's house adjoining to Newgate; but as it would have been very dangerous to have jumped to such a depth, he went back for the blanket with which he used to cover himself, when he slept in the castle; and he endeavoured to fasten his stockings to the blanket, to ease his descent; but not being able to do so, he was compelled to use the blanket alone; wherefore he made it fast to the wall of Newgate with the spike that he took out of the chapel; and sliding down, he dropped on the turner's leads just as the clock was striking nine.

It happened that the door of the garret next the turner's leads was open, on which he stole softly down two pair of stairs, and heard some company talking in a room. His irons clinking, a woman cried, What noise is that? and a man answered, Perhaps the dog or cat.

Sheppard, who was exceedingly fatigued, returned to the garret, and laid down for more than two hours; after which he crept down once more, as far as the room where the company were, when he heard a gentleman taking leave of the family and saw the maid light him down stairs. As soon as the maid returned, he resolved to venture at hazards; but in stealing down the stairs, he stumbled against a chamber door: but instantly recovering himself, he got into the street.

At this time it was after twelve o'clock, and passing by the watch house of St. Sepulchre, he bid the watchman good morrow, and going up Holborn, he turned down Gray's Inn Lane, and about two in the morning got into the fields near Tottenham-Court, where he took shelter in a place that had been a cow house, and slept soundly about three hours. His fetters being still on, his legs were greatly bruised and swelled, and he dreaded the approach of day light, lest he should be discovered. He had now above forty shillings in his possession, but was afraid to send to any person for any assistance.

At seven in the morning it began to rain hard, and continued to do so all day, so that no person appeared in the fields; and during this melancholy day he would, to use his own expression, have given his right hand for ' a hammer, a chissel,

d a punch.' Night coming on, and being pres-
ed by hunger, he ventured to a little chandler's
shop in Tottenham-court-road, where he got a
supply of bread and cheese, small beer, and some
other necessaries, hiding his irons with a long
great coat. He asked the woman of the house
for a hammer; but she had no such implement;
on which he retired to the cow-house, where he
kept that night, and remained all the next day.

At night he went again to the chandler's shop,
supplied himself with provisions, and returned to
his hiding place. At six the next morning, which
was Sunday, he began to beat the basils of his
fetters with a stone, in order to bring them to an
oval form, to slip his heels through. In the afternoon the master of the cow-house coming thither,
and seeing his irons, said, For God's sake who
are you? Sheppard said he was an unfortunate
young fellow, who having had a bastard child
born to him, and not being able to give security
to the parish for its support, he had been sent to
bridewell, from whence he had made his escape.
The man said if that was all it did not much
signify, but he did not care how soon he was gone,
for he did not like his looks.

Soon after he was gone, Sheppard saw a journeyman shoemaker, to whom he told the same
story of the bastard child, and offered him twenty
shillings if he would procure a smith's hammer
and a punch. The poor man, tempted by the reward, procured them accordingly, and assisted
him in getting rid of his irons, which work was
completed by five o'clock in the evening.

When night came on, our adventurer tied a

handkerchief about his head, tore his woollen cap in several places, and likewise tore his coat and stockings, so as to have the appearance of a beggar; and in this condition he went to a cellar near Charing cross, where he supped on roasted veal, and listened to the conversation of the company, all of whom were talking of the escape of Sheppard.

On the Monday he sheltered himself at a public house of little trade in Rupert street, and conversing with the landlady about Sheppard, he told her it was impossible for him to get out of the kingdom; and the keepers would certainly have him again in a few days; on which the woman wished that a curse might fall on those who should betray him. Remaining in this place till evening, he went into the Haymarket, where a crowd of people were surrounding two ballad singers, and listening to a song made on his adventures and escape.

On the next day he hired a garret in Newport-market and soon afterwards, dressing himself like a porter, he went to Black friars, to the house of Mr. Applebee, printer of the dying speeches, and delivered a letter, in which he ridiculed the printer, and the Ordinary of Newgate, and enclosed a letter for one of the keepers of Newgate.

Some nights after this he broke open the shop of Mr. Rawlings, a pawnbroker in Drury lane, where he stole a sword, and a suit of wearing apparel, some snuff boxes, rings, watches, and other effects to a considerable amount. Determining to make the appearance of a gentleman among his old acquaintance in Drury-lane and

Clare-market, he dressed himself in a suit of black
and a tye-wig, wore a ruffled shirt, a silver hilted
sword, a diamond ring, and a gold watch ; though
he knew that diligent search was making after
him at that very time.

On the 31st of October. he dined with two women at a public house in Newgate-street, and
about four in the afternoon, they all passed under
Newgate in a hackney coach, having first drawn
up the blinds. Going in the evening to a public
house in May-pole Alley, Clare-market, Sheppard
sent for his mother, and treated her with brandy,
when the poor woman dropped on her knees and
begged he would immediately quit the kingdom,
which he promised to do, but had no intention of
keeping his word.

Being now grown valiant through an excess of
liquor, he wandered from ale house to gin shops
in the neighbourhood till near twelve o'clock at
night, when he was apprehended in consequence
of the information of an alehouse boy who knew
him. When taken into custody he was quite
senseless, from the quantity and variety of liquors
he had drunk, and was conveyed to Newgate in a
coach, without being capable of making the least
resistance, though he had two pistols then in his
possession.

His fame was now so much increased by his
exploits that he was visited by great numbers of
people, and some of them of the highest quality.
He endeavoured to divert them by a recital of the
particulars of many robberies in which he had
been concerned ; and when any noblemen came
to see him, he never failed to beg that they would

intercede with the king for a pardon, to which he thought that his singular dexterity gave him some pretensions.

Having been already convicted, he was carried to the bar of the court of King's Bench, on the 10th of November, and the record of his conviction being read, and an affidavit being made that he was the same John Sheppard mentioned int he record, sentence of death was passed on him by Mr. Justice Powis, and a rule of court was made for his execution on the Monday following.

He regularly attended the prayers in the chapel ; but though he behaved with decency there, he affected mirth before he went thither, and endeavoured to prevent any degree of seriousness in the other prisoners on their return.

Even when the day of execution arrived, Sheppard did not appear to have given over all expectations of eluding justice ; for having been furnished with a penknife, he put it into his pocket with a view, when the melancholy procession came opposite Little Turnstile, to have cut the cord that bound his arms, throwing himself out of the cart among the crowd, to have run through the narrow passage where the sheriff's officers could not follow on horseback ; and he had no doubt but he should make his escape by the assistance of the mob.

It is not impossible but this scheme might have succeeded ; but before Shepherd left the press-yard, one Watson, an officer, searching his pockets, found the knife, and was cut with it so as to occasion a great effusion of blood.

Sheppard had a further view to his preservation, even after execution; for he desired his acquaintance to put him into a warm bed as soon as he should be cut down; and to try to open a vein, which he had been told would restore him to life.

He behaved with great decency at the place of execution, and confessed to having committed two robberies, for which he had been tried and acquitted. He suffered in the 23d year of his age. He died with difficulty, and was much pitied by the surrounding multitude. When he was cut down, his body was carried to a public house in Long acre, whence he was removed in the evening, and buried in the church yard of St. Martin in the fields.

The following account was written by Sheppard during his confinement in the Middle stone-room, and left with the Ordinary for publication :—

As my last escape from Newgate, out of the strong-room, called the Castle, has made a greater noise in the world than any other action of my life, I shall relate every minute circumstance thereof, as far as I can remember, intending thereby to satisfy the curious, and to do justice to the ignorant.

After I had been made a public spectacle for many days, with my legs chained together, loaded with heavy irons, and stapled down to the floor, I thought it was not altogether impracticable to escape, if I could be furnished with implements ; but as every person that came near me was carefully watched, there was no possibility of any such

assistance; till one day, in the absence of my
gaolers, looking about on the floor. I espied a
small nail within reach; and with that, after a
little practice, I found the great horse padlock,
that went from the chain to the staple in the
floor, might be unlocked; which I did afterwards
at pleasure, and was frequently about the room,
and had several times slept on the barracks,
when the keeper imagined I had not been out of
my chair. But being unable to pass up the chimney, and void of tools, I remained where I was;
till being detected in these practices by the keepers, who surprised me one day before I could fix
myself to the staple in the manner they left me, I
showed Mr. Pitt, Mr. Rouse, and Mr. Parry, my
art; and before their faces unlocked the padlock
with the nail; and though people made such an
outcry about it, there is scarce a smith in
London but what may easily do the same thing;
however, this called for a further security of me;
and till now I remained without handcuffs. A
jolly pair was provided for me, and Mr. Kneebone
was present when they were put on. I, with
tears begged his intercession with the keepers to
preserve me from these dreadful manacles; telling him my heart was broken, and that I should
be much more miserable than before. Mr. Kneebone could not refrain from shedding tears, and
used his utmost endeavours with the keepers to
keep me from them, but to no purpose: on they
went, though at the same time I despised them,
and well knew that, with my teeth only, I could
take them off at pleasure; but this was to lull
them into a firm belief that they had effectually

frustrated all attempts to escape for the future.—I was still far from despairing. The turnkey and Mr. Kneebone had not been gone down stairs an hour, ere I made an experiment, and got off my handcuffs, and before they visited me again I put them on, and industriously rubbed and fretted the skin on my wrists, making them appear bloody, as thinking, if such a thing were possible to be done, not to move the turnkeys to compassion, but rather to confirm them in their opinion; but though this had no effect upon them, it wrought much more upon the spectators, and drew down from them not only much pity, but quantities of silver and copper: but I wanted a still more useful metal—a crow, a chisel, and a file, and a saw or two; those weapons being more serviceable to me than than the mines of Mexico: but there was no expecting any such things in my circumstances.

Wednesday, the 14th of October, the sessions beginning, I found there was not a moment to be lost; and the affair of Jonathan's Wild's throat, together with the business of the Old Bailey, having sufficiently engaged the atention of the keepers, I thought that then was the time to make a push.

On Thursday the 15th (as near as I can remember), just before three in the afternoon, I went to work, taking off first my handcuff; next, with main strength, I twisted a small link of the chain between my legs asunder, and the broken pieces proved extremely useful to me in my design; the feet locks I drew up to the calves of my legs, first taking off my stockings, and with my garters made them fast to my body, to prevent their jingling.

I then proceeded to make a hole in the chimney of the castle, three feet wide, and six feet high from the floor; and with the help of the broken links aforesaid, wrenched an iron bar out of the chimney, of about two feet and a half in length, and an inch and a half square—a most notable implement. I immediately entered the bed room directly over the castle, where one of the Preston rebels had been confined a long time ago, the keepers said, the door of which had not been unlocked for seven years; but I intended not to be seven years in opening it, if they had.

I went to work upon the nut of the lock, and with little difficulty got it off, and made the door fly before me; in this room I found a large nail, which proved of great use in my further progress. The door of the entry between the bed room and the chapel proved a hard task, it being a laborious piece of work; for here I was obliged to break away the wall, and dislodge the bolt, which was fastened on the other side. This occasioned a noise, and I was fearful of being heard by the master-side debtors. Being got into the chapel, I climbed over the iron spikes, and with much ease broke one of them off for my purpose, and opened the door on the inside.

I stripped the nut from off the lock of the door, going out of the chapel to the leads, as I had done before to that of the bed room, and then got into the entry, between the chapel and the leads, and came to another strong, door, which being fastened by a very strong lock, there

I had like to have stopped; and it being quite dark, my spirits began to fail me, as greatly doubting of succeeding; but cheering up, I wrought on with great diligence; and in less than half an hour with the main help of the nail from the bed room, and the spike from the chapel, wrenched the box off, and so made it my humble servant.

A little further on my passage, another stout door stood in my way; and this was a difficulty with a witness to it, being gnarled with more bolts, bars, and locks than I had hitherto met with; I had by this time great encouragement as hoping soon to be rewarded for all my toil and labour. The clock at St. Sepulchre's was then going the eighth hour, and this proved a very useful hint to me soon after. I went to work first upon the box and the nut, but found labour in vain; and then proceeded to attack the fillet of the door; this succeeded beyond expectation, for the box of the lock came off with it from the main post. I found my work was near finished, and that my fate would soon be determined.

I now got to a door opening on the lower leads which being only bolted on the inside, I opened with ease, and thus climbed from the top of it to the higher leads, and went over the wall. I saw the streets lighted, the shops being still open, and therefore began to consider what was necessary to be further done, as knowing the smallest accident would spoil the whole workmanship. I was, therefore, doubtful on which of the houses

I should alight. I found I must go back for the blanket, which had been my covering at nights in the castle, which I accordingly did, and endeavoured to fasten my stockings and that together to shorten my descent, but wanted necessaries so to do, and was therefore forced to make use of the blanket alone; I fixed the same with the chapel spike into the wall of Newgate, and dropt from it on the turner's leads, a house adjoining to the prison; it was then nine o'clock and the shops not shut in.

It fortunately happened that the garret door on the leads was open. I stole softly down about two pair of stairs, and then heard company talking in a room, the door being open. My irons gave a small clink which made a woman cry, Lord what noise is that? a man replied, perhaps the dog or cat, and so it went off. I returned to the garret, and laid myself down being terribly fatigued, and continued there for about two hours, and then crept down once more to the room where the company were and heard a gentleman taking his leave, being very importunate to be gone, saying he had disappointed some friends by not going home sooner. In about three quarters more, the gentleman took leave and went, being lighted down stairs by the maid, who, when she returned, shut the chamber door. I then resolved at all hazards to follow, and slipped down stairs, but made a stumble against a chamber door. I was instantly in the entry, and out at the street door, which I was so unmannerly as not to shut after me, and I was once more contrary to my expectation, and that of all mankind, a free man.

I passed directly by St. Sepulchre's watch-house, bidding them good morrow, it being after twelve, and down Snow-hill, up Holborn, leaving St. Andrew's watch on my left, and then again passed the watch-house at Holborn bars, and made down Gray's inn-yard into the fields, and and at two in the morning came to Tottenham-court, and there got into an old house in the fields, where cows had sometimes been kept, and laid me down to rest, and slept well for three hours. My legs were very much swelled and bruised, which gave me great uneasiness, and still having my fetters on, I dreaded the approach of day, fearing that then I should be discovered. I began to examine my pockets, and found myself master of between forty and fifty shillings. I had no friend in the world that I could send to, or trust with my condition. About seven on Friday morning it began raining, and continued so the whole day, insomuch, that not one creature was seen in the fields. I would freely have parted with my right hand for a hammer, a chisel, and a punch. I kept snug in my retreat until evening, when after dark, I ventured into Tottenham, and got to a little blind chandler's shop, and there furnished myself with cheese, bread, and small beer, and other necessaries, hiding my irons with my great coat as much as possible ; I asked the woman for a hammer, but there was none to be had, so I went very quietly back to my dormitory, and rested pretty well that night, and continued there till Sunday. At night I went again to the chandler's shop, and got provisions, and slept till about six the next day, which being Sunday, I began with a stone to batter the basils of the fetters, in order to beat them into an ovil, and then to slip my heels through. In the afternoon, the master of the shed came in, and seeing my irons, asked me, For God's sake who are you? I told him, An unfortunate young man, who had been sent to bridewell about a bastard child, as not being able to give security to the parish, and had made my escape. The man replied, If that be the case it was a small fault indeed, for he had been guilty of the same himself formerly; and withal said, however, he did not like my looks, and cared not how soon I was gone.

After he was gone, I observed a poor looking man, like a joiner, and made up to him, telling him the same story, assuring him that twenty shillings should be at his disposal, if he could furnish me with a smith's hammer and a punch. The man proved a shoemake by trade, but willing to obtain the reward, immediately borrowed the tools of a blacksmith his neighbour; and likewise gave me great assistance, and before five o'clock in the evening, I had entirely got rid of those troublesome companions, my fetters, which I gave to the fellow, besides the twenty shillings, if he thought fit to make use of them.

That night I came to a cellar at Charing cross and refreshed myself comfortably with roast veal &c., where a dozen people were all discoursing about Sheppard, and nothing else was talked of whilst I staid among them. I had a handkerchief about my head, tore my woollen cap in many places, as likewise my coat and stockings, and exactly like what I designed to represent—a beggar fellow.

The next day I took shelter at an ale house of little or no trade in Rupert street, near Piccadilly. The woman and I discoursed much about Sheppard. I assured her it was impossible for him to escape out of the kingdom, and the keepers would have him again in a few days. The woman wished a curse might fall on those who should betray him. I continued there until the evening, when I stept towards the Haymarket, and mixed in a crowd round two ballad singers, the subject being concerning Sheppard, and I remember the company were very merry about the matter.

On Thursday, I hired a garret for my lodgings, at a poor house in Newport-market, and sent for a sober steady young woman, who for a long time past had been the real mistress of my affections, who came and rendered me all the assistance she was capable of affording. I made her the messenger to my mother, who lodged in Clare-street; she likewise visited me in a day or two after, begging on her knees, I would make the best of my way out of the kingdom which I faithfully promised; but I cannot say it was my intention heartily so to do.

I was oftentimes in Spitalfields, Drury lane, Parker's lane, St Thomas's street, &c., these having been the chief scenes of my rambles and pleasures.

I had once formed a design to have opened a shop or two in Monmouth street for some necessaries, but let that drop, and came to a resolution of breaking open the house of the two Mr. Rawlin's, brokers, and pawnbrokers, in Drury lane, whice I accordingly put into practice, and succeeded ; they both heard me rifling their goods, as they lay in a bed together in the next room, and though there was none to assist me, yet I pretended there was, by loudly giving out directions for shooting the first person through the head that presumed to stir, which effectually quieted them, while I carried off my booty ; with part thereof, on the fatal Saturday following, being the 31st of October, I made an extraordinary appearance, and, from a carpenter and butcher, was now transformed into a perfect gentleman ; and in company with my sweetheart aforesaid, and another young woman, of her acquaintance, went into the city, and were very merry together at a public house not far from the place of my old confinement.

At four in the afternoon, we all passed under Newgate in a hackney coach, the windows drawn up ; and in the evening sent for my mother to the Shears ale-honse, in Maypole-alley, near Clare-market, and with her drank three quarterns of brandy and after leaving her, I drank in one place or other about that neighbourhood all the evening till the hour of twelve, having been seen and known by many of my acquaintance, all of them cautioning me, and wondering at my presumption to appear in that manner. At length my senses were quite overcome with the quantity and variety of the liquors I had all the day been drinking, which paved the way for my fate to meet me : and when apprehended, I do protest I was altogether incapable of resisting, I scarce knew what they were doing to me, and had but two second hand pistols, scarce worth carrying about me.

A clear and ample account I have now given of the most material transactions of my life, and do hope the same will prove a warning to all young men.

Nothing now remains but to return my hearty thanks to the Rev. Dr. Bennet, the Rev. Mr. Burney, the Rev. Mr. Wagstaff, the Rev. Mr. Hawkins, the Rev. Mr. Flood, and the Rev. Mr. Edwards, for their charitable visits and assistance to me; as also my hearty thanks to those gentlemen who so generously contributed towards my support in prison.

I hope none will be so cruel as to reflect on my poor distressed mother, the unhappy parent of two miserable wretches, myself and brother; the last gone to America for his crimes, and myself going to the grave for mine.

I beseech the Supreme Being to pardon my numberless and enormous crimes, and to have mercy on my poor departing soul.

JOHN SHEPPARD.

Middle stone-room,
Newgate, Nov. 10, 1724.

P. S. After I had escaped from the castle, concluding that Blueskin would have been decreed for death, I did fully purpose to have gone and cut down the gallows the night before his execution.

BENJAMIN TAPNER, JOHN COBBY, &c.,

(SMUGGLERS AND MURDERERS,)

Executed at Colchester, June 18th, 1794.

THE smugglers, on the sea coast, formerly went in parties sufficiently strong to oppose the officers of the excise, and sometimes even to menace parties of the military, sent to apprehend them. Whenever a custom house officer unfortunately fell into their hands, he was barbarously and cruelly tortured, and often murdered. Such a cruel murder as this we are about to detail, is not to be found in this volume; and we much question whether the annals of Europe can furnish a parallel.

The two unfortunate sufferers who were murdered by this desperate gang, were William Galley, the elder, a custom house officer of Southampton, and Daniel Chater, a shoemaker, of Fordingbridge. These men, having been sent to give information, respecting some circumstances attending the daring burglary into the custom house of Poole, and not returning to their respective homes, a suspicion arose that they had been way laid and murdered by the smugglers, and a search for them was therefore instituted.

Those employed for this purpose, after every inquiry, could hear no certain tidings of them, for fear of the smugglers' resentment silencing such inhabitants on the road over which they had carried the unfortunate men, as were not in connection with them. At length a Mr. Stone, following his hounds, came to a spot which appeared to have been dug not long before, and the publicity of the circumstances of the men above mentioned being missed, he conjectured that there they might have been buried, and therefore he gave immediate information. Upon digging there, nearly seven feet in the earth, were found the remains of Galley, but in so putrid a state, as not to be known, except by the clothes. The search after Chater was now pursued with redoubled vigilance, and found in a well, six miles distant from Galley, in Harris Wood, near Lady Holt Park, with a quantity of stones, wooden rails, and earth upon it.

Benjamin Tapner, John Cobby, John Hammond, William Barter, Richard Mills the Elder, and Richard Mills the younger, were indicted for the murder of Daniel Chater; the first three as principals, and the other as accessories before the fact; and William Jackson, and William Carter were indicted for the murder of William Galley.

Benjamin Tapner was a native of Aldington in Sussex and worked for some time as a bricklayer; but being of an idle disposition, he soon quitted his business, and associated with a gang of smugglers, who had rendered themselves formidable to the neighbourhood by their lawless depredations.

John Cobby was an illiterate country fellow, the son of James Cobby, of the county of Sussex, labourer, and joined the smugglers a little time before he was thirty years of age.

John Hammond was a labouring man, born at Berstead in Sussex, and had been a smuggler for some time before he was apprehended for the above mentioned murder, which was when he was almost forty years old.

William Jackson was a native of Hampshire, and had a wife and large family. He was brought up to the business of husbandry ; but the hope of acquiring more money in an easier way induced him to engage with the smugglers, which at length ended in his ruin.

William Carter, of Rowland's Castle, in Hampshire, was the son of William Carter, of Eastmean, in the same county, thatcher. He was about the age of thirty-nine, and had practised smuggling a considerable time before the perpetration of the fact which led to his destruction.

Richard Mills, the elder, was a native of Trotton in Sussex, and had been a horse dealer by profession ; but it is said, that a failure in that business induced him to commence smuggler, and he had been long enough in that illicit practice to become one of the most hardened of the gang.

Richard Mills, the younger, lived at Stredham in Sussex, and for some time followed his father's profession of horse dealing ; but unfortunately making a connection with the smugglers. he came to the same igominious end as his companions, in the thirty-seventh year of his age,

The two men, Galley and Chater, went on Sunday, February 14th, 1748, to Major Batten, a justice of the peace, at Stanstead in Sussex, with a letter written by Mr. Shearer, collector of the customs at Southampton, requesting him to make an examination of Cheater concerning one Diamond or Dymar, who was committed to Chichester jail, on suspicion of being one who broke the ng's warehouse at Poole. Chater was engaged give evidence, but with some reluctance, having declared that he saw Diamond and shaked nds with him, who with many others was coming from Poole, loaded with tea, of which he rew him a bag. Having passed Havant, and ming to the New Inn, at Leigh, they enquired eir way, when George Austin, his brother, and other-in-law, said that they were going the me road, and would accompany them to Rowd's Castle, where they might get better direcns, it being just by Stanfield Park.

A little before noon shey came to the White rt at Rolland's Castle, kept by Mrs. Elizabeth yne, widow, who had two sons, blacksmiths, in e same village. After some talk she told orge Austins privately, she was afraid that these o strangers were come to hurt the smugglers. e said, No, sure, they were only carrying a letter Major Batten. Upon this, she sent one of her ns for William Jackson and William Carter, o lived near her house. Meanwhile Chater d Galley wanted to be going, and asked for eir horses; but she told them, that the major s not at home, which indeed was true.

As soon as Jackson and Carter came she told em her suspicions, with the circumstances of e letter. Soon after she advised George Austin go away lest he should come to any harm; he so, leaving his brothers.

Paye's other son went and fetched in William eele and Samuel Downer, otherwise little Sauel, Edmund Richards, and Henry Sheermen, otherwise Little Harry, all smugglers belonging to the same gang.

After they had drank a little while, Carter, who had some little knowledge of Chater, called him into the yard, and asked him where Diamond was. Chater said, he believed he was in custody, and that he was going to appear against him, which he was sorry for, but he could not help it. Galley came into the yard to them, and asking Chater why he would stay there? Jackson, who followed him, said with a horrid imprecation, what's that to you? Galley immediately struck him a blow in the face which knocked him down, and set his nose and mouth a bleeding; soon after they all came into the house, when Jackson reviving, Galley offered to strike him again, but one of Payne interposed.—Galley and Chater now began to be very uneasy, and wanted to be going; but Jackson, Carter and the rest of them, persuaded them to stay and drink some more rum, and make it up, for they were sorry for what had happened: they sat down again: Austin and his brother-in-law being present. Jackson and Carter desired to see the letter, but they refused to shew it. The smugglers then drank about plentifully, and made Galley and Chater fuddled; then persuaded them to lie down on a bed, which they did, and fell asleep; the letter was then taken away, read, and the substance of it greatly exasperating them, it was destroyed.

One John Royce, a smuggler, now came in, and Jackson and Carter told him the contents of the letter, and that they had got the old rogue the shoemaker of Fording-bridge; who was going inform against John Diamond, the shepherd, then in custody a Chichester. Here William Steele proposed to take them both to a well, about two hundred yards from the house, and to murder and throw them in.

This proposal did not take, as they had been seen in their company by the Austins, Mr. Garret, and one Mr. Jenks, who was newly come into the house to drink. It was next proposed to send them to France; but that was objected against, as there was a possibility of their coming over again. Jackson's and Carter's wives being present, cried out, Hang the dogs, for they came here to hang you. It was then proposed and agreed. to keep them confined till they could know Diamond's fate, and whatever it was, to treat these in the same manner; and each to allow three pence a week towards keeping them.

Galley and Chater continuing asleep, Jackson went in, and began the first scene of cruelty! for having put on his spurs, he got upon the bed, and spurred their foreheads, to wake them, and afterwards whipped them with a horse-whip so that when they came out they were both bleeding. The above named smugglers then took them out of the house, but Richards returned with a pistol, and swore he would shoot any person who should mention what had passed.

Meanwhile the rest put Galley and Charter on one horse, tied their legs under the horse's belly, and tied both their legs together; they now set forward all but Race, who had no horse. They had not gone above two hundred yards before Jackson called out, Whip 'em, cut 'em, slash 'em,

d—n 'em; upon which all began to whip exc
Steele, who led the horse, the roads being ve
bad. They whipped them for half a mile, ti
they came to Woodash, where they fell off wi
their heads under the horse's belly, and the
legs, which were tied, appeared over the hor
back. Their tormentors soon set them uprigh
again, and continued whipping them over th
head, face, shoulders, &c., till they came to Dea
upwards of half a mile farther; here they bo
fell again as before, with their heads under th
horse's belly, which were struck at every step
the horse's hoofs.

Upon placing them again in the saddle the
found them so weak, that they could not sit, upo
which they separated them, and put Galley be
fore Steele, and Chater before Little Sam, an
then whipped Galley so severely, that the lash
coming upon Steele, at his desire they desiste
They then went to Harris's well, near Lady-ho
park, where they took Galley off the horse, an
threatened to throw him into the well. Upo
which he desired them to dispatch him at on
and put an end to his misery. No, says Jackso
cursing, if that's the case, we have more to say t
you; then put him on a horse again, and whip
ped him over the Downs, till he was so wea
that he fell off; when they laid him across th
saddle, with his breast downwards, and Litt
Sam got up behind them, and as they went on, h
squeezed Galley's testicles, so that he groane
with the agony, and tumbled off; being then pu
on astride, Richards got up behind him, but soo
the poor man cried out, I fall, I fall, I fall: an

Richards pushing him, said, Fall and be d—d. Upon which he fell down, and the villains thinking this fall had broke his neck, laid him again on the horse, and proposed to go to some proper place, where Chater might be concealed till they heard the fate of Diamond.

Jackson and Carter called at one Peascod's house, desiring admittance for two sick men; but he absolutely refused it.

Being now one o'clock in the morning, they agreed to go to one Scardefield's at the Red Lion, at Rake, which was not far. Here Carter and Jackson got admittance after many refusals. While Scardefield went to draw liquor, he heard more company come in; but though they refused to admit him into the room, he saw one man stand up very bloody, and another lie as dead. They said they had engaged with some officers, lost their tea, and several of them were wounded if not killed.

Jackson and little Harry now carried Chater down to one old Mills', which was not far off. and chained him in a turf house, and Little Harry staying to watch him. Jackson returned again to the company,—After they had drank gin and rum, they all went out, taking Galley with them. Carter compelled Scardefield to shew them the place where they used to bury their tea, and to lend them spades and a candle and lanthorn; there they began to dig, and it being very cold he helped to make a hole, where they buried something that lay across a horse like a dead man.

They continued at Scardefield's drinking all that day, and in the night went to their own homes, in

order to be seen on Tuesday, agreeing to m
again on Thursday at the same house, and br
more of their associates. They met according
and brought old Richard Mills, and his s
Richard and John, Thomas Stringer, John Cob
Benjamin Tapner, and John Hammond, who wi
the former made fourteen. They consulted n
what was to be done with Chater; it was una
mously agreed that he must be destroyed. Rich
Mills, jun. proposed to load a gun, clap the muz
to his head, tie a long string to the trigger, th
all pull at it, that all might be equally guilty
his murder. This was rejected, because it wou
put him out of his pain too soon; and at leng
they came to a resolution to carry him up
Harris's well, which was not far off, and to thro
him in.

All this while Chater was in the utmost horr
and misery, being visited by one or other of the
who abused him both with words and blows. A
last they all came, and Tapner and Cobby goin
into the turf house, the former pulled out a clasp
knife and said, with a great oath, down on you
knees, and go to prayers, for with his knife I'll b
your butcher. The poor man knelt down, and a
he was at prayers Cobby kick'd him, calling hi
an informing villain. Chater asking what the
had done with Mr. Galley, Tapner slashing hi
knife across his eyes, almost cut them out, an
the gristle of his nose quite through; he bore i
patiently, believing they were putting an end t
his misery; accordingly Tapner struck at him
again, and made a deep cut in his forehead. Upon
this old Mills said, Do not murder him here, but

ewhere else. Accordingly they placed him
n a horse, and all set out together for Harris's
l, except Mills and his sons, they having no
ses ready, and saying in excuse, that there
s enough without them to murder one man.
the way Tapner whipped him till the blood
ne, and then swore that if he blooded the
dle he would torture him the more: as he
uld not stop his wounds from bleeding, this was
incredible instance of barbarity.
When they were come within two hundred
ds of the well, Jackson and Carter stopped,
ing to Tapner, Cobby, Stringer, Steele, and
mmond, "Go on and do your duty upon Cha-
, as we have ours upon Galley." In the dead
the night, of the 18th, they brought him to the
ll, which was near thirty feet deep, but dry,
paled round. Tapner having fastened a noose
nd Chater's neck, they bid him get over the
es to the well. He was going through a bro-
place, but though he was covered with blood,
fainting through the anguish of his wounds,
y forced him to climb up, having the rope
nd his neck, one end of which being tied to
pales, they pushed him into the well, but the
e being short, he hung no farther within it
n his thighs, and leaning against the edge, he
ng above a quarter of an hour, and was not
angled. They then untied him, and threw him
d foremost into the well. They tarried some
e, and hearing him groan, they concluded to
to one William Comleah's, a gardener, to bor-
w a rope and ladder, saying, they wanted to re-

M

lieve one of their companions, who had fallen int
Harris's well.   He said they might take them
but they could not manage the ladder, in the
confusion, it being a long one.

They then returned to the well, and still find
ing him groan, and fearing that he might b
heard, so as to make a discovery, the place bein
near the road, they threw upon him some of th
rails and gate posts fixed about the well, al
great stones ; when finding him silent, they le
him.

The next consultation was how to dispose
their horses, when they killed Galley's, whi
was grey, and took his hide off, cut it into sm
pieces, and hid them so as to prevent any di
covery ; but a bay horse that Chater rode on, g
from them.

This daring gang now broken, a number of w
nesses came forward on their trial, and two
their accomplices being pardoned, were admitt
evidence against them.   The charge, in all i
horror, was fully proved ; whereupen the judg
Sir Michael Foster, pronounced sentence up
the convicts, in one of the most pathetic address
that ever was heard ; representing the enormi
of the crime, and exhorting them to make imm
diate preparation for the awful fate that awaite
them ; adding, " Christian charity obliges me
tell you, that your time in this world will be ve
short.

The heinousness of the crime which these m
had been convicted of, rendering it necessary th
their punishment should be exemplary, the jud
ordered that they should be executed the follo

ing day; and the sentence was accordingly carried into execution against all but Jackson, who died in prison, on the evening that he was condemned. They were attended by two ministers, and all but Mills and his sons (who took no notice of each other, and thought themselves not guilty, because they were not present at the finishing of the inhuman murder,) shewed great marks of penitence. Tapner and Carter gave good advice to the spectators, and desired diligence might be used in apprehending Richards, whom they charged as the cause of their being brought to this wretched end. Young Mills smiled several times at the executioner, who was a discharged marine, and having ropes far too short for some of them, was puzzled to fit them. Old Mills being forced to stand on tip-toe to reach the halter, desired that he might not be hanged by inches. The Mills' were so rejoiced at being told that they were not to be hanged in chains after execution, that death seemed to excite in them no terror; while Jackson was so struck with horror, at being measured for his irons, that he soon expired.

They were hanged at Chichester, on the 18th of January, 1749, amidst such a concourse of spectators as is seldom seen on the occasion of a public execution.

Carter was hung in chains, near Rake, in Sussex: Tapner on Rock's-hill, near Chichester; and Cobby and Hammond at Cesley Isle, on the beach where they sometimes landed their smuggled goods, and where they could be seen at a great distance east and west.

The body of Jackson was thrown into a hole near the place of execution; so were the bodies of Mills, the father and son, who had no friends to take them away; and at a short distance from this spot is erected a stone, on which is the following inscription :—

Near this place was buried the body of William Jackson, who upon special commission of Oyer and Terminer, held at Chichester, on the 16th day of January, 1748-9, was, with William Carter, attained for the murder of William Galley, custom house officer; and who likewise was, together with Benjamin Tapner, John Cobby, John Hammond, Richard Mills the elder, Richard Mills the younger, his son, attained for the murder of Daniel Chater; but dying in a few hours after sentence of death was pronounced upon him, he thereby escaped the punishment which the heinousness of his complicated crimes deserved, and which was, the next day, most justly inflicted upon his accomplices.

LAWRENCE EARL FERRERS,

Who was Hanged for Murder.

LAWRENCE EARL FERRERS was a man of an unhappy disposition. Though of clear intellects and acknowledged abilities, when sober, yet an early attachment to drinking greatly impaired his faculties, and when drunk, his behaviour was that of a madman.

Lord Ferrers married the youngest daughter of Sir William Meredith, in the year 1752; but behaved to her with such unwarrantable cruelty, that she was obliged to apply to parliament for redress: the consequence of which was that an act passed for allowing her a separate maintenance, to be raised out of his estates.

At Derby races in the year 1756, Lord Ferrers ran his mare against Captain M——'s horse for £50. and was the winner. When the race was ended, he spent the evening with some gentlemen, and in the course of conversation the Captain (who heard that his lordship's mare was with foal) proposed, in a jocose manner, to run his horse against her at the expiration of seven months. Lord Ferrers was so affronted by this circumstance, which he conceived to have risen from a pre-concerted plan to insult him, that he quitted Derby at three o'clock in the morning, and went immediately to his seat at Stanton Harold in Leicestershire.

He rang his bell next morning; and a servant attending, he asked if he knew how Captain M. came to be informed his mare was with foal. The servant declared that he was ignorant of the matter, but the groom might have told it; and the groom being called, he denied having given any information respecting the matter.

Previous to the affront presumed to have been given on the preceding evening, Lord Ferrers had invited the captain and the rest of the company to dine with him on that day; but they all refused their attendance, though he sent a servant to remind them that they had promised to come.

Lord Ferrers was so enraged at this disappointment, that he kicked and horsewhipped his servants, and threw at them such articles as lay
within his reach.

The following will afford a specimen of the
brutality of Lord Ferrers' behaviour. Some oys-
ters had been sent from London, which, not
proving good, his lordship directed one of the servants to swear that the carrier had changed them
—but the servant declining to take such an oath,
the earl flew on him in a furious rage, stabbed
him in the breast with a knife, cut his head with
a candlestick, and kicked him on the groin with
such severity, as to render him incapable of a re-
tention of urine for several years afterwards.

Lord Ferrers brother and his wife paying a visit
to him and his countess at Stanton-Harold, some
dispute arose between the parties ; and Lady Ferrers being absent from the room, the earl ran up
stairs with a large clasp knife in his hand, and
asked a servant whom he met where his lady was.
The man said, *In his own room ;* and being directed to follow him thither, Lord Ferrers ordered him to load a brace of pistols with bullets.—
This order was complied with ; but the servant,
apprehensive of mischief, declined priming the
pistols—which Lord Ferrers discovering, swore
at him, asked him for powder, and primed them
himself. He then threatened that if he did not
immediately go and shoot his brother the captain,
he would blow his brains out. The servant hesitating, his lordship pulled the trigger of one of
the pistols, but it missed fire. Hereupon the
countess dropped upon her knees, and begged him

to appease his passion ; but in return he swore at
her, and threatened her destruction if she opposed,
him. The servant now escaped from the rooms
and reported what had passed to his lordship's
brother, who immediately called his wife from her
bed room, and they left the house, though it was
then two o'clock in the morning.

The unfortunate Mr. Johnson, who fell a sacrifice to the ungovernable passion of Lord Ferrers,
had been bred up in the family from his youth,
and was distinguished for the regular manner in
which he kept the accounts, and for his fidelity as
a steward.

When the law had decreed a separate maintenance for the countess, Mr. Johnson was proposed
as receiver of the rents for her use ; but he declined this office, till urged by the earl himself.—
It appears that Johnson now stood high in his
lordship's opinion : but a different scene soon ensued ; for the earl having conceived an opinion,
that Johnson had combined with the trustees to
disappoint him of a contract for coal mines, he
came to the resolution to destroy the honest steward !

The earl's displeasure was first evinced by his
sending notice to Johnson to quit a beneficial
farm which he held under him ; but Johnson
producing a lease granted him by the trustees, no
farther steps were taken in the affair.

After this, Lord Ferrers behaved in so affable
a manner to Johnson, that the latter imagined all
thoughts of revenge had subsided ; but on the
3th of January, 1760, his lordship called on
Johnson, who lived about half a mile from his

seat, and bid him come to Stanton between three and four in the afternoon of the Friday following. His lordship's family now consisted of a gentle-woman named Clifford, with four of her natural children, three maid servants, and five members, exclusive of an old man and a boy. After dinner on the Friday, Lord Ferrers sent away all the men servants out of the house, and desired Mrs. Clifford to go with her children to the house of her father, at the distance of about two miles.

Johnson coming to his appointment, one of the maids let him in, and, after waiting some time, he was admitted to his lordship's room, and being ordered to kneel down, was shot with a pistol, the ball from which entered his body just beneath his ribs.

Lord Ferrers, alarmed at the crime he had committed, now called for the maid-servant, and directed them to put Mr. Johnson to bed. He likewise sent to Mr. Kirkland, a surgeon, who lived at Ashby-de-la-Zouch, two miles from his seat. At the request of the wounded man; a person was also sent for his children.

Miss Johnson, the eldest daughter, soon came, and was followed by the surgeon. to whom Lord Ferrers said, I intended to have shot him dead; but since he is still alive, you must do what you can for him.

The surgeon soon found that Johnson had been mortally wounded; but knowing the Earl's fiery disposition, and dreading similar consequences to himself, he dissembled the matter, and told him that there was no danger in the case.

Hereupon Lord Ferrers drank himself into a

tate of intoxication, and then went to bed; after which Mr. Johnson was sent to his own house in a chair, at two o'clock in the morning, and died at nine.

Mr. Kirkland being convinced that Johnson could not live. procured a number of persons to secure the murderer. When they arrived at Stanton Harold, Lord Ferrers was just arisen, and going towards the stables, with his garters in his hands; but observing the people, he retired to the house, and shifted from place to place, so that it was a considerable time before he was taken.

This happened on a Saturday, and he was conveyed to Ashby de-la-Zouch, and confined at a public house till the Monday following, when the coroner's jury sat on the body, and delivering a verdict of Wilful Murder, his lordship was committed to the gaol of Leicester.

After remaining in the above place about a fortnight, he was conveyed to London in his own landeau. He behaved with the utmost composure during the journey, and being taken before the House of Peers, the verdict of the coroner's jury was read; on which he was committed to the Tower.

His Lordship's place of confinement was the Round Tower, near the Draw Bridge. Two wardens constantly attended in his room, and one waited at the door, At the bottom of the stairs two soldiers were placed, with their bayonets fixed; and a third was stationed on the drawbridge; and the gates of the Tower were shut an hour before the usual time, in consequence of his imprisonment.

Mrs. Clifford now brought her four children to London, and taking lodgings in Tower street, she sent messages to his lordship several times in the day, and answers being sent, the communication became troublesome; so that their messages were forbid to pass more than once in the day.

While in the Tower, Lord Ferrers lived in a regular manner. His breakfast consisted of a muffin, and a bason of tea, with a spoonful of brandy in it. After dinner and supper, he drank a pint of wine mixed with water. His behaviour in general was decent, but he sometimes exhibited evident proofs of discomposure of mind. His natural children were permitted to be with him sometimes: but Mrs. Clifford was denied admittance, after repeated applications.

Preparations being made for Lord Ferrers' trial and Lord Henley (the Chancellor) being created High Steward on the occasion, the trial came on before the House of Peers, in Westminster hall, on the 16th of April, 1760. The proof of the fact was sufficiently clear; but Lord Ferrers cross examined the witnesses in such a manner as gave sufficient proof of the sanity of his mind, of which some doubts had been entertained.

Being found guilty by the unanimous voice of the Peers of Great Britain, the Lord High Steward passed sentence that he should be executed on the 21st of April, but his sentence was respited to the 5th of May.

While in the tower, Lord Ferrers left sixty pounds a year to Mrs. Clifford, a thousand pounds to each of his natural daughters, and thir

en hundred pounds to the children of Mr. John-
on.

This unhappy nobleman petitioned to be behead-
d within the Tower: but, as the crime was so
trocious, the king refused to mitigate the sen-
ence. A scaffold was erected under the gallows
t Tyburn, and covered with baize: and a part of
he scaffold, on which he was to stand, was raised
bout eighteen inches above the rest.

About nine o'clock, the sheriffs attended at the
ower gate; and Lord Ferrers being told that
hey were, come, requested that he might go in
is own landau, instead of a mourning coach,
hich had been prepared for him. No objection
eing made to this request, he entered the landau,
ttended by the Rev. J. Mumphries, chaplain of
he Tower. His Lordship was dressed in a white
uit richly embroidered with silver, and when he
ut it on, he said. This is the suit in which I was
arried, and in which I will die.

Mr. Sheriff Vaillant joined them at the Tower-
ate, and taking his seat in the landau, told his
ordship how disagreeable it was to wait on him
n so awful an occasion, but that he would endea-
our to render his situation as little irksome as
ossible.

The procession now moved slowly through an
mmense crowd of spectators. On their way,
ord Ferrers asked Mr. Vaillant, if ever he had
een such a crowd? the Sheriff answered in the
egative: to which the unhappy peer replied, I
uppose it is because they never saw a Lord hang-
d before.

The chaplain observing that the public would

be naturally inquisitive about his Lordship's reli
gious opinion; he'replied, that he did not think
himself accountable to the world for his sentiment
on religion; but that he always believed in one
God, the maker of all things; that whatever were
his religious notions, he had never propagated
them; that all countries had a form of religion
by which the people were governed, and whoever
disturbed them in it, he considered them as an
enemy to society: that he thought Lord Boling
broke to blame, for permitting his sentiments of
religion to be published to the world. And h
made other observations of a like nature.

Respecting the death of Mr Johnson, he said
he was under particular circumstances, and he
met with so many crosses and vexations, that h
scarce knew what he did; but declared that h
had no malice against the unfortunate man.

So immense was the crowd, that it was near
three hours before the procession reached the plac
of execution, on the way to which Lord Ferrer
desired to stop to have a glass of wine and water
but the sheriff observing that it would only draw
a greater crowd about him, he replied, that is true
I say no more; let us by no means stop. He
likewise observed that the preliminary apparatus
of death produced more terror than death itself.

At the place of execution, he expressed a wis
to take a final leave of Mrs. Clifford; but the
Sheriff advised him to decline it, as it would dis
arm him of the fortitude he possessed; to which
he answered, If you, Sir, think I am wrong,
submit; after which he gave the sheriff a pocket
book, containing a bank note. with a ring and

urse of guineas ; which were afterwards delivered
the unhappy woman.

The procession was attended by a party of horse-
grenadiers, and foot-guards, and at the place of
execution was met by another party of horse,
which formed a circle round the gallows.

His Lordship walked up the steps of the scaffold
with great composure, and having joined with the
chaplain in repeating the Lord's Prayer, which he
called a fine composition, he spoke the following
words with great fervency, "O God, forgive me
all my errors ! pardon all my sins !"

He gave five guineas to the executioner's assist-
ant by mistake, instead of giving it to himself.
The master demanding the money, a dispute arose
between the parties, which might have discompos-
ed the dying man, had not the Sheriff exerted his
authority to put an end to it.

The executioner now proceeded to do his duty.
Lord Ferrer's neck cloth was taken off, a white
cap, which he had brought in his pocket put on
his head, his arms secured with a black sash, and
the halter put round his neck.   He then ascended
the raised part of the scaffold, and the cap being
pulled over his face, the Sheriff gave a signal, on
which the raised scaffold was struck, and remained
level with the rest,

After hanging an hour and five minutes, the
body was put into a coffin lined with white satin,
and conveyed to surgeon's hall, where an incision
was made from the neck to the bottom of the
breast, and the bowels were taken out : on inspection of which, the surgeons declared that they had

never beheld greater signs of long life in any subject who had come under their notice.

His Lordship's hat and halter lay near his feet
in the coffin, on the lid of which were these words:
Lawrence Earl Ferrers, suffered May 5th, 1760.
After the body had remained some time at surgeon's halls, for inspection, it was delivered to his
friends for interment : but it would be unjust to
his memory not to mention, that during his imprisonment, he made pecuniary recompense to several persons whom he had injured during the extravagance of those passions to which he was un-
happily subject.

His Lordship gave his gold watch to Sheriff
Vaillant, who kept it in his possession. Upon the
subject of the subsequent part of his punishment,
viz. that of dissection, was strenuously opposed by
his friends, many of whom petitioned the throne,
as well as the master and wardens of the corpora-
tion of surgeons. The late Selina, Countess of
Huntingdon, was in the foremost rank in her endeavours to obtain a remittance of the posthumous
part of his punishment : but Counsellor Murray,
afterwards Lord Chief Justice, gave it as his opinion, that the act of Parliament respecting the
capital punishment of murder, was not to be tri-
fled with.

Reflections —Lord Ferrers appears to have been
uninfluenced by the mild doctrines of Christianity.
If these had held their proper weight on his mind
it would have been impossible that he could have
acted as he did; but when religion fails to produce its natural, its genuine effects, then may

ceases to appear as such, and becomes an object of compassion, if not contempt!

WILLIAM HONEYMAN,

(THE YOUNG SWINLDER,)

Convicted for forgery at the Lent Assixes, 1806. for Kent, and executed upon Pennenden Heath.

THIS young adept was born at Portsmouth, of creditable parents. and who, after giving him a good education. placed him as midshipman in the royal navy. However, he had not been long on board the man of war to which he was appointed, then stationed at Sheerness, ere he deserted, and began his career of vice at a tavern called the Silver Oar, at Rochester. before he had completed his sixteenth year. There he was invited by some gentlemen to partake of their dinner, which was no sooner over than they perceived he had no money. and appeared dejected, and upon interrogation, he confessed his name and needy circumstances; the company, much to their credit, agreed to supply him with money, and he was kept there till his friends were made acquainted with his situation : when, according to their desire, he was forwarded to London.

He returned some time after to the Silver Oar, saying he had been to see, ordered a dinner, and treated his former friends.

Afterwards he took a route to the West of England, following his nefarious practices. However, on the 18th of November, 1805, under the name of Alexander Innes, captain in the navy, he was brought to Marlborough-street Police-office, in custody of an officer belonging to Surrey, to answer a charge preferred against him by a Mr. Jeff, a liveryman, in Silver-street, Golden-square.

Mr. Jeff stated, that the prisoner called at his stables on the ninth day of November, representing himself as the person above described, and residing at No. 49, Howland-street, and hired a chesnut mare to go to Richmond. The mare was never returned to the owner; and after a week had elapsed, Mr. Jeff suspected he had been swindled. He consequently went to the given address, and had there further cause of suspicion; for the house was a brothel, and he was only known to have slept there one night.

In consequence of some information Mr. Jeff had received, he went to the house of an eminent tradesman in the Borough, where, it was said, the prisoner was known, having drawn money by bills, &c. Mr. Jeff was there informed of the circumstances alluded to, and that Captain Innes had sent thither a mare from the country, which had been attended with unpleasant circumstances. The parties, however said, they knew but little of the prisoner.

He was detected by calling at the Gloucester coffee house, Piccadilly, which house he had frequented with a person of the name of Kennesley, who left it without discharging his bill. The prisoner called to enquire after his friend, on leaving the house, two of the waiters followed him, suspecting him to be the person advertised by Mr. Jeff. At a convenient spot near Vauxhall, the waiters gave him into the charge of an officer.

It was stated to the magistrate, that the prisoner had been at the Castle, at Richmond, where the waiter was refused his bill; but by assistance the visitors were detained, and a watch was left as a security for the bill.

Mr. Jeff had never heard of his mare, but it was reported she was at Andover, Hants. When at Richmond, on Sunday, at the Castle Inn, he was informed that a mare, answering the description of the one hired, was sold on Wednesday last, at Croydon, to a butcher at Richmond; but he had not an opportunity of seeing her, the butcher being from home. On the prisoner being questioned respecting what he had done with the mare, he merely answered, he had spoken to Mr. Jeff on that subject. He was dressed in the first style of fashion, and his person was very well known in the lobby at the theatres.

The next day the concourse of people that assembled at Marlborough street Office was immense. Several naval officers attended, for the purpose of proving that there were only two captains in the navy of the names of Innes: they are brothers, and gentlemen of the highest respectability; the one, Alexander, being captain on board the Eurus frigate in the Cove of Cork; and the other, John, prisoner in France, having been taken in the Ranger.

I

Several persons intimated their intentions of exhibiting charges against the prisoner on the next examination, which took place November 21st. Numerous fresh charges were adduced against him; and it appeared by the evidence, that an insinuating confident address, with a commanding person, had enabled him to enter the circles of gentlemen, whom he is said to have defrauded, as well as trades-people, inn keepers, &c., in town and country.—The horses he hired of Mr. Jeff had been traced to George-yard, Drury lane.

John Rich, ostler to Mr. Cartwright, Camden-place, Piccadilly, stated, that the prisoner hired a brown gelding six weeks since, in the absence of his master. He said he resided in St. James-street; that he merely wanted to ride out for two or three hours, and on his return he would send the horse home by his servant. He, however, never returned, nor had the horse ever been heard of. A person in the office (Mr. Nuns) informed Mr. Cartwright, that a horse answering the description he had given, was left at his Livery stables, Vauxhall, on the 14th of October, and he believed by the prisoner. He hired a horse and chaise of Mr. Nuns, and left the horse in his care, until he should return, which event never took place. The prisoner said his name was Becket, and that he resided at Gravesend. Mr. Nuns, finding the prisoner did not return, went to Gravesend, and Mr. Becket proved to be a banker, who informed him that a person answering the description of the prisoner, had forged on his bank. Mr. Nuns had travelled three or four hundred miles after his horse and chaise; and at length by an advertisement, he received a letter, stating, that the horse was at Alton, in Hampshire, and the chaise was at Honiton, in Devonshire, the prisoner having left the horse as he had done at other places, and hired a fresh one.

It was proved by another witness, that the prisoner had committed depredations in the West of England, by representing himself as a Mr. Pigeon, son of Mr. Pigeon belonging to a distillery firm in the Borough. By this imposition, affecting to be travelling on account of the firm, he was very successful in obtaining money, by swindling, bills, &c. In this part of the country he drove about in a postchaise and pair, associated with the best company, joined their hunting parties, and became the complete man of fashion. At Exeter the he drove through the city a week before the news of victory over the combined fleet, as a naval officer with despatches from the fleet. The gentlemen belonging to a subscription house, and the leading men of the city, desirous of hearing good news, politely requested to be informed if the news was good. The prisoner, who represented himself as the son of the Lord Mulgrave, assured them that it was good news, and that it was from the hero, Nelson. The gentlemen were desirous of further information; but fearing to put the question too pointedly, they asked, if it equalled the business of the Nile? The prisoner replied, The Nile is a fool to it; and he immediately drove off, having diffused joy throughout the ancient city of Exeter.

A number of other charges were brought against him. A gentleman positively proved the prisoner to be an impostor, in representing himself as Capt.

Innes. The prisoner said his name was Innes, and he was addressed as a captain by naval characters. On being questioned by the magistrates, if he was ever in the navy, and what rank he held? the prisoner replied, He was a midshipman in the Magnunime, of sixty-four guns, but had not been in the service since last war. He was before that in the Active, of thirty-two guns. He was remanded again, in order to give country people an opportunity to attend: and on the day appointed, the office was crowded so excessively, that many who repaired thither to take a view of the prisoner, were disappointed.

Among other circumstances, Hamilton, the officer, said that he was authorized by the gentlemen of the Gravesend Bank, to state a circumstance that recently occurred there, the complainants being unable to attend this examination; the prisoner in the name of Charles Young, presented to them a bill of exchange for eighty pounds, purporting to have been drawn upon Simmons and Co. at the Canterbury Bank, for which he received cash and notes, and they soon afterwards discovered it to be a forgery.

There was also another serious charge against the prisoner, for a transaction during his tour in the west of England. It had been stated that the prisoner diffused joy throughout the city of Exeter, by proclaiming a victory, said to have been gained by the departed hero, Nelson, a week before that of Trafalgar. He also, it appeared, represented himself as the bearer of joyful tidings, when the glorious victory was obtained. Being on the Portsmouth road when Lord Fitzroy was travelling to the Admiralty, with the important news, and having obtained some slight information respecting it, or at least that his lordship was going with despatches to town, he immediately ordered a post chaise and four, and was driven after the messenger at full speed. On his entering the town of Basingstoke, his chaise was surrounded by the multitude, who were more ready to be imposed on, a ray of hope having spread itself that a victory had been gained. In the habit of a naval officer, the prisoner went to the bank, called himself Lord Fitzroy, drew 100l. in his name, and gave a forged draft. He apologized to the gentlemen of the bank for the sudden intrusion, and alleged that his cash was insufficient to carry him to the Admiralty. This imposition was soon detected, the prisoner was followed, and the money recovered. On his being asked if he had any thing to say, he replied, he had not, in his present disagreeable situation. The magistrates observed, that it would be necessary to remand the prisoner again, in order to give time for the people to attend; when a gentleman, from the Gravesend Bank attended, and the prisoner was fully committed to take his trial, and soon after removed to Maidstone (the forgery having been done in Kent,) where he was indicted March 12, 1809, for feloniously and falsely making, forging, and counterfeiting, and feloniously uttering and publishing as true, at Gravesend, a certain false, forged, and counterfeited bill of exchange, for the sum of eighty pounds, purporting to have been drawn by one Charles Young, and to be directed to Messrs. Simmonds, Poley, and Co. at Canterbury, with intent to defraud John Brenchley,

Charles Becket, and George Rich, of Gravesend aforesaid.

He also stood indicted upon the oaths of John Rich, and others, with stealing one brown gelding, the property of Edward Cartwright.

He also stood indicted, upon the oath of Richard Nuns, with stealing at Lambeth, in the county of Surrey, one black mare, a chaise, and harness, his property.

On the first indictment, it appeared he came to the Gravesend Bank, and represented himself as a person under the tuition of Mr. Stevenson, (steward to the Earl of Darnley,) for a knowledge of agricultural improvement, which afterwards proved to be false. The fraud on the Bank being substantiated by the clerk, the jury, after a little deliberation, found the prisoner guilty; and being found guilty upon the first charge, the judge would not try him on the others.

From the time of the judge's passing sentence on him, and informing him he could not expect mercy, the crime being so great an offence, he became much dejected, and behaved himself in a very becoming manner.

On the 28th of March, the unfortunate prisoner wrote a letter from the cell to the Gravesend, Bank, acknowledging the crime laid to his charge, thanking the prosecutors for their humanity in recommending him to the Judge for mercy, and requesting they would sign a petition to the king; which had been done before, but which the prisoner was not aware of. He stated in his letter, that he was deranged at the time of committing the act. He also said, it had ever been his father's wish to train him in the world to friendly society. He made the following speech at the place of execution, from a written paper, which he gave to a friend, upon his request :

For my own part, I confess, with the greatest contrition, the crime which has brought me to this horrid place. and admit the justice of my sentence, while I am sinking under its severity; and I earnestly exhort you all, my fellow-prisoners, and young men at liberty, to acknowledge the offences you have been guilty of, and to bequeath to your country that confidence in public justice, without which there cannot be either peace or safety in this world.

As few of you suffer for the first offences, it is necessary to enquire how far confession ought to be extended. Whatever good remains in our power we must diligently perform. We must prevent, to the utmost of our power, all the evil consequences of our crimes. We must forgive all who injure us. We must, by fervent prayer, and always praying to God, in constancy and meditation, endeavour to repress all worldly passions; and generate in our minds that love of goodness, and hatred of sin, which may fit us for the society of heavenly minds; and finally, we must commend and entrust our souls to him that died for the sins of men, with earnest wishes and humble hopes that he will admit us with the labourers who entered the vineyard at the last hour, and associate us with the thief he pardoned on the cross.

Thus. we humbly trust, our sorrowful petitions and prayers will be acceptable in his sight. Thus shall we be qualified through Christ, to exchange this dismal body and these uneasy fetters. for the glorious liberty of the sons of God, and then our legal doom on earth will be changed into a comfortable declaration of mercy in the highest heaven, and all through the most precious and all sufficient merits of the blessed Saviour of mankind.

I wish you all the happiness that this land affords, and the enjoyment of life in all its branches. You, my brothers and sisters, will, I hope, take caution of so young a man as I am, whose years are only eighteen, and to think that I should suffer this ignominious and awful death before so many of you. Our happiness or misery only begins when we die.

It is but your sins that can make you afraid of dying. It concerns us more than our life is worth, to know what will become of us when we die.

This speech which was spoken in a manly and distinct tone, made a deep impression on an unusual number of spectators (many of whom were soldiers). Shortly after he seemed to reflect on the jury, and the severity of the law of this country, by saying, So young a man as he was, might have been useful in being sent abroad; because the petition had been presented, and interest made in vain, to his majesty to save his life. He behaved however, with the greatest decorum at

e place of execution, praying in most penitent
anner, till the platform fell under him.

EORGE KENNEDY, MARTIN MOODY, AND RICHARD BARTON,

(SOLDIERS OF THE FOOT GUARDS.)

*nvicted of a Robbery, attended with circum-
stances of cruelty.*

HESE men to the disgrace of the character of
e soldier, were indicted for assaulting and dan-
rously wounding, on the 14th of November,
04, on the king's highway between Sandwich
d Deal, George John Piercy Leith, and feloni-
sly robbing him of a quantity of bank notes, a
ver watch, and some money. .

Mr. Leith deposed that he lived at Walmer, and
the 14th of November he had been at Sandwich
arket: in the evening he was returning home to
house, which was about six miles from Sand-
ch. It was a fine evening and the moon shone
y bright. When he came to Shoudham Downs
ere the road turns off towards Fowlney chalk-
, he observed three soldiers walking before him ;
e was in a red jacket faced with blue, the uni-
m of the guards ; and the other two had forag-
dresses. When he came up with them, he
eived a violent blow on the left cheek, which
ocked out one of his teeth, and swelled his eye
as to blind him. At the same instant, the man

who gave the blow called out to the other in
Comrade stop him. His horse started out of
road, and went a little way over the plough
ground, but the bridle was seized by the man
the round frock. One of them said, your mon
another said, yes and soon. Whether he recei
another blow at this instant he could not tell,
whether he was pulled off, but he fell from
horse which ran away. They left him for a
ment as he lay upon the ground ; but seeing th
approach him again, he put his hand in his poc
and gave them the bag containing the notes
money. One of them, with great dexterity, put
finger into his fob, and hooked out his wa
which he wore without a chain. They then
ran away. The prosecutor then got up, and
the moon shine very bright on the turnpike ro
he soon after met a James Wyburn, and with
assistance got home. He would not swear to
person of any of the prisoners, but he thought
Barton was the man in red, and Kennedy the
who stood at the head of his horse. He had t
day at Sandwich received sixteen five-guinea
sixteen one guinea notes.

Serjeant John Rutter, of the third battalion
the first regiment of guards, deposed that, Bar
and Moody belonged to the same company as hi
self, and Kennedy to the same regiment.
Thursday the 15th of November, as the witn
was visiting the quarters of the married m
who lived out of the barracks, he saw Moo
come into a public-house in Deal. Moody ask
another soldier if he would drink, and offered
treat him with half-a-pint of gin if he would

h him. The sergeant said, he had seen the
nd-bills that morning, which gave an account
the robbery, and he knew that Moody had no
ney the day before, because the witness had
t him a shilling. Finding that he was appa-
ntly flush of money, it raised his suspicion; he
wever said nothing, but went home to the bar-
cks. Barton had been sent to the guard-house
t evening, for coming drunk to the parade;
d about eight o'clock, Moody came in, and ask-
, If all was well? The witness supposed he
ant to ask, whether he was home in time, and
swered, Yes. He then inquired why Barton
s in custody, and was told for being drunk at
rade. He next asked the witness, if he had any
jection to let a comrade sing a song, as they
re undressing; the sergeant replied that it was
t nine, he had no objection to the song. He
tched Moody as he was undressing, and obser-
d him to take the jacket from under the head
his bed-fellow, who was asleep, and substitute
own, putting Austin's, the other man's, under
own head. The witness was then obliged to
ve them to attend the roll-call of non-commis-
ned officers. He then concerted with Sergeant
ung, and it was agreed that the latter should
me into Moody's room, and say that he had or-
rs to search all men in liquor. In consequence
this plan, Sergeant Young came in shortly af-
and searched Moody's bed: he took his jacket
m under Austin's head and between the cloth
d the lining they found the watch, and three
-guinea notes, answering the description in the
nd-bill.

Sergeant Aylesbury deposed, that Barton
committed to custody that day for being drunk
parade. Moody came in that day about four,
he observed that he had some private talk
with Barton. At a quarter before nine, the
ness received orders to search Barton, which
did, and between the lining and cloth of his ja
sleeves, he found several Bank notes, all of wh
corresponded in number and value with those
scribed in the hand-bills advertising the robb
He delivered them all over to sergeant-major
quboun.

The sergeant-major was called who corrobo
ed the testimony of the last witness, and depo
that he delivered them over to the constable
the presence of the magistrate.

Thomas Simmons a victualler at Walmer,
posed that the morning after the three prison
were taken into custody, he went to the gu
room about half-past seven, to carry the serge
on guard some beer. Moody complained that
was uncomfortable, and begged the sergeant
take his handcuffs off for awhile, that he mi
tighten himself up. The sergeant said he co
not do that, but if he would sit on the table,
would button his jacket and gaiters for him.
did so ; and as he was buttoning his jacket abo
his breast, he said, Moody, you have no collar
Moody replied, Never mind, we shall soon hav
hempen collar that will fit us all. Barton sa
If you have one, I shall have one too, for I sto
ped his horse. Kennedy joined and said, But
was he who demanded his money ; and as he did n
give it, I brought him down with a topper of

geon; I thought the horse had stamped upon
head when he was down. They then said, af-
he was down they robbed him of a handful of
s, his watch, half a guinea, and a crown piece.
ton said to Kennedy, I am sorry you beat him:
n we went out I ordered you to rob, but not
murder. They then described what they had
rally done after the robbery. They had all
e the best of their way to the barracks, pass-
Deal Castle, and then buried the notes that
ht under a large stone between the Castle and
beach. Moody and Barton said, that they
t home to bed. Kennedy said he went to the
teen, where he got a roll, a herring, and a
t of beer to refresh himself.

ergeants Aylesbury and Young both corrobor-
d this account of the last witness, and said the
oners described what they had done in a kind
bravado manner.

William Wyburn, the constable, produced the
es and watch, which was sworn to by Mr.
ith: and he added, that he had also lost half a
nea and a crown piece, as stated by the pri-
ers, although they were not stated in the in-
ctment.

Mr. Hodgson, a partner in the Sandwich Bank,
amined the notes, and comparing them with his
ok, deposed that they were all paid by him to
. Leith, at Sandwich, on the day of the rob-
ry.

The jury found all the prisoners guilty.

Barton who was a very handsome man, pleaded
uch with the judge for his life; and from its
ving appeared that he was the least cruel of

the three he received a respite, and was sent to serve his country the remainder of his life in some distant settlement; but Kennedy and Moody were executed.

LAURENCE JONES,

(A NOTORIOUS SWINDLER,)

Sentenced to death in 1763, but who hanged himself three days previous to that appointed for his execution.

THOUGH many writers have attempted some moral excuse for suicide, yet we find it inexcuseable in any point of view. Hamlet says,

The Almighty fix'd his cannon 'gainst self murder.

The prince, therefore, though robbed of succession to the throne of Denmark, and with the knowledge that his father was basely murdered by his uncle, yet he would not, after mature deliberation, take away his own life, which belonged to God alone.

In examining the crime of self murder with the eyes of a philosopher, we find it a cowardly dereliction from the firmness of a great mind.

People can be restrained from sin only by religion or the dread of death; and when both these ties are broken, what crimes may we not expect to be committed? Where laws nor religion no longer prevail, kings will totter on their thrones,

nisters will knock off their perch of power,
d the people in one general wreck, again sink
to the barbarity of the earliest times.

The self murderer Jones, was born in London,
respectable parents, whose too great indulgence
wards him in his early years, probably led to
s untimely end. He received a genteel educa-
n, and possessing a good address, he introduced
mself into the first company, which unfortun-
ely led him into habits of extravagance his in-
me was not equal to: though he enjoyed a lu-
ative employment in one of the public offices,
here being detected in some mal-practices, he
s discharged. His means of subsistence being
w entirely gone, and his character also, he
nd himself under the necessity of doing some-
ing, in order to support himself and a lady of
sy virtue, with whom he cohabited, to whose
travagance there was no end.

He next determined to commence swindler,
hich he continued for some time with the great-
t success, till being suspected, he was at length
prehended and committed to Newgate, where
e contracted an acquaintance with the noted
eorge Barrington who was then in confinement,
evious to his transportation to Botany Bay. A
arrel once arising between Barrington and
nes, a battle ensued in which Barrington came
conqueror, and Jones was beat in a shocking
anner, and for which, it appearing Barrington
as the aggressor, he was confined in the cells of
ewgate.

The session arriving when Jones was to be
ied he was acquitted for want of evidence.

Once again at liberty, and having a considerable sum of money left him by a relation about this time, he resolved to set up in his old trade, on a very extensive scale, for which purpose he took a very handsome house in St. James's, which he had elegantly furnished, kept his carriage and servants, who, by the bye, were accomplices to carry on the deception, which he did with great success for some months.

During his abode in this place, he defrauded Mr. Hudson, a silversmith, of plate, to the value of near three thousand pounds; Mr. Kempton, a mercer, of silks and other goods, to a very large amount; and Mr. Bailey, a watch maker and jeweller, of a gold repeater, &c. &c. to the value of three hundred pounds

The time of payment coming on, and suspicion being entertained of his pretensions to property, he thought it time to decamp. which he effected just in time to escape a warrant out against him,

After this he lived privately for some time, that suspicion might die away, before he again began his fraudulent practices, which he carried on with his usual success, till the affair in Hatton Garden for which he was condemned; the particulars of which are as follow :—

Mr. Campbell was the collecting clerk to Vere, Lucadou, and Co., bankers, in Lombard street, and in the course of his business, he called at a house (which was hired for the express purpose of preying upon the unwary) for the payment of a bill, a scheme concerted before by the villains.

No sooner had he knocked at the door than it was opened by a person, in the appearance of a gentleman, who desired him to walk into the counting-house, and when he came there, a man came behind him, and covered his head and face over with a thick cap, so that he could see nothing. They then threw him on the floor, and wrapped him up in a green baize, in which condition they bound him hand and foot, and carried him down stairs, when they proceeded to rob him.

They took from him his pocket book, with bank notes and bills to the amount of £900. They next took measures to prevent a discovery before they should receive the money for the bills, &c., with which one of the gang immediately went out to turn them into cash, while the rest, in the mean time, handled the unfortunate young man in the following manner:—

They first laid him flat on his back on a board, and chained him hand and foot, and then carried him down stairs into a back kitchen, where they chained him to the bar of a copper grate, threatening that if he made a noise they would blow his brains out.

They then left him after placing before him some bread, some ham, and some water.

In this condition he remained for about eight hours, not daring to make the least noise, expecting every moment to be murdered if he spoke: but Providence preserved him from this dreadful fate; for hearing no more of them for so many hours, he at last had the courage to call out, thinking it better to have his brains blown out at once than perish in that miserable condition.

After crying out with all his might for near

K

three hours, his cries were at last heard by a man who was at work in a house behind that in which Mr. Campbell was confined. The man had the resolution to break open the door of the house from whence the noise proceeded. when, directed by the cry, he went down stairs, and there discovered the unfortunate man almost expiring, exhausted with struggling and crying out so long.

It was not long before he was set at liberty, and restored to his friends, to their great joy, and infinite satisfaction to his employers.

Jones was apprehended by Jealous and Kennedy, officers of Bow-street, at the King's Arms, in Bridge street, Westminster. Kennedy seeing that he agreed with the description of his person, as lodged at Bow-street, respecting the man that opened the door to Campbell. he took him into custody, with the assistance of Jealous.

Before they attempted to search him, it was judged expedient to call in some assistance, Jones being of rather a refractory disposition, and fearing a rescue might be attempted, there being a great concourse of people in Palace-yard, some of whom might have been his companions.

For that purpose Jealous went out, and left the prisoner with Kennedy till he should return. During Jealous's absence, Jones became very importunate with Kennedy, respecting the cause of his being apprehended.

On Jealous's arrival with a reinforcement of four, viz. M'Manus, Carpmeal, Townsend, and Lavendar, Jones was searched, but nothing of consequence found upon him, except a direction to his lodgings, which he attempted to snatch from Townsend's hand, but failed.

They then proceeded to conduct him to a place of safety; but just as they left the room, Kennedy desired Carpmeal to return, look into the fire-place, and see if there was any thing there, the prisoner having stood with his back against that place: which he did, and returned with a handfull of bills and notes: and then proceeded to a place of security, where they left him, and immediately set off for his lodgings in Peckham Rye-lane, which was the place specified on the paper found in Jones's pocket: and, on their arrival there, found his wife, his brother and two other persons, all of whom were brought together with a great quantity of papers, among which was a letter to Mr. Pitt, the contents of which were not ascertained. On his examination he behaved very insolently.

Being committed to Newgate, he was afterwards tried and found guilty, when he received sentence and was ordered for execution on Wednesday, Dec. 8, 1793, in Hatton Garden, near the house where he committed the robbery; but on Saturday previous thereto, about six o'clock in the morning, when the turnkey entered the cell to prepare him to hear the condemned sermon and receive the sacrament, he found him dead. It appears that he had made several attempts on his life before, but was prevented; and the manner in which he accomplished this worst of all crimes was very extraordinary; he had taken the knee-strings with which his fetters were supported, and tied them round his neck, then tying the other end to the ring which his chain was fastened to, he placed his feet against the wall and strangled himself. The coroner's jury pronounced a verdict of ' Felo de se.'

In consequence of the above verdict, the body was, on Wednesday morning, carried out of Newgate, extended upon a plank on the top of an open cart, in his clothes, and fettered, his face covered with a white cloth, to the brow of Holborn hill, directly opposite to the end of Hatton Garden. The procession was attended by the sheriffs, city-marshals, and near 500 constables. Being arrived at what may be called the place of execution, the body was deposited in a deep pit, and a stake driven through it, according to the coroner's verdict.

JOHN LANCASTER,

Executed at Tyburn, Sept. 24th, 1748.

WE could wish, seriously, to caution all young people against attending fairs. They constitute an assemblage of idle people; and where there is indiscriminately mixed thieves and pickpockets who go from fair to fair, loose women, strolling players, and vagabonds of every description, waiting to plunder the honest part of the people. Saint Bartholomew's fair, from its long continuance, is a school of vice, which has initiated more youth into the habits of villany, than even Newgate. It is but lately, that a numerous gang infant thieves, of both sexes, were detected in committing depredations of every description which they could accomplish. They had, in imitation of Macbeth's gang, their captain and the receiver of the stolen property, who, though the eldest of the confederacy, was not more than thirteen or fourteen years of age!

The parents of John Lancaster were poor but honest people, who put him to school to be instructed in reading, writing, and arithmetic, and, when about fourteen years of age, apprenticed him to a velvet weaver, who, as well as his parents, lived in Whitechapel.

After the term of his servitude expired, he for some time followed his trade as a journeyman.— He was naturally inclined to vicious practices, and constantly associated with the most profligate company. He was known to have committed several offences against the laws, for one of which, however, he was apprehended and secured in Newgate, where he contracted an acquaintance with a man named Lewis. They were both acquitted at the same sessions—Lewis in defect of evidence, and Lancaster because no prosecutor appeared.

They went together to Rumford, predetermined to obtain money by violence. At Stratford they stopped a gentleman, and robbed him of his watch, a guinea, and some silver. Their success in this attempt giving them a great flow of spirits, Lewis (who had long been a notorious thief) said, Come along with me, my boy, and we shall soon get money enough to live like gentlemen: and they agreed to seek no means of support but that dangerous and unjustifiable one of making depredations on the public.

They now determined to go to Smithfield, it being the time of Bartholomew fair, where they stole a silver mug. Leaving the fair, they went to Duke's place, in order to sell the mug to a Jew named Levi Chitty; but he not being at home, they adjourned to a neighbouring alehouse, to wait till his return; but they had not been long there before Lancaster broke open a drawer, and from thence stole several valuable articles. They now paid for the beer they had drunk, and escaped without suspicion.

On the following day they stole a quantity of brass candlesticks, which they sold for fifty shillings to the Jew, who told them that he would not have given so high a price, but that he was desirous of encouraging them to steal articles of greater value. They made a booty of a number of silk handkerchiefs, and the money received for them from the Jew, they spent in the company of a number of prostitutes, among whom was Sarah Cock, the widow of George Cock, who was executed for robbery.

Lancaster, Lewis, and Sarah Cock, went the following evening to the Royal Exchange, where they picked the pockets of several passengers, of watches, pocket-books, purses of money, and other property. They frequented all the places of public resort; and during divine service on a Sunday evening at the Foundery near Moorfields, they picked the pockets of several of the congregation. On their return from the place of worship, they came to the house of a velvet weaver; and Lancaster knowing him to be reputed as a man of considerable property, it was determined to break open and rob the house. Having effected an entrance, they secured a quantity of plate, and then went into the warehouse, whence they sole velvet, to the amount of more than £100. Having obtained this considerable booty, they went to Sarah Cock, and giving her the velvet, adjourned to an alehouse in Houndsditch, to wait till she had disposed of it to the Jew.

The sum Cock demanded for the velvet, the Jew said was more than he could really afford to give, as the colour was very indifferent, and he should be put to expence in sending it to Holland, where all his stolen goods were exported for sale. During their conversation they were observed by a weaver and constable, who suspected the velvet to have been stolen; the woman was interrogated as to the manner of its coming into her possession. She acknowledged having received the property from Lancaster and Lewis, and mentioned the house where they were then waiting: in consequence of which, they were both apprehended, and secured in Newgate.

Lewis being admitted an evidence for the crown, Lancaster was convicted of stealing the silver mug and other property, and sentenced to die. While under sentence of death, the ordinary endeavoured to give him a proper idea of his Creator; but to the very moment of his death he obstinately persisted in a refusal to make what atonement was yet in his power for the many offences he had committed.

MARTIN NOWLAND,

Executed at Tyburn, on the 24th of February, 1742, for High-Treason.

THE folly of a man's attempting to recruit the French army in London, is more to be wondered at, than the commission of the crime. This man, before he attempted to corrupt the allegiance of an Englishman must surely have been apprized of the conviction and execution of Thomas Henning, for enlisting a man for the King of Prussia, which took place just before he accepted a French commission, to commit a similar crime. Little more can be said of Nowland's case, than that it is treasonable in the highest degree, aiming a mortal blow at the constitution of our country, by enticing us to join our enemy. Yet we cannot, however, pass on to particulars, without expressing admiration at the loyalty of the brave soldiers whom he endeavoured to corrupt.

This traitor was a native of Ireland, and while a youth was decoyed from his parents, conveyed to Dunkirk, and entered into the regiment of Dillon. In this station he continued fourteen years, at the end of which time he was sent to London to enlist men into the French service; and was promised a promotion on his return, and a recompence for the diligence he might exert.

On his arrival in London he endeavoured to connect himself with people of the lower ranks, whom he thought most likely to be seduced by his

rtifices: and one day going on the quays near
ondon-bridge, he met with two brothers, named
Meredith, both of them in the army, but who oc-
sionally worked on the quays, to make an addi-
on to their military pay.

Having invited these men to a house in the Bo-
ough, he treated them with liquor, representing
he emoluments that would arise from their enter-
g into the French service; and, among other
hings, said that, exclusive of their pay, they would
ceive four loaves of bread every week.

When they were thus refreshed, Nowland pre-
ailed on them to go to his lodgings in Kent-street,
here he farther regaled them, and then said he
oped they would enter into the service. They
xpressed their readiness to do so: and said they
ould aid him in enlisting several other men, if he
ould spend the evening with them at a public-
ouse in the Strand.

This proposal being assented to, they took him
o a famous alehouse near the Savoy, called the
oal hole, where Nowland was terrified at the
ight of several soldiers of the guards; but on
Meredith's saying they were intimate acquaintance
he parties adjourned to a room by themselves.
Here the brothers asked Nowland how much they
ere to receive for enlisting, which he told them
ould be four guineas; and that he was commis-
ioned to pay their expences till they should join
he regiment.

The intention of the brothers seems to have
een to obtain some money of Nowland; but
nding it was not in his power to advance any
hile they remained in England, one of them went

to the serjeant at the Savoy, informing him
what had past, and asked him how he must di
pose of Nowland.   The serjeant said he must b
detained for the night, and taken before a magi
trate on the following day

On his return to the public-house, Nowlan
produced a certificate, signed by the lieutena
colonel of the regiment, as a proof that he wi
actually in the service of France.   He likewi
said, that the soldiers must dispose of their clothe
and purchase others, to prevent their being detect
ed at Dover ; and he repeated his promise of th
bounty money, and other accommodations prope
for a soldier, on their reaching the regiment.

When the Merediths, and other soldiers, ha
drank at Nowland's expence till they were sati
fied, they conveyed him to the round house, an
on the following day, took him before a magistrat
to whom, after some hesitation, he acknowledge
that he had been employed to enlist men for th
Irish brigades in the service of France

Enquiry being made respecting his accomplice
he acknowledged that a captain belonging to hi
regiment was in London, and that some othe
agents were soon expected in the kingdom : o
which he was informed that he should be admitte
an evidence if he would impeach the accomplice
He replied, that " he was a man of honour, an
would never be guilty of hanging any other perso
to save his own life."

He was committed to Newgate in consequene
of this confession, and being brought to his tri
he was convicted at the following sessions at th
Old Bailey, and received sentence of death.

Nowland being of the Roman Catholic persua-
on, it is not possible to give a particular account
his behaviour after conviction ; as he declined
holding any correspondence with the ordinary of
Newgate. When he came to the fatal tree, he
performed his devotions in his own way, and being
executed, his body was carried to St. Giles's, and
son afterwards buried in St. Pancras churchyard,
by some of his Roman Catholic friends.

MARTHA TRACEY,

*executed at Tyburn, February 16th, 1745, for a
street Robbery.*

THE fate of this unfortunate malefactor adduces
another instance of the melancholy effects of female seduction. The man who robs an innocent
girl of her virtue, and then abandons her to shame
and want, though the law has not made provision
for an adequate punishment, yet surely, he never
more can taste the sweets of a contented mind.

This much injured but vain woman was a native
of Bristol, and descended from poor parents, who
educated her in the best manner in their power.
Getting a place in the service of a merchant, when
she was sixteen years of age, she lived with him
three years, and then came to London.

Having procured a place in a house where
lodgings were let to single gentlemen, and being
a girl of very elegant appearance, and particularly

fond of dress, she was liable to a variety of temptations.

Her vanity being even more than equal to her beauty, she at length conceived that she had made a conquest of one of the gentlemen lodgers, and was presumptious enough to imagine he would marry her.

With a view of keeping alive the passion she thought she had inspired, she sought every pretence of going into his chamber, and he having some design against her virtue, purchased for her some new clothes, in which she went to church on the following Sunday, where she was observed by her mistress.

On their return from church, the mistress immediately enquired how she came to be possessed of such fine clothes; and having learnt the real state of the case. she was discharged from her situation on the Monday morning.

As she still thought the gentleman intended marrying her, she wrote to him, desiring that he would meet her at a public house; and on his attending, she wept incessantly, and complained of the treatment she had received from her mistress, which she attributed to the presents she had received from him.

The seducer advised her to calm her spirits, and go to lodgings which he would immediately provide for her, and where he could securely visit her till the marriage should take place.

Deluded by this artifice, she went that day to lodge at a house in the Strand, which he said was kept by a lady who was related to him. In this place he visited her on the following day, and several successive days; attended her to public places, and making her presents of elegant clothes, which effectually flattered her vanity, and lulled asleep the small remains of her virtue.

It is needless to say that her ruin followed. After a connection of a few months, she found him less frequent in his visits; and informing him that she was with child, demanded that he would make good his promise of marriage: on which he declared that he had never intended marrying her, and that he would not maintain her any longer and hinted that she should seek another lodging.

On the following day the mistress of the house told her that she must not stay there any longer; unless she would pay for her lodgings in advance, which, being unable to to, or perhaps unwilling to remain in a house where she had been so unworthily treated, she packed up her effects, and removed to another lodging.

When she was brought to bed, the father took away the infant, and left the wretched mother in a very distressed situation. Having subsisted for some time by pawning her clothes, she was at length so much reduced as to listen to the advice of a woman of the town, who persuaded her to procure herself a subsistence by the casual wages of prostitution.

Having embarked in this horrid course of life, she very soon became a common street-walker, and experienced all the bitter calamities incident to so deplorable a situation. Being sometimes tempted to pick pockets for a subsistence, she became an occasional visitor at Bridewell, where her mind grew only the more corrupt by the conversation of the abandoned wretches who were confined in that place.

We come now to speak of the fact, the commission of which forfeited her life to the violated laws of her country.

At the sessions held at the Old Bailey, in the month of January, 1745, she was indicted for robbing William Humphreys of a guinea on the king's highway.

The fact was, that being passing, at midnight near Northumberland-house in the Strand, she accosted Mr. Humphreys, who declining to hold any correspondence with her, two fellows with whom she was connected came up, and one of them knocking him down, they both ran away; when she robbed him of a guinea which she concealed in her mouth: but Mr. Humphreys seizing her, and two persons coming up, she was conducted to the watch-house, where the guinea was found in her mouth, as above mentioned, by the constable of the night.

At her trial, it was proved that she had called the men, one of whom knocked down the prosecutor; so that there could be no doubt of her being an accomplice with him; whereupon the jury brought her in guilty.

After conviction she appeared to have a proper idea of her former guilt, and the horrors of her present situation. In fact she was a sincere penitent, and lamented that pride of heart which had first seduced her to destruction.

She behaved with the greatest decency and propriety to the last moment of her life.

ROBERT RAMSEY,

(HIGHWAYMAN AND A SINGULAR CHEAT,)

Executed at Tyburn, on the 13th of June, 1742.

In the trick which this man played upon a clergyman, we know not which of them the most to despise: whether the avarice and gluttony of the latter, or the knavery of the cheat preponderates, we leave to the reader: the one would have defrauded the church, and the other robbed the clergyman! In this assumed character of quack doctor we have a proof of the credulity of mankind: and we are somewhat relieved from the odium which arises at the recital of his deceptions, by the escape of an unsuspicious female's honour, though purchased by the neprivation of a part of her fortune. This man's fate deserves little commiseration; and more especially as a liberal education might have taught him to lead a life of virtue.

This offender was born of respectable parents near Grosvenor square, and apprenticed to an apothecary, after being liberally educated at Westminster school. His master's circumstances becoming embarrassed, Ramsey left him, and went into the service of another gentleman of the same profession.

He now became a professed gamester. The billiard and hazard tables engrossed his time; and his skill being great, he often stripped his companions: yet the money he thus obtained, he squandered away in the most extravagant manner.

Having made an acquaintance with one Carr, they singled out a clergyman who frequented the coffee house they used, as a proper object to impose upon: and having ingratiated themselves into his good opinion, Ramsey took the opportunity of Carr's absence to tell the clergyman that he had a secret of the utmost consequence to impart: the clergyman having promised secresy, the other said that Carr was in love with a young widow, who was very rich, and inclined to marry him; but that the match was opposed by her relations.

He added that the lady herself was averse to being married at the Fleet, even if she could escape the vigilance of her relations so far as to reach that place. The clergyman listening to the story, Ramsey offered him twenty guineas to marry the young couple: and it was agreed that the parties should meet at a tavern near the Royal Exchange on the following day.

Ramsey, having told Carr what had passed, went to the clergyman the next morning; and observing that if the lady took her own footman he might be known, said he would disguise himself in livery, and attend the priest.

This being done, a hackney coach was called for the clergyman, and Ramsey getting up behind it, they drove to the tavern, where rich wines were called for, of which Ramsey urged the clergyman to drink so freely that he fell asleep when Ramsey picked his pocket of his keys.

The clergyman awaking, enquired for the couple that were to be married; on which Ramsey, calling for more wine, said he would go in search of them; but immediately calling for a coach, he went to the clergyman's lodgings, and producing the keys, said he had been sent by the gentleman for some papers in his cabinet.

The landlady of the house, seeing the keys, permitted him to search for what he wanted; on which he stole a diamond ring of the value of forty pounds, and about a hundred pounds in money, and carried off some papers.

This being done, he returned to the clergyman, said the young couple would attend in a short time, and desired him to order a genteel dinner: but this last injunction was unnecessary, for the parson had taken previous care of it: and while he was at dinner, said he would go and order a diamond, and a plain gold ring, and would return immediately.

He had not been long absent, when a jeweller brought the rings, which he said were for a baronet and his lady who were coming to be married. The clergyman asked him to drink the healths of the young couple; and just at this juncture Ramsey came in and told the jeweller that he was instantly wanted at home: but that he must return without loss of time, as his master's arrival was immediately expected.

The jeweller was no sooner gone than Ramsey, taking up the diamond ring, said that he had brought a wrong one, and he would go back and rectify the mistake. In the interim the jeweller, finding that he had not been wanted at home, began to suspect that some undue artifice had

been used ; on which he hurried to the tavern,
and thought himself happy to find that the parson
had not decamped.

Having privately directed the waiter to procure a constable, he charged the clergyman with
defrauding him of the rings. The other was
naturally astonished at such a charge : but the
jeweller insisted on taking him before a magistrate ; where he related a tale that, some days
before, those rings had been ordered by a man
whom he supposed to be an accomplice of the
person now charged ; but the clergyman being a
man of fair character, sent for some reputable
people to bail him ; while the jeweller returned
home, cursing his ill fortune for the trick that
had been put upon him.

London being an unsafe place for Ramsey
longer to reside in, he went to Chester, where he
assumed the character of an Irish gentleman,
who had been to study physic in Holland, and
was now going back to his native country.
During his residence at Chester he insinuated
that he was in possession of a specific cure for
the gout ; and the landlord of the inn he put up
at being ill of that disorder, took the medicine;
and his fit leaving him in a few days, he ascribed
the cure to the supposed nostrum.

Ramsey having gone by the name of Johnson
in this city, now dressed himself as a physician,
and having printed and dispersed hand-bills, giving an account of many patients whose disorders
had yielded to his skill, and promising to cure the
poor without expense, no person doubted either

the character or the abilities of Doctor John-son.

A young lady who was troubled with an asthma became one of his patients; and Ramsey presuming that she possessed a good fortune, insinuated himself so far into her good graces that she would have married him; but that her uncle, in whose hands her money was, happened to come to Chester at that juncture.

The young lady acquainted the uncle with the proposed marriage; on which the old gentleman observed that it would be imprudent to marry a man with whose circumstances and character she was wholly unacquainted; on which she consented that the necessary enquiries should be made; but to this her consent was reluctantly obtained as she was entirely devoted to her lover.

Hereupon Ramsey put into the uncle's hands copies of several letters which he said he had written to some people of distinction, who would answer for his character. By this finesse he hoped to get time to prevail on the lady to marry him privately, which, indeed, she would readily have done, but through fear of offending her uncle.

During this situation of affairs, while Ramsey was walking about the city, he happened to see the clergyman above mentioned, whom he had so much injured in London; on which he hastily retired to a public house in Chester, and sent a person to Park-gate, to enquire when any ship would sail for Ireland: and the answer brought was, that a vessel would sail that very night.

On receiving this intelligence, Ramsey went

and drank tea with the young lady; and taking the opportunity of her absence from the room, he opened a drawer, whence he took a diamond ring, and fifty guineas, out of eighty, which were in a bag.

Some little time afterwards he asked the lady to spend the evening at his lodgings, and play a game at cards; and having obtained her consent, they spent some time with apparent satisfaction; but Ramsey going down stairs, returned in great haste, and said that her uncle was below. As she appeared frightened by this circumstance, he locked her in the room, first giving her a book to read, and said that if her uncle should desire to come up, he would pretend to have lost the key of the door.

The intent of this plan was to effect his escape while she was confined; and having got on board the ship the same evening, he sent her a letter, of which the following is a copy;—

Dear Madam,

I doubt not but you will be extremely surprised at the sudden disappearance of your lover, but when you begin to consider what a dreadful precipice you have escaped, you will bless your stars. By the time this comes to hand, I shall be pretty near London, and as for the trifle I borrowed of you, I hope you will excuse it, as you know I might have taken the whole, if I would; but you see there is still some conscience among the doctors.

The ring I intend to keep for your sake, unless the hazard table disappoints me, and if so fortune puts it in my power, I will make you a suitable return ; but till then, take this advice, never let a strange doctor possess your affections any more.

I had almost forgot to ask pardon for making you my prisoner ; but I doubt not but old Starch-face your uncle, would detain me a little longer, if he could find me. Adieu !

R. JOHNSON.

This letter he committed to the care of a person who was to go to Chester in a few days : and in the interim, Ramsey reached Dublin, where, having dissipated his money in extravagance, he embarked in a ship bound to Bristol, whence he travelled to London.

On his arrival in the metropolis, he found his younger brother, who had likewise supported himself by acts of dishonesty : and the two brothers agreed to act in concert.

His brother was a snuff box maker, and they now went out together genteelly dressed, early in the morning in order to commit their depredations, when they found the door of a genteel house open, and while the servant woman was washing the steps, or gone on a short errand, leaving the door a-jar, one of them slipt in and seized the plate on the side-board, or whatever he could lay his hands on, while the other remained to prevent surprise : and then he would receive and run off with the prize, while the actual robber, with apparent unconcern, walked off another way.

They committed a variety of robberies in conjunction, confining their depredations chiefly to the stealing of plate; but we proceed to the narrative of that for which Ramsey suffered the utmost rigour of the law.

Having taken a previous survey of Mr. Glyn's house at the corner of Hatton Garden, the brothers broke into it in the night, and carried off a quantity of plate; but hand-bills being immediately circulated, they were taken into custody while offering the plate for sale to a Jew in Duke's Place. The lord mayor, on examining the prisoners, admitted the younger brother as an evidence against the elder.

At the next sessions at the Old Bailey it was an affecting scene to behold the one brother giving evidence against the other, who was capitally convicted, and received sentence of death.

After conviction Ramsey seemed to entertain a proper idea of the enormity of the offences of which he had been guilty; and in several letters to persons whom he had robbed, he confessed his crimes, and entreated their prayers. He did not flatter himself with the least hope of pardon; sensible that his numerous offences must necessarily preclude him from such favour.

A letter, which he wrote to a friend at Bristol, contains the following pathetic expressions:—O! blame me not: I am now by the judgment of God and man, under sentence of death. Whatever injuries I have committed, with tears in my poor eyes, I ask forgiveness. Oh! my friend, could you but guess or think what agonies I feel, I am sure you would pity me: may my Father, which is in heaven, pity me likewise!

At the place of execution Ramsey made an

affecting address to the surrounding multitude: entreating the younger part of the audience to avoid gaming, as what would infallibly lead to destruction.

After the customary devotions on such melancholy occasions, he was turned off, and the body having hung the usual time, was conveyed in a hearse to Giltspur-street, whence it was taken and decently interred by his friends, at the expiration of two days from the time of his execution.

———

JEREMIAH READING,

(THE SCAPE GOAT OF SWINDLERS,)

Convicted of Forgery at the Old Bailey, the judgment arrested, and the condemned pardoned.

THE forgery for which this man was tried, was supposed to have been committed by two swindlers, John King and one White.

There was much hard swearing to bolster up a respectability to the character of the former, but the learned judge seemed to be of opinion, that the prisoner was, to use his own words, ' a scapegoat in their hands.'

Jeremiah Reading was tried for forging the name of John King, as an acceptor to a bill of exchange for £831 with intent to defraud William Dolben and Richard Brown, linen-drapers, in Bishop-gate street.

William Dolben being sworn, deposed that in

the month of February, 1792, the prisoner, who had been for a considerable time indebted to them for £9 applied to him saying, he had now the means of discharging the arrears, having received a note, which he wished to have discounted. For that night he wished to receive only £10 which he had immediate occasion for. He described White, the drawer of the bill, to be a reputable merchant in Bristol: and King, the acceptor, a man of opulence, who resided in a large house in Berkeley street, Portman-square, and kept a carriage, livery servants, &c.

The witness remarked, that the acceptance in the bill appeared in the place where indorsements are usually made. To this the prisoner replied, that when he took the bill, he made the same observation; but that Mr. King assured him he always accepted his bills in that way, and that it should be regularly honoured when it became due. He then gave him 30l. for which he took his receipt.

The prisoner not returning for the remainder of the money, excited suspicion, and induced the witness to make inquiry after the drawer and acceptor. The result was, that White had once resided in Bristol, but had disappeared for two years; but as to King, no such person was to be found in Berkeley street. The witness having occasion to pay a visit to the King's bench, found Reading a prisoner there, and brought him on his trial.

A servant in the prosecutor's house corroborated the testimony; and the collector of the taxes said, that no person of the name of King was a early housekeeper in Berkeley street, otherwise he must have known him.

This was the case for the evidence of the prosecution.

In defence, one Clark appeared, who swore, that he lived as clerk in the house of White, in Bristol, and recollected having copied the note in question, and its being forwarded to King in Berkeley street. The witness underwent an examination of two hours, in which he was required to give an account of himself. This he did in a very extraordinary manner, beginning at the time when he was only three years old; but it was found impossible to extract from him the manner in which he employed himself for the last eighteen months.

Allen, a hair-dresser, deposed, that he lived near Soho-Square, in good business; and that, in the year 1792, he dressed a Mr King, in Berkeley-street, Portman-square. He recollected, that about the end of February, the prisoner came to Mr. King, while he was dressing him, and presented a bill which he accepted. He added, that all the conversation took place relative to the extraordinary mode of indorsement, &c., which was related by the prisoner when passing the bill upon Dolben. He also stated a circumstance of King's receiving a letter addressed to him under the name of Nugent.

Several witnesses gave the prisoner a good character, amongst whom was a Miss Davis, whose mother's house in Berkeley street he frequented for three years.

Mr. Justice Grosse summed up this very intricate evidence in a very able and circumstantial manner. He commented upon all the points, and when he came to that which regarded King's passing by the name of Nugent,

Miss Davis requested the liberty of interrupting him. She said, that the mention of the name of Nugent brought a circumstance to her remembrance, which as it may affect the case before court, she thought it her duty to state, though she could not have done so in her direct evidence; the whole having been suggested by the testimony of another witness. She then related, that a person named Nugent had taken lodgings at her mother's and refused to give any reference for character, saying, there was no occasion for it, as he was a regular man, and would pay weekly. He afterwards absconded in the night; and on sweeping the room one morning, she found a pawnbroker's duplicate of an article pledged in the name of John King. Having never seen a pawnbroker's ticket before, she showed it to a gentleman, and their mutual curiosity led them to pay a visit to the pawnbroker. The latter told them, that he had directions to stop any person who should apply with the ticket; and that the instruction was given by the person who deposited the pledge. On the affair being explained the pawnbroker gave a description of the man, who perfectly corresponded with the person of Nugent.

She was desired to produce the ticket; but, said, that having no idea that such a circumstance would apply in evidence to this case, she had not brought it with her, as she otherwise would have done.

The learned judge, after a short hesitation, proceeded to his charge. He remarked, that hat they had last heard went in a great measure to confirm the evidence of Allen. If the jury should be led to attribute the whole to a foul and fraudulent conspiracy of White and King as an expedient for raising money, and that the prisoner was only a scape-goat in their hands, it was not forgery, as was charged in the indictment, and they must of course acquit him. They were not to convict upon doubt, inference, probability, or conjecture. The question to be considered was, whether the prisoner uttered this instrument knowing it to be forged? If they believed the evidence of Allen and Clark, corroborated by that of Davis, the charge was fully rebutted; but, if not, the other evidence was not sufficient to convict him.

The jury, after retiring for a considerable time, returned with a verdict, finding the prisoner guilty on the second count of the indictment; "Guilty of uttering the bill, knowing it to be forged." Death.

The learned judge, however, thought proper to reserve the case for the opinion of the judges; and accordingly, at the Sessions House in the Old Bailey, 1794, the judges were of opinion, that as the indictment stated the bill to be directed to John King, by the name and description of John King, and as there was no such person to be found as John King, that their description was erroneous, and repugnant to the precision of the law required in the form of indictments, and that therefore, the judgment ought to be arrested.

The case, however, being of great public importance, the judges were of opinion that the prisoner ought not to be discharged, as the prosecutor was at liberty to prefer a new indictment against him. The prisoner was of course detained in custody. However, in the succeeding month, he received his Majesty's free pardon.

ELIZABETH BROWNRIGG,

Executed at Tyburn, on the 14th September, 1767, for Murder.

ELIZABETH BROWNRIGG, having been a servant to a merchant in Goodman's Field, became the wife of James Brownrigg, a plumber, who, after being several years in Greenwich, came to London, and took a house in Flower-de-Luce Court, Fleet-street, where he carried on a considerable share of business, and had a little house at Islington, for an occasional retreat. This woman had been the mother of sixteen children, and having practised midwifery, was appointed, by the overseers of the poor of St. Dunstan's parish, to take care of the poor women who were taken in labour at the workhouse; which duty she performed to the satisfaction of her employers. Mary Mitchell, a poor girl of the precinct of White Friars, was put apprentice to Mrs. Brownrigg in the year 1765; and about the same time Mary Jones, one of the children in the Foundling Hospital, was likewise placed with her, in the same capacity;

nd she had other apprentices. At first the poor orphans were treated with some degree of civility, but this was soon changed for the most savage barbarity. Having laid Mary across two chairs in the kitchen, she whipped her with such wanton cruelty, that she was occasionally obliged to desist from mere weariness. This treatment was frequently repeated; and Mrs. Brownrigg used to throw water on her when he had done whipping her, and sometimes she would dip her head into a pail of water. The room appointed for the girl to sleep in adjoined to the passage leading to the street door, and as she had received many wounds on her head, shoulders, and various parts of her body, she determined not to bear such ill treatment any longer, if she could effect her escape. Observing that the key was left in the street door when the family went to bed, she opened the door cautiously one morning, and escaped into the street. Thus freed from her horrid confinement, she repeatedly inquired her way to the Foundling Hospital till she found it, and was admitted, after describing in what manner she had been treated. and describing the bruises she had received. The child having been examined by a surgeon, who found her wounds to be of the most alarming nature, the governors of the hospital ordered Mr. Plumtree, their solicitor, to write to James Brownrigg, threatening a prosecution, if he did not give a proper reason for the severities exercised towards the child. No notice of this having been taken, and the governors of the hospital thinking it imprudent to indict at common law, the girl was discharged, in consequence of an age

plication to the chamberlain of London. The
other girl, Mary Mitchell, continued with her
mistress for the space of a year, during which she
was treated with equal cruelty, and she also resolved to quit her service.   Having escaped out of
the house, she was met in the street by the younger
son of Brownrigg, who forced her to return home,
when her sufferings were greatly aggravated on
account of her elopement.   In the interim, the
overseers of the precinct of White Friars bound
Mary Clifford to Brownrigg; nor was it long before she experienced similar cruelties to those inflicted on the other poor girls, and probably still
more severe.   She was frequently tied up naked,
and beaten, with a hearth-broom, a horse-whip,
or a cane, till she was absolutely speechless.   This
poor girl having a natural infirmity, the mistress
would not permit her to lie in a bed, but placed
her on a mat, in a coal hole that was remarkably
cold: however, after some time, a sack and a
quantity of straw formed her bed, instead of the
mat.   During her confinement in this wretched
situation, she had nothing to subsist upon but
bread and water; and her covering during the
night consisted only of her own clothes, so that
she sometimes lay almost perished with cold.

On a particular occasion, when she was almost
starving through hunger, she broke open a cupboard in search of food, but found it empty: and
on another occasion, she broke down some boards,
in order to procure a draught of water.   Though
she was thus pressed for the humblest necessaries
of life, Mrs. Brownrigg determined to punish her
with rigour for the means she had taken to supply

herself with them. On this, she caused the girl to strip to the skin, and, during the course of a whole day, while she remained naked, she repeatedly beat her with the but-end of a whip. In the course of this most inhuman treatment, a jack chain was fixed round her neck, the end of which was fastened to the yard door, and then it was pulled as tight as possible without strangling her. A day being passed in the practice of these savage barbarities, the girl was remanded to the coal-hole at night, her hands being tied behind her, and the chain still remaining about her neck. The husband having been obliged to find his wife's apprentices in wearing apparel, they were repeatedly stripped naked, and kept so for whole days, if their garments happened to be torn. The elder son had frequently the superintendance of these wretched girls; but this was sometimes committed to the apprentice, who declared, that she was totally naked one night when he went to tie her up. The two poor girls were frequently so beaten, that their heads and shoulders appeared as one general sore; and when a plaister was applied to their wounds, the skin used to peel away.

Sometimes Mr. Brownrigg, when resolved on uncommon severity, used to tie their hands with a cord, and draw them up to a water pipe which ran across the ceiling in the kitchen; but that giving way, she desired her husband to fix a hook in the beam, through which a cord was drawn, and their arms being extended, she used to horsewhip them till she was weary, and till the blood followed at every stroke. The elder son having one day directed Mary Clifford to put up a half-tester bed-

stead, the poor girl was unable to do it ; on which
he beat her till she could no longer support his
severity ; and, at another time, when the mother
had been whipping her in the kitchen till she was
absolutely tired, the son renewed the savage treatment Mrs. Brownrigg would sometimes seize
the poor girl by the cheeks, and forcing the skin
down violently by her fingers, caused the blood to
gush from her eyes. Mary Clifford, unable to
bear these repeated severities, complained of her
hard treatment to a French lady who lodged in
the house : and she having represented the impropriety of such behaviour to Mrs Brownrigg
the inhuman monster flew at the girl, and cut her
tongue in two places with a pair of scissors.

On the morning of the 13th of July, this barbarous woman went into the kitchen, and, after
obliging Mary Clifford to strip to the skin, drew
her up to the staple, and, though her body was
an entire sore, from former bruises, yet this
wretch renewed her cruelties, with her accustomed severity. After whipping her till the blood
streamed down her body she let her down, and
made her wash herself in a tub of cold water;
Mary Mitchell, the other poor girl, being present
during this transaction. While Clifford was
washing herself, Mrs. Brownrigg struck her on
the shoulders, already sore with former bruises
with the butt end of a whip; and she treated the
child in this manner five times in the same day.
The poor girl's wounds now began to shew evident
signs of mortification : her mother in law, who
had resided some time in the country, came
about this time, to town to town and enquired of

ter her. Being informed that she was placed at Brownrigg's, she went thither, but was refused admittance by Mr. Brownrigg, who even threatened to carry her before the lord mayor, if she came there to make further disturbances. Hereupon the mother-in-law was going away, when Mrs. Deacon, wife of Mr. Deacon, baker, at the adjoining house, called her in, and informed her, that she and her family had often heard moanings and groans issue from Brownrigg's house, and that she suspected the apprentices were treated with unwarrantable severity. The good woman likewise promised to exert herself to ascertain the truth. At this juncture, Mr. Brownrigg, going to Hampstead on business, bought a hog, which he sent home. The hog was put into a covered yard, having a sky-light, which it was thought necessary to remove, in order to give air to the animal. As soon as it was known that the sky light was removed, Mr. Deacon ordered his servants to watch, in order, if possible, to discover the girls. Deacon's servant maid, looking from a window, saw one of the girls stooping down; on which she called her mistress, and she desired the attendance of some of the neighbours, who having been witnesses of the shocking scene, some men got upon the leads, and dropped bits of dirt, to induce the girl to speak to them: but she seemed wholly incapable. Hereupon, Mrs. Deacon sent to girl's mother-in-law, who immediately called upon Mr. Grundy, one of the overseers of St. Dunstan's and represented the case. Mr. Grundy and the rest of the overseers, with the woman,

M

went and demanded a sight of Mary Clifford;
but Brownrigg, who had nick-named her Nan,
told them that he knew no such person, but if
they wanted to see Mary, (meaning Mary Mitchell)
they might, and accordingly produced her. Upon
this, Mr. Deacon's servant declared that Mary
Mitchell was not the girl they wanted. Mr.
Grundy now sent for a constable to search the
house; but no discovery was then made. Mr.
Brownrigg threatened highly; but Mr. Grundy,
with the spirit that became the officer of a parish,
took Mary Mitchell with him to the work-house,
where, on the taking off her leathern boddice, it
stuck so fast to her wounds, that she shrieked
with the pain : but, on being treated with great
humanity, and told that she should not be sent
back to Brownrigg's, she gave an account of the
horrid treatment that she and Mary Clifford had
sustained and confessed that she had met the
latter on the stairs just before they came to the
house. Hereupon, Mr. Grundy and some others
returned to the house, to make a stricter search:
on which, Brownrigg sent for a lawyer, in order
to intimidate them, and even threatened a pro-
tsecution, unless they immediately quitted the
premises.

Unterrified by the threats, Mr. Grundy sent for
a coach to carry Brownrigg to the compter; on
which the latter promised to produce the girl in
half an hour, if the coach was discharged. This
being consented to, the girl was produced from a
cupboard, under a beaufet in the dining-room,
after a pair of shoes, which young Brownrigg
had in his hand during the proposal, had been

put upon her. It is not in language to describe the miserable appearance this poor girl made; almost her whole body was ulcerated. Being taken to the workhouse, an apothecary was sent for, who pronounced her to be in danger. Brownrigg was conveyed to Wood-street compter; but his wife and son made their escape, taking with them a gold watch and some money. Mr. Brownrigg was now carried before Mr. Alderman Crosby, who fully committed him, ordered the girls to be taken to St. Bartholomew's hospital, where Mary Clifford died, within a few days; and the coroner's inquest being summoned, found a verdict of Wilful Murder against James and Elizabeth Brownrigg, and John their son. In the mean time, Mrs. Brownrigg and her son shifted from place to place in London, bought clothes in Rag-fair to disguise themselves, and then went to Wandsworth, where they took lodgings in the house of Mr. Dunbar, who kept a chandler's shop. This chandler happening to read a newspaper on the 15th of August, saw an advertisement which so clearly described his lodgers, that he had no doubt but they were the murderers. On this, he went to London the next day which was Sunday, and going to church, he sent for Mr. Owen, the churchwarden, to attend him in the vestry, and gave such a description of the parties that Mr. Owen desired Mr. Deacon and Mr. Wingrave, a constable, to go to Wandsworth, and make the necessary enquiry. On their arrival at Dunbar's house they found the wretched mother and son in a room by themselves who evinced great agitation at this discovery. A coach being procured, they were conveyed to London, without any person in Wandsworth having knowledge of the affair, except Mr. and Mrs. Dunbar. At the ensuing sessions at the Old Bailey, the father, mother, and son were indicted; when Elizabeth Brownrigg, after a trial of eleven hours, was found guilty of murder, and ordered for execution; but the man and his son, being acquitted of the higher charge, were detained, to take their trials for the misdemeanor, of which they were convicted, and imprisoned for six months. After sentence of death was passed on Mrs. Brownrigg, she was attended by a clergyman, to whom she confessed the enormity of her crime, and acknowledged the justice of the sentence by which she had been condemned. The parting between her and her husband and son, on the morning of her execution, was affecting beyond description. The son falling on his knees, she bent herself over him and embraced him; while the husband was kneeling on the other side. On her way to the fatal tree, the people expressed their abhorrence of her crime in terms which, though not proper at the moment, testified their destination of her cruelty. Before her exit she joined in prayers with the ordinary of Newgate, whom she earnestly desired to declare to the multitude, that she confessed her guilt, and acknowledged the justice of her sentence. After execution, her body was put into a hackney-coach, conveyed to Surgeon's hall, dissected and anatomized; her skeleton is still in preservation.

THURTELL, HUNT, AND PROBERT,

Tried at Hertford Assizes, 1824, for Murder.

IT is impossible to give any idea of the intense interest which the trial of these unfortunate men excited. The town of Hertford was crowded with strangers from all the country round, and long before daylight appeared on the morning of the trial, numerous vehicles of every description poured into the town.

On the 7th of January, 1824, the indictment against the prisoner Thurtell, charging him with the murder of Mr. Weare, and Hunt and Probert as being accessaries in the deed, was read over. Mr. Gurney opened the case by stating it was not his intention to offer any evidence against the prisoner Probert, and a verdict of acquittal was consequently pronounced. Mr. Gurney then proceeded to state that the crime with which the prisoners stood charged, was, undoubtedly one of the most enormous magnitude; its perpetration had been attended with no common ferocity. It was imputed to one of the parties, that he had actually committed the murder; and to the other that he had assisted with his previous counsel and concert, and co-operated in the promotion of the premeditated act. But in proportion to the great enormity of the crime ought to be the strength of the proof; and he did not mean to ask of them to pronounce a verdict of guilty, unless on such evidence as left no rational doubt on their minds of the fact. He repeated, that when they considered the nature of the case, and the violent aggravation with which it was attended, they were bound to call for very strong proof to convince them that any man was capable of so dreadful an atrocity; for if the evidence he had to adduce were substantiated and believed, one of the prisoners at the bar had been guilty, not only of the crime of murder in all its atrocity, but with the murder of a man with whom he had been living in habits of acquaintance, if not of intimacy. It was said (whether true or not, he knew not), that the deceased had provoked one of the prisoners, by doing him some wrong at play; and that the other had never been injured by the man whose death he had concerted to aid in inflicting.

These persons, under the specious pretences of friendship, had invited the deceased to accompany them upon a short country excursion; but they had invited him into their company to deprive him the same night of his life. It was emphatically said. that murder was a crime to be perpetrated in darkness. The hour of night was mostly chosen as the opportune time for its infliction: because it was in that moment of solitude they thought that no human eye could see, nor hear the struggles of the dying; darkness rendered detection more difficult. It was therefore the peculiar feature of crimes of this kind that their proof often depended upon circumstantial evidence, which, however, was frequently found to convey, by its character and combination, a demonstration as conclusive as any which could arise from the operation of positive testimony. There was another species of evidence, which was sometimes of necessity resorted to in cases of this nature —he meant the evidence of an accomplice, nor even to get that species of testimony, without compounding in some measure with acknowledged guilt. Upon a very full and anxious deliberation of the whole of this case, those who conducted the prosecution had maturely decided upon the admission of an accomplice into their evidence. The deceased, whose murder was the subject of the present enquiry, was the late Mr. William Weare—a man, it was said, addicted to play, and, as he had been informed, connected with gaming houses. Whether he was the best, or the least amiable individual in society, was no part of their present consideration. The prisoner at the bar, John Thurtell, had been his acquaintance, and in some practices of play, had, it was said, been wronged by him, and deprived of a large sum of money. The other prisoner, Hunt, was described as being a public sinner, and was also known to Mr. Weare, but not, as he believed, in habits of friendship. Probert, who was admitted as an accomplice, had been in trade a spirit dealer, and rented a cottage in Gill's hill lane, near Elstree. It was situate in a bye lane, going out of the London road to St. Alban's, and two or three miles beyond Elstree. The cottage of Probert was, it would appear, selected from its seclusion, as the fit spot for the perpetration of the murder. Probert was himself much engaged in London, and his wife generally-resided at the cottage, which was a small one, and pretty fully occupied in the accommodation of Mrs. Probert, her sister, (Miss Noyes,) some children of Thomas Thurtell's (the prisoner's brother,) and a maid and boy servant. It would seem, from what had taken place, that the deceased had been invited by John Thurtell, to this place to enjoy a day or two's shooting. It would be proved that the prisoner Thurtell met the deceased at a billiard room, kept by one Rex-worthy, on the Thursday night (that previous to the murder). They were joined by Hunt.

On the forenoon of the Friday, the deceased was with Rexworthy at the same place, and said he was going for a day's journey into the country. Weare went from the billiard rooms between three and four o'clock to his chambers in Lyon's inn, where he partook of a chop dinner, and afterwards packed up, in a green carpet bag, some clothes, and a mere change of linen, such as a journey for the time he had specified might require. He also took with him when he left his chambers, in a hackney coach, which the laundress had called, a double-barrelled gun, and a backgammon-box; dice, &c. He left his chamber in this manner before four o'clock, and drove first to Charing-cross, and afterwards to Maddox-street, Hanover square, from thence he proceeded to the New road, where he went out of the coach, and returned after some time, accompanied by some other person, and took his things away. Undoubtedly the deceased left town on that evening with the expectation of reaching Gill's hall cottage; but it had been previously determined by his companions, that he should never reach that spot alive. Here he would beg to state a few of the circumstances

which had occurred antecedent to the commission
of the crime. Thomas and John Thurtell were
desirous of some temporary concealment, owing to
their inability to provide the bail requisite to meet
some charge of misdemeanour, and Probert had
procured for them a retreat at Testall's, the sign
of the Coach and Horses, in Conduit-street, where
they remained for two or three weeks previous to
the murder.

On the morning of Friday, the 24th of October,
two men answering in every respect to the description of John Thurtell and Hunt, went to a pawnbroker's in Mary-le-bone, and purchased a pair of
pocket-pistols. In the middle of the same day,
Hunt hired a gig, and afterwards a horse, under
the pretence of going to Dartfort in Kent; he also
inquired where he could purchase a sack and a
rope, and was directed to a place over West-
minster-bridge, which he was told, was on his
road into Kent. Somewhere, however, it would
be found that he did procure a sack and a cord,
and he met the same afternoon, at Testall's,
Thomas Thurtell and Noyes. They were all assembled together at the Coach and Horses in Conduit street. When he made use of the names of
the two last individuals, he begged to be understood as saying that he had no reason to believe
that either Thomas Thurtell or Noyes were privy
to the guilty purpose of the prisoners. Some conversation took place at the time between the parties, and Hunt was heard to ask Probert if he
would be in what they (Hunt and John Thurtell)
were about. Thurtell drove off from Testall's between four and five o'clock to take up a friend, as

he said to Probert, to be killed as he travelled with him ; an expression which Probert said at the time he believed to have been a piece of idle bravado. He requested Probert to bring down Hunt in his own gig. In the course of that evening, the prisoner Thurtell is seen in a gig with a horse of a very remarkable colour. He was a sort of iron grey, with a white face and white legs—very particular marks for identity. He was first seen by a patrole near Edgeware ; beyond that part of the road he was seen by the landlord ; but from that time of the evening until his arrival at Probert's cottage on the same night, they had no direct evidence to trace him. Probert, according to Thurtell's request, drove Hunt down in his gig, and, having a better horse, on the road they overtook Thurtell and Weare in the gig, and passed them without notice.

They stopped afterwards at a public house on the road to drink grog, where they believe Thurtell must have passed them unperceived. Probert drove Hunt until they reached Philimore-lodge, where he (Hunt) got out, as he said by Thurtell's desire, to wait for him. Probert from thence drove alone to Gill's hill-cottage, in the lane near which he met Thurtell on foot, alone. Thurtell inquired, Where was Hunt, had he been left behind ? he then added, that he had done the business without his assistance, and had killed his man. At his desire, Probert returned to bring Hunt to the spot, where he (Probert) went to Hunt for that purpose. When they met, he told Hunt what happened. Why, it was to be done here, said Hunt, pointing to nearer Philimore

odge, admitting his privity, and that he had got
out to assist in the commission of the deed.

When Thurtell rebuked Hunt for his absence,
Why, said the latter, you had the tools. They
were not good, replied Thurtell, the pistols were
not better than pop guns. I fired at his cheek
and it glanced off—that Weare ran out of the
gig, for mercy, and offered to return the money
he had robbed him of—that he (Thurtell) pursued
him up the lane when he jumped out of the gig.
Finding the pistol unavailing, he attempted to
reach him by cutting the penknife across his
throat, and ultimately finished him by driving the
barrel of the pistol into his head, and turning it
in his brains, after he had penetrated the forehead. Such was the manner in which Thurtell
described he had disposed of the body of the deceased, and they would hear from Probert what
he said on the occasion. A gig was about that
time heard to drive very quickly past Probert's
cottage. The servants expected their master and
thought he had arrived; but he did not make
his appearance. Five minutes after that period,
certain persons who would be called in as evidence, and who happened to be on the road, distinctly heard the report of a gun or pistol, which
was followed by voices, as if in contention. Violent groans were next heard, which however, became fainter and fainter, and then died away altogether.

The spot where the report of the pistol and the
sound of groans were heard, was Gill's hill lane,
and near it was situated the cottage of Probert.
They had now therefore, to keep it in mind that

Thurtell arrived at about nine o'clock in
evening at Probert's cottage, having set off t
Conduit street, at five o'clock; and though
had been seen on the road in company with
other person in the gig, yet it appeared that
arrived at the cottage alone, having in his po
sion the double barrelled gun, the green ca
bag, and the backgammon board, which
Weare took away with him. He gave his ho
to the boy, and the horse appeared in a cool st
which corroborated the fact that he had stopp
a good while on his way. He left Cond
street it should be observed at five, and arrive
nine—a distance which, under ordinary circu
stances would not have occupied more than
hour. The boy enquired after Probert and Hu
and was told that they would soon be at
cottage. At length a second gig arriv
and those two persons were in it. They ro
while Thurtell who went to meet them, walk
with them. The boy having cleaned his maste
horse, then performed the same office for
horse of Thurtell, which occupied a good deal
time. Probert went into the house. Neith
Thurtell nor Hunt was expected by Mrs. Probe
With Thurtell she was acquainted; but Hu
was a stranger, and was formally introduced
her. They then supped on some pork chop
which Hunt had brought down with him fro
London. They then went out, as Probert said
visit Mr. Nicholls, a neighbour of his: but the
real object was to go down to the place whe
the body of Weare was deposited. Thurtell to
them to the spot down the lane, and the bo

dragged through the hedge into the adjoin-
field. The body was, as he had previously
cribed it to be, enclosed in a sack. They then
ctually rifled the deceased man, Thurtell hav-
informed his companions that he had, in the
t instance, taken the fourth part of his pro-
ty. They then went back to the cottage.

It ought to be stated, that Thurtell, before he
nt out, placed a large sponge in the gig; and
en he returned from this expedition, he went
the stable and sponged himself with great care.
endeavoured to remove the spots of blood, ma-
of which were distinctly seen by Probert's boy:
d certainly such marks would be observable on
person of any one who had been engaged in
ch a transaction. In the course of the evening,
urtell produced a gold watch, without a chain,
ich occasioned several remarks. He also dis-
yed a gold curb chain, which might be used
a watch when double, or, when single, might
wore round a lady's neck. On producing the
in, it was remarked that it was more fit for a
ly than a gentleman; on which Thurtell press-
it on Mrs. Probert, and made her accept of it.
offer was afterwards made that a bed should
given to Thurtell and Hunt, which was to be
complished by Miss Noyes giving up her bed,
d sleeping with the children. This was refused,
urtell and Hunt observing, that they would
ther sit up. Miss Noyes, therefore, retired to
r own bed.

Something, however, occurred, which raised
spicion in the mind of Mrs. Probert; and, in-
ed, it was scarcely possible, if it were at all pos-

sible, for persons who had been engaged in
transaction of this kind, to avoid some disorder
mind — some absence of thought that was calc
lated to excite suspicion. In consequence of o
serving those feelings, Mrs Probert did not go
bed, or undress herself. She went to the wind
and looked out, and saw that Probert, Hunt, a
Thurtell, were in the garden. It would be pro
that they went down to the body, and finding
teo heavy to be removed, one of the horses we
taken from the stable. The body was then thro
across the horse ; and stones having been put in
the sack, the body, with the sack thus render
weighty by the stones, was thrown into the pon
Mrs. Probert distinctly saw something hea
drawn across the garden where Thurtell w
The parties then returned to the house ; and M
Probert whose fears and suspicions were me
powerfully excited, went down stairs and listen
behind the parlour door. The parties now pr
ceeded to share the booty ; and Thurtell divid
with them to the amount of £6 each. The pur
the pocket book, and certain papers which mig
lead to detection, were carefully burned. Th
remained up late ; and Probert, when he went
bed, was surprised to find that his wife was n
asleep. Hunt and Thurtell still continued to
up in the parlour.

The next morning, as early as six o'cloc
Hunt and Thurtell were seen out, and in the la
together. Some men who were at work ther
observed them, as they call it " grabbing " f
something in the hedge. They were spok
to by these men, and as persons thus accost

ust say something, Thurtell observed ; That it
is a very bad road, and that he had nearly been
upsized there last night. The men said, I hope
you were not hurt. Thurtell answered, Oh no,
the gig was not upset. They then went away.
These men, thinking something might have been
lost on the spot, searched after Thurtell and
Hunt were gone. In one place, they found a
quantity of blood, further on they found a bloody
knife, and next they found a bloody pistol—one
of the identical pair which he would show were
purchased by Hunt. That pistol bore marks of
blood and of human brains. The spot was still
further examined afterwards, and more blood was
discovered, which had been concealed by branches and leaves, so that no doubt could be entertained that the murder had been committed in
his particular place.

On the following morning, Saturday, the 25th
of October, Thurtell and Hunt left Probert's cottage in the gig which Hunt had come down in,
carrying away with them the gun, the carpet bag,
and the backgammon-board, the property of Mr.
Weare. These articles were taken to Hunt's
lodgings, where they were afterwards found.
When Hunt arrived in town on Saturday, he appeared to be unusually gay. He said, We Turpin
lads can do the trick, I am able to drink wine
now, and I will drink nothing but wine. He
seemed to be very much elevated at the recollection of some successful exploit. It was observed, that Thurtell's hands were very much
scratched, and some remark having been made on
the subject, he stated, That they had been cut

netting partridges, and that his hands had got scratched in that occupation. On some other points, he gave similarly evasive answers. On Sunday, John Thurtell, Thomas Thurtell, Noyes and Hunt, spent the day at Probert's cottage. Hunt went down dressed in a manner so very shabby as to excite observation. But in the course of the day he went up stairs, and attired himself in very handsome clothes. There was very little doubt that those were the clothes of the deceased Mr. Weare.

He had now to call the attention of the jury to a very remarkable circumstance. On the Saturday, Hunt had a new spade sent to his lodgings, which he took down to the cottage on Sunday. When he got near Probert's garden, he told that individual, that he had brought it to dig a hole to bury the body in. On that evening, Probert did really visit Mr. Nicholls; and the latter said to him, that some persons had heard the report of a gun or pistol in the lane, on Friday evening; but he supposed, it was some foolish joke. Probert on his return, stated this to Thurtell and Hunt, and the information appeared to alarm the former, who said, he feared he should be hanged. The intelligence, however, inspired them all with a strong desire to conceal the body effectually. Probert wished it to be removed from his pond; for, had it been found there, he knew it would be important evidence against himself. He declared that he would not suffer it to remain there; and Thurtell and Hunt promised to come down on the Monday, and remove it. On Monday, Thurtell and Hunt went out in the gig, and in furtherance of that scene of villainy which they meditated, they took with them Probert's boy. They carried him to various places, and finally lodged the boy at Mr. Testalt's in Conduit street.

On the evening of the same Monday, Hunt and Thurtell came down to the cotage. Hunt engaged Mrs. Probert in conversation, while Thurtell and Probert took the body out of the pond, put it into Thurtell's gig, and then gave notice to Hunt that the gig was ready. In this manner they carried away the body that night: but where they took it, Probert did not know. It appeared, however, that the body was carried to a pond near Elstree, at a considerable distance from Probert's cottage, and there sunk, as it had before been in Probert's pond, in a sack containing a considerable quantity of stones. Hunt and Thurtell then went to London ; and the appearance of the gig the next morning clearly told the way in which it had been used over night; a quantity of blood and mud being quite perceptible at the bottom. The parties heard that the report of a pistol in the lane on Friday evening, and the discovery of the blood in the field, had led to great alarm amongst the magistracy. Inquiry was set on foot, and Thurtell, Hunt, and Probert were at length apprehended. It was found that Hunt had adopted a peculiar mode for the purpose of concealing his identity: for when he was hiring the gig, and doing various other acts connected with this atrocious proceeding he wore very long whiskers; but on the Monday after the murder, he had taken them off; and they all knew that nothing could

N

possibly alter the appearance of a man more than
the taking away of large bushy whiskers. Strict
enquiries were made by the magistrates, but nothing was ascertained to prove to a certainty who
was murdered. The body, was, however, found
on the Thursday, Hunt having given evidence as
to the place where the body was deposited. The
evidence which Hunt gave, and which led to the
finding of the body, he would use ; but no other
fact coming out of his mouth, save that, would he
advert to. He was entitled, in point of law, to
make use of that. If a person tells me, under any
promise of mercy, where stolen goods are to be
found, and on searching I find them, I am entitled
to adduce the fact of finding against the criminal
party ; and for this reason—because persons may,
from hope or fear, be induced to state what is not
true. But the finding proves the truth, and on
that point I have a right to proceed.

The fact only of the disclosure by Hunt, in consequence of which the body was discovered, was
he permitted to make use of; and to that alone, so
far as Hunt's confession went, he would confine
himself. But by reference to his conversations
with others, and to various circumstances not ad-
verted to by him, he was convinced that he should
be enabled to establish a perfect and complete chain
of evidence. He had now stated the principal part
of the facts which it would be his duty to lay before the jury. Some of them, they must observe,
would depend on the evidence of an accomplice ;
for Probert, though not an accomplice *before* the
murder, was confessedly privy to a certain part of
the transaction—to the concealment of the body

—to the concealment, consequently, of the murder. He must be looked upon as a bad, a very bad man. He was presented to the jury in that character. What good man could ever lend himself, in the remotest degree, to so revolting a transaction! An accomplice must always be, to a greater or less extent, a base man. The jury would therefore receive the evidence of Probert with extreme caution, and they would mark, with peculiar attention, how far his evidence was confirmed by testimony that could not be impeached. But he would produce such witnesses in confirmation of Probert's statement—he would so confirm him in every point, as to build up his testimony with a degree of strength and consistency which could not be shaken, much less overturned. He would prove by other witnesses besides Probert, that Thurtell set out with a companion from London, who did not arrive at the ostensible end of his journey; he would prove that he had brought the property of that companion to Probert's house, the double-barrelled gun, the backgammon-board, and the green carpet-bag; he would prove, that some time before he arrived at the cottage, the report of a gun or pistol was heard in Gill's hill-lane, not far from the cottage; he would prove that his clothes were in a bloody state; and that, when he was apprehended, even on the Wednesday, after the murder, he had not been able to efface all the marks from his apparel. Besides all this, they would find, that in his pocket, when apprehended, there was a penknife which was positively sworn to as having belonged to Mr. Weare, and also the fellow-

pistol of that which was found adjoining the
place where the murder was committed,—the
pair having been purchased in Mary-le-bone
street by Hunt.   These circumstances brought
the case clearly home to Thurtell.   Next as to
Hunt.   He was charged as an accomplice before
the fact.   It was evident that he advised this
proceeding.   For what purpose, but to advise,
did he proceed to the cottage? He was a stranger
to Mrs. Probert and her family ; he was not expected at the cottage.   There was not for him
as there was for Thurtell, an apology for his
visit.   He hired a gig. and he procured a sack—
the jury knew to what end and purpose.   They
would also bear in mind, that the gun, travelling-
bag, and backgammon-board, were found in his
lodging.   These constituted a part of the plunder
of Mr. Weare, and could only be possessed by
a person participating in his crime.   Besides,
there was placed about the neck of Probert's
wife, a chain which had belonged to Mr. Weare,
and round the neck of the murdered man there
was found a shawl, which belonged to Thurtell,
but which had been seen in the hands of Hunt.
In giving this summary of the case, he had not
stated every circumstance connected with it.
His great anxiety was, not to state that which
he did not firmly believe would be borne out
by evidence.   One circumstance he had omitted,
which he felt it necessary to lay before the jury.
It was, that a watch was seen in possession of
Thurtell, which he would show belonged to
Mr. Weare.   After Thurtell was apprehended,
and Hunt had said something on the subject

of this transaction, one of the officers asked Thurtell what he had done with the watch ? He answered that, when he was taken into custody, he put his hand behind him, and chucked it away. Thurtell also made another disclosure. He said, when questioned, that other persons, near the spot, were concerned in it, whom he forebore to mention. As to Thurtell, the evidence would, he believed, clearly prove him to have been the perpetrator of the murder ; and with respect to Hunt, it was equally clear that he was an accessory before the fact. If, however, the jury felt any conscientious doubt, the prisoner ought certainly to receive the benefit of it ; but where a case was clearly and satisfactorily made out, they would perform fearlessly that duty which they owed to heaven, and to the due administration of justice.

Several witnesses were now examined on the part of the prosecution, and at the conclusion of the evidence, Thurtell delivered the following defence.

My lord and gentlemen of the Jury—Under greater difficulties than ever man encountered I now rise to vindicate my character, and defend my life. I have been supported in this hour of trial, by the knowledge that my cause is heard before an enlightened tribunal, and that the free institutions of my country have placed my destiny in the hands of twelve men, who are uninfluenced by prejudice, and unawed by power. I have been represented by the press, which carries its benefits or curses on rapid wings from one extremity of the kingdom to the other, as a man more depraved, more gratuitously and habitually profligate

and cruel, than has ever appeared in modern
times. I have been held up to the world as a
perpetrator of a murder, under circumstances of
greater aggravation, of more cruel and premeditated atrocity, than it ever before fell to the lot
of man to have seen or heard of. I have been
held forth to the world as a depraved, heartless,
remorseless, prayerless villain, who had seduced
my friend into a sequestered path, merely in order
to dispatch him with the greater security—as a
snake who had crept into his bosom only to strike
a surer blow—as a monster, who, after the perpetration of a deed from which the hardest heart
recoils with horror, and at which humanity stands
aghast, washed away the remembrance of my guilt
in the midst of riot and debauchery. You, gentlemen, must have read the details which have
been daily, I may say hourly, published regarding
me. It would be requiring more than the usual
virtue of our nature to expect that you should
entirely divest your minds of those feelings, I may
say those creditable feelings, which such relations
must have excited: but I am satisfied, that as far
as it is possible for men to enter into a grave investigation, with minds unbiassed, and judgments
unimpaired, after the calumnies with which the
public mind has been deluged—I say, I am satisfied, that with such minds and judgments, you
have this day assumed your sacred office. The
horrible guilt which has been attributed to me, is
such as could not have resulted from custom, but
must have been the innate principle of my infant
mind, and have grown with my growth, and
strengthened with my strength. But I will call

before you gentlemen, whose characters are unimpeachable, and whose testimony must be above suspicion, who will tell you, that the time was when my bosom overflowed with all the kindly feelings ; and even my failings were those of an improvident generosity and unsuspecting friendship. Beware, then, gentlemen, of an anticipated verdict. Do not suffer the reports which you have heard to influence your determination. Do not believe that a few short years can have reversed the course of nature, and converted the good feelings which I possessed into the spirit of malignant cruelty to which only demons can attain.

A kind, affectionate, and religious mother, directed the steps of my infancy, in the paths of piety and virtue. My rising youth was guided in the way it should go by a father whose piety was universally known and believed—whose kindness and charity extended to all who came within the sphere of its influence. After leaving my parental roof, I entered the service of our late revered monarch, who was justly entitled the father of his people. You will learn from some of my honourable companions, that while I served under his colours, I never tarnished their lustre. The country which is dear to me I have served— I have fought for her—I have shed my blood for her. I feared not in the open field to shed the blood of her declared foes. But oh! to suppose that on that account I was ready to raise the assassin's arm against my friend, and with that view to draw him into secret places for his

destruction—it is monstrous, horrible, incredible,
I have been represented to you as a man given to
gambling, and the constant companion of gamblers.   To this accusation, in some part, my heart
with feeling penitence pleads guilty.   I have
gambled—I have been a gambler—but not for the
last three years, During that time I have not
attended or betted upon a race-horse, or a fight,
or any public exhibition of that nature. If I
have erred in these things, half the nobility of the
land have been my examples; some of the most
enlightened statesmen of the country have been
my companions in them.   I have, indeed, been a
gambler—I have been an unfortunate one.   But
whose fortune, or whose family suffered from it?
My own family were the only sufferers—my own
fortune was the only sacrifice.   At this I feel
the distress of my situation.   But, gentlemen, let
not this misfortune entice your verdict against
me.   Beware of your own feelings, when you are
told by the highest authority, that the heart of
man is deceitful above all things.   Beware, gentlemen, of an anticipated verdict.   It is the remark of a very sage and experienced writer, that
no man becomes wicked all at once.   And with
this which I earnestly request you to bear in
mind, I proceed to lay before you the whole career
of my life.   I will not tire you with tedious re-
petitions, but I will disclose enough of my past
life to inform your judgments; leaving it to your
clemency to supply whatever little defects you
may observe.   You will consider my misfortunes,
and the situation in which I stand—the deep
anxiety that I must feel—the object for which I

ave to strive. You may suppose some thing of
ll this ; but oh ! no lines, no pen, though dipped
n the hues of Heaven, can pourtray my feelings
t this crisis. Recollect, I again entreat you, my
situation, and allow something for the workings
of a mind little at ease ; and pity and forgive the
aults of my address. The conclusion of the late
war, which threw its lustre upon the fortune of
the nation generally, threw a gloomy shadow over
mine. I entered into a mercantile life with
feelings as kind, and with a heart as warm, as I
ad carried with me in the service. I took the
ommercial world as if it had been governed by
the same regulations as the army. I looked upon
the merchants as if they had been my mess-com-
anions. In my transactions I had with them my
urse was open, my heart was warm, to answer to
their demands, as they had been to my former
ssociates. I need not say that my fortune, however ample, would have been insufficient to meet
uch a course of conduct. I, of course, became
the subject of a commission of bankruptcy. My
olicitor, in whom I had foolishly confided as my
articular friend, I discovered, too late, to have
een a traitor—a man who was foremost in the
ank of my bitterest enemies. But for that man
should still have been enabled to regain a sta-
on in society, and I should have yet preserved
the esteem of my friends, and, above all, my own
elf respect. But how often is it seen that the
varice of one creditor destroys the clemency of
ll the rest, and for ever dissipates the fair pro-
ects of the unfortunate debtor? With the kind
assistance of Mr. Thomas Oliver Hingfield, I ob-

tained the signature of all my creditors to
petition for superseding my bankruptcy. B
just then, when I flattered myself that my ill fo
tune was about to close—that my blossoms we
ripening—there came a frost—a nipping fro
My chief creditor refused to sign unless he w
paid a bonus of 300l. upon his debt beyond
other creditors.   This demand was backed by th
man who was at that time his and my solicitor,
spurned the offer—I awakened his resentment,
was cast upon the world—my all disposed of—i
the deepest distress.

My brother afterwards availed himself of m
misfortune, and entered into business.   His war
houses were destroyed by the accident of a fire,
has been proved by the verdict of a jury on a tri
at which the venerable judge now present pr
sided.   But that accident, unfortunate as it wa
has been taken advantage of, in order to insinua
that I was guilty of crime, because his proper
was destroyed by it, as will be proved by th
verdict of an honest and upright jury in an actio
for conspiracy, which will be tried ere long b
fore the chief justice of the King's Bench.
conspiracy there was—but where ?   Why, in th
acts of the prosecutor himself, Mr. Barber Bea
mont, who was guilty of suborning witnesses, an
will be proved to have paid for false testimon
Yes; this professed friend of the aggrieved—th
pretended prosecutor of public abuses—this sel
appointed supporter of the laws, who panders
rebellion, and had the audacity to raise its stand
ard in the front of the royal palace—this ma
who has just head enough to contrive crime, b

t heart enough to risk its consequences—this
the real author of the conspiracy which will
ortly undergo legal investigation. To these
rticulars I have thought it necessary to call
ur attention, in language which you may per-
ps think too warm—in terms not so measured,
t that they may incur your reproof. But

The flesh will quiver where the pincers tear,
The blood will follow where the knife is driven.

You have been told that I intended to decoy
oods to his destruction : and he has said that
saw me in the passage of the house. I can
ove, by honest witnesses, fellow-citizens of my
tive city of Norwich, that I was there at the
ne; but, for the sake of an amiable and inno-
t female, who might be injured, I grant to Mr.
oods the mercy of my silence. When, before
is, did it ever fall to the lot of any subject to be
rne down by the weight of calumny and obloquy
ich now oppresses me? The press, which
ght to be the shield of public liberty, the
enger of public wrongs—which, above all, should
ve exerted itself to preserve the purity of its
ourite institution, the trial by jury—has direct-
its whole force to my injury and prejudice ; it
heaped slander upon slander, and whetted
public appetite for slanders more atrocious :
more, what in other men would serve to re-
and repel the shaft of calumny, is made to
in with a deeper dye the villanies ascribed to
. One would have imagined, that some time
nt in the service of my country would have
tled me to some favour from the public under

a charge of this nature. But no; in my case the
order of things is changed—nature is reversed.
The acts of times long since past have been
made to cast a deeper shadow over the acts attributed to within the last few days: and the pursuit
of a profession, hitherto held honourable among
men, has been turned to the advantage of the accusation against me. You have been told that
after the battle, I boasted of my inhumanity to a
vanquished, yielding, wounded enemy—that I
made a wanton sacrifice of my bleeding and sup-
plicating foe, by striking him to the earth with
my cowardly steel; and that, after this deed of
blood, I coldly sat down to plunder my unhappy
victim. Nay, more—that with folly indescribable
and incredible, I boasted of my barbarity as of a
victory. Is there an English officer, is there an
English soldier, or an Englishman, whose heart
would not have revolted with hatred against such
baseness and folly? Far better, gentlemen, would
it have been for me, rather than have seen this
day, to have fallen with my honourable companions, stemming and opposing the tide of battle
upon the field of my country's glory. Then my
father and my family, though they would have
mourned my loss, would have blessed my memory,
and shame would never have darkened me with a
suspicion. Before I recur to the evidence brought
against my life, I wish to return my most sincere
thanks to the high sheriff and the magistrates for
their kindness shown to me. I cannot but express
my unfeigned regret at a slight misunderstanding
which as occurred between the Rev. Mr Lloyd, the
visiting magistrate, and my solicitor. As it was

nothing more than a misunderstanding, I trust the
bonds of friendship are again ratified between us
all. My most particular gratitude is due to the
Rev. Mr. Franklin, whose kind visits and pious
consolations have inspired me with a deeper sense
of the awful truths of religion, and have trebly
armed my breast with fortitude to serve me on
this day. Though last, not least—let me not
forget Mr. Wilson, the governor of the prison,
and the fatherly treatment which he hath shown
me throughout. My memory must perish ere
I can forget his kindness. My heart must be
cold ere it can cease to beat with gratitude to
him, and wishes for the prosperity of his family.
(This effusion of gratitude which the prisoner acknowledged moved him to tears; the emotion to
which it gave rise, spread its influence round the
court in a manner which we are wholly unable to
describe.) I will now proceed to make a few observations on the evidence brought against me in
this case, which is so far like other cases which I
shall have to cite, that it is full of caution, and
subject to manifold doubts, and that it is derived
principally from persons who come forward anxious to save their own lives, which are in jeopardy
from this charge. In the first place, however,
Beeson says that there are several roads leading
out of Gill's hill lane; the inference drawn from
this circumstance, and that of my horse's head
being turned towards Battler's green, is futile,
because, in fact, that is the nearer road. But
what consistency was there in the testimony?
The whole party admit that they were ignorant of

the body and the place where it lay, until pointed
out by Hunt. How did Hunt get at this particular knowledge? The inference must be, that he
put it there himself. The constable said, that
one man could not have thrown it there. What
proof is there that the body was at any time
thrown into Probert's pond? None, but what is
furnished by Probert himself. Men would have
thought, indeed, that the pond being deep, would
have been the most convenient place for it. You
have learnt that it was much deeper than the
ditch in which it was found. Who but Probert
could have known that the large pond was dry at
times, and that the shallower ditch was never so.
Then, again, as to the cord and sack. You learn
that they were brought by Hunt. Was he ignorant of the purpose for which they were designed?
I pass by Field and Upson, and come to Rexworthy. This witness admitted that he was connected
with gamblers, and the supporter of gamblers.
Now I will proceed to a remark or two upon
Ruthven's evidence. He speaks of the dress that
had been worn by Hunt two days previously?
On the search which took place afterwards, knife
and pistol were found in the pockets. When
Ruthven came to me, he admits that there was no
concealment—that he found me with unclosed
doors: with drawers unlocked. Was this the
conduct of a person fearing conviction? What
did he find on searching the premises? A shirt
and cravat marked with blood, just as Hunt left
them. I forgot, my lord, and gentlemen of the
jury, to call the attention of my brother to that
circumstance. The cravat was a white one—a

thing which unto that time and since my confinement I never wore.

It was proved that another person was in the room with me. Was it prudence, was it common caution in me to allow this person to be with me, who might disclose my guilt? Ruthven admits that he found nothing of that openness on going to apprehend Hunt. Simmons says, that he took a red shawl and handkerchief, which are proved to have been given to Hunt on the evening previous to the murder. The sack and cord were given to Hunt previous to the murder. I come now to the only man whose evidence tends, in any way to convict me. What is the worth of his testimony? Who is he? The answer to either question is that he is a murderer. He did not refuse, even of his own account, to admit a man to his house hot from slaughter, and to introduce him as a companion for his wife. Where was the murder done? Within a quarter of a mile of his own house. Where was the body taken? To his own pond. Who took it there? He himself. His family, at this time, consisted of eight persons, and yet he invited us down, knowing that he had no accommodation for us. You will learn from respectable, witnesses what was the real cause of my visiting Mr. Testall's. Probert gave a true account of the affair of the money which was borrowed, at the first examination; but he gave a totally different one yesterday. Are you to doom me to ignominy and death upon the evidence of such a man? Forget not, I beseech you, the difference which appears in the evidence of the two men who are engaged in running a race,

as it were, to determine which shall best deser
the character of approver, with a bridle on the
tongues which is only in the proportion to th
length of their consciences.   This is the evidenc
to prove that I was the murderer of Mr. Wear
Probert tells you that I was going to kill him, be
cause he had robbed me of some hundreds. Ca
you believe me to be so egregiously foolish? H
says that I told the man to stop for me at a ce
tain place.   He admits that the man was a strange
both to him and his wife, and that he had neve
stopt at the cottage before.   Yet he put him dow
at a proposed place, where it was intended t
commit the murder.   Would Probert have allow
ed Hunt to get out of his gig to meet a man with
out asking whom?   Is it credible that Prober
would receive a stranger, unless he knew how an
when he was to receive him.   You learn tha
Probert desired that twenty shillings might b
given to Hunt, in case he went in his own gig
You also hear that he gave him money to procur
a loin of pork on his way down.   Is this not th
conduct of men engaged in a joint business?
believe, though I cannot speak with certainty
that Weare was designed to be the sacrifice of th
fatal spirit which then possessed them, and that
also was to become their victim.   They had we
prepared themselves for the deed by the quantit
of brandy and water which they had taken.

Probert tells you that I and Hunt slept on th
sofa, at Gill's-hill-lane. Be it so.   Probert ba
admitted that he invited us down without havin
sufficient accommodation to receive us. Why w
put up with the sofa is clear. Miss Noyes wa

sleeping in the only spare bed.   What else could
we have done, under the circumstances?   As to
the evidence of what was taken out of the bag, I
have no observations to make upon it, because if
true, it is perfectly consistent with my evidence.
The evidence of the conversation spoken to by
Probert carries its own refutation.   Was it likely
that I should trust a matter of so great and awful
danger to Probert, who says he had no knowledge
of my design?   Probert adds. that I confessed my
intention to murder Mr. Barber Beaumont and
Mr. Woods, the latter being on the verge of marriage with Mrs. Probert's sister.   Is it credible
that I should entrust such a secret to Probert,
above all men on earth?   Observe, too, the con-
tradiction in their testimony.   He says that
Wardle's field was the place where the body was
first deposited.   Mrs. Probert says that it was
taken to the stable, and then dragged to the pond.
He says that there was a lantern.   Mrs. Probert
says that it was fine moonlight, which is contrary
to all the evidence of all the other witnesses.
What will be your surprise when you learn that
the garden gate is on one side of the house, the
stable on the other, and that the walk from the
stable to the pond is not to be seen from any part
of the house.   Probert says that he did not get up
next morning till nine o'clock.   What truth is
there in this?   Probert says, that on telling me
what he had heard at Mr. Nichol's, I said Then
I am baked.   And yet it appears that I returned
to town and lived where I did the preceding week,
with doors and drawers unlocked; actually post-

ing the marks of my guilt. Probert says that Hunt came down in dirty clothes; and it was proved that he was afterwards seen in clothes belonging to my brother. Probert tells you that the boy was sent away, which is the truth, and that because he might not be in the way to answer questions. What truth is there in this? You learn that Probert was going next day to quit the cottage, and that regular notice had been given. I have no more remarks to offer on this cold-blooded witness. You will receive with caution the evidence of such a man, when in his cross-examination he confesses that he did not think of giving evidence until Hunt had confessed. Then commenced the strife between them which should make out the strongest case to deserve and obtain the mercy of the crown. After much prevarication, Probert said that he did not come down till nine o'clock the next morning. He then refused to swear that it was so late as eight o'clock: his boy swears that it was not seven. You will not fail to remark the character of this witness, as it was wrung from him by the cross-examination of Mr. Andrews—that he had been committed to jail six or seven times, and that he had been frequently remanded by the commissioners in his bankruptcy. He proved himself that he had introduced Hunt to me: for what purpose is now only too plain. The evidence of Mrs. Probert, gentlemen, is no less open to discredit. You cannot have forgotten the account she gave of seeing the horse come from the stable, when, from the subsequent part of her examination, she admitted that she could not see the stable door. That

witness has also detailed a long conversation
which she says she heard, although it was conducted in whispers, and although the door which
intervened was shut. Now, gentlemen, I entreat
you to mark what follows: in answer to a question put to her by the learned judge, she said,
that the conversation, which she heard in whispers, was after she had seen her husband dragging
something across the water ; in this she is directly contradicted by her husband, who says, that
immediately after leaving the pond, he went up
stairs to bed. Is it not plain, then, gentlemen,
from this remarkable discrepancy, if from no other
circumstance, that the pretended whispering is a
scheme which has been arranged between Probert
and his wife, and which has broken down in their
attempt to execute it? I know not—I cannot
know; but I most firmly believe that the body
was never in Probert's pond at all. Mrs. Probert's account of the situation of the garden proves
nothing that should contravene this presumption.
The appearance of the ground is accounted for,
because she has said that potatoes were grown
there; and they would of course be dug up before she left the premises, as she was about to do
when the circumstances to which she speaks
are supposed to have taken place. It has been
stated, too, that the body was stripped, and taken
out at the side of the pond. I could not learn
from the evidence at which side ; but an en-
graving in the *Observer* newspaper of the 9th
of November last, represents it as being on
that side opposite to which Mrs. Probert said
she heard the body dragging. The evidence given

by Probert, the horse-keeper, seems to me, gentlemen, to deserve your most serious consideration.
From his testimony, you will perceive it is beyond
all doubt that Hunt hired the horse and gig; it
is proved no less clearly that he provided every
thing which was necessary for the occasion on
which he was to employ himself. The witness
Flect, has proved, too, that Hunt took the shawl;
and Probert has himself told you that he supplied
him with the sovereign which was to pay his expenses.

I now call your attention to the evidence of
Clark, the person keeping the White Lion at
Edgeware; and this I beg you to examine most
scrupulously. You will remember he stated, that
as he was returning home at night, he met a gig
on the wrong side of the road; that a coach was
at the same moment passing along, by the lamps
of which he was enabled to distinguish my person. Now, gentlemen, I ask you whether your
own experience does not convince you that this is
altogether false? I know, and every other man
who will take the trouble of reflecting for a moment on the statement, must also know, that it
must be false. On a wide dark road as this is
stated to have been, in a dark night, it would be
impossible for a person passing between a coach's
lamp and a gig on the wrong side of the road, to
distinguish the features of a man in the gig. You
know very well, that under such circumstances
the lamps would rather have been an hinderance
than otherwise.. And yet, in the face of this absolute impossibility, the witness Clark has sworn
that he was able to discern my person, and to see

that a gentleman was sitting upon my left hand.
This is in my humble opinion conclusive as to
the credit which you are to give to this witness's
testimony. It is, you know, commonly said, that
witnesses who endeavour to prove too much, commonly fail in every particular; and the observation was never more strikingly illustrated than in
the case of this Clark, whose demeanour alone is
sufficient to show that no reliance can be placed
upon him, and whose character is such, that no
individual who knows him would believe him on
his oath. The testimony of the hackney coachman, to which I must now call your attention,
proves that he set down Mr. Weare at half-past
four o'clock. This he has sworn to positively;
he said also that a man in a light shaggy coat met
the deceased when he set him down, and assisted
in carrying away the luggage. All the witnesses
agree that I did not leave Testall's until five
o'clock. I therefore could not have been the
person alluded to. That the evidence of the
coachman has been such as it is, I am indebted, I
believe, to the caution of my solicitor; for if the
witness had been allowed to see me alone, and as
others were introduced to me, I have no doubt
that he, as well as they, would have identified me,
and would thus have been the means of strength-
ening the conspiracy of which I am the victim.
Upon the evidence, I have to observe, to you,
gentlemen, that although he says now he never
stated the gig he saw to have been a yellow gig,
my recollection is quite clear that he did so state
it before the magistrates. Clark's hostler proves

that the night was so dark, it was impossible to distinguish colours.

Mr. Field, the landlord of the Artichoke, at Elstree, has proved that Probert and Hunt did not reach his house until past nine o'clock. Clark says they left his house at seven; thus, you see, gentlemen, there was ample time for Hunt and Probert to have gone to Gill's hill-lane, and to have perpetrated this atrocious deed, and to have returned to the Artichoke in time to be seen by Mr. Field. That they did so, I have no doubt, and it is also most consistent with that desire which they have manifested throughout, to shift the blame from their own shoulders to those of any other person. Can you believe, gentlemen, the story which has been told you, of Hunt leaving his companion in the dark, within a mile and a half of Probert's cottage; Can you believe the evidence which has been given you by Probert? I am sure you cannot; and if you disbelieve that man, there is no testimony whatever tending to fix upon me the horrid crime with which I am charged. Clark's hostler has stated that he saw two gentlemen in the gig at half past seven, and that it was then so dark that he could not discern the countenances of either; and yet, notwithstanding this assertion, the laundry-maid has been brought to swear, that she believed Mr. Weare to have been one of the persons, but you are still uninformed, gentlemen, in spite of all this effort in swearing, who was the other person. Why, I ask, and I am sure you will ask too, why did not this hostler, when the business was first under investigation, go before the magistrates on the coroner's jury, and state there what he has now been induced to depose before you? His evidence and that of his master, so far as it can be at all credited, go distinctly to prove that it was impossible for me to have been seen by either of them. Upon the evidence of the man who sold the pistols, I do not think it necessary to say anything, because I am satisfied, gentlemen, that you cannot suppose that any thing can be collected from that by which I am to be convicted. With respect to the conversation of which you have heard, and which is said to have taken place between me and an officer at St. Alban's, all I have to observe, is, that although some such conversation did occur, the nature of it has been much mistaken. I said nothing more than that even if I were guilty as Hunt had represented me to be, he must nevertheless be a great scoundrel; for that if I had been in his place, I would have died rather than have betrayed my companion. Enough has been said to you about the watch; it has been most minutely and circumstantially described, and yet it is not forthcoming. Have you not a right, and have I not still a greater right to ask, Where is it? what has become of it? why do they not produce it?

I ought to rejoice, gentlemen, that these circumstances, upon which my prosecutors have relied to prove my guilt, will, when fairly and dispassionately considered, furnish evidence of my innocence. Gentlemen, your verdict must be formed entirely upon circumstances. Those circumstances. I think, I have satisfactorily shown, do not point at me as the perpetrator of this horrid deed; but circumstantial evidence is at best a fearful guide for human judgment, as the annals of our own and of foreign jurisprudence too frequently show. The imperfection of human judgment, aided only by circumstantial evidence, devoted a father to death for the supposed murder of his son, and a servant for a crime of which she was afterwards proved to be innocent. The names of Calas and Palaisea present an awful lesson to judges and to jurors who have decided upon the lives of their fellow creatures. In our own happy country, instances of incorrect judgment have been less frequent, but still they have occurred often enough to inspire jurors with the utmost caution. Mr. Justice Hale, in his Pleas of the Crown, vol. 2, p. 290, declares in the most impressive manner, that he would never sanction a verdict against a prisoner charged with murder, unless evidence of the most satisfactory nature respecting the body of the deceased, and the nature of the wounds which had caused his death, should be produced in aid of the circumstances by which the accusation was to be supported. The same learned judge quotes a cause showing the necessity of such a resolution, which he states to have happened in Staffordshire, within his own recollection. A. was missing, and there having been a strong presumption that he had been dispatched by B., who was suspected of having consumed his body to ashes in his own oven, B. was indicted for the murder, convicted, and executed. About a year afterwards A. returned home from beyond the seas, whither he had been sent by B. against his will : so that, although perhaps B. really deserved death, he was clearly innocent of the crime for which he suffered. Another case was that of a nobleman, who had the care of bringing up his niece, to whom he was next in succession to certain property. The child it seems had committed some offence, for which her uncle had found it necessary to correct her, and she had been overheard saying, Good uncle, don't kill me. The child was afterwards not to be found ; the uncle was committed for the murder, and the judge, before whom he was tried, admonished him to find the child against the next assizes. When that period arrived, the uncle did not find the child, but produced another like his niece, in years and in figure. On examination it was discovered that this child was not the one that had disappeared, and the uncle was found guilty and executed. It appeared afterwards that the child had been terrified, and had run away, and had been received by a stranger who had maintained her ; and when she became of age she claimed her land, and was put in possession of it, having satisfactorily proved herself to be the true child.

The prisoner read the cases with a firm voice, and in a most distinct manner. At their conclusion he said, I shall not trouble you, gentlemen of the jury, with any more cases. (Here Thurtell's solicitor said something to him in an under tone, and he then cited one more case from the *Newgate Calendar*.)—As the case is long, I shall not detain you by reading it all. I shall give only

the heads of it.   It is the trial of a man named
Holman, in 1748, at Kingston, for the murder of
a young woman.   The young woman lived ten
weeks after receiving the wounds that eventually
caused her death.   She stated before her death,
that she had been attacked by a man named Holman.   Holman was taken up : and a strong case
of circumstances being made out against him, he
was executed, protesting his innocence to the last
moment.   In about three years after this, two
persons were tried for another murder, and found
guilty : they then confessed that Holman had died
undeservedly, that he was wholly ignorant of the
murder.   They acknowledged that it was committed by one of them, who had assumed the name
of Holman, in order that he (Holman) might afterwards be charged with it.   Thurtell then resumed his paper and read.—And now, gentlemen,
having read those cases to you, am I not justified
in saying, that unless you are thoroughly convinced
that the circumstances before you are actually
inconsistent with my innocence, I have a claim to
your verdict of acquittal ?   Am I not justified in
saying, that you might come to the conclusion,
that all the circumstances stated might be true,
and yet I be innocent.   I am sure, gentlemen,
you will banish from your minds any prejudice
which may have been excited against me, and act
upon the principle, that every man is to be deemed
innocent, until he is proved guilty.

Judge of my case, gentlemen, with mature consideration, and remember that my existence de-
pends upon your breath. If you bring in a verdict
of guilty, the law afterwards allows no mercy. If

upon a due consideration of all the circumstances you shall have a doubt, the law orders, and your own conscience will teach you to give me the benefit of it. I implore you, gentlemen, to give my case your utmost attention. I ask not so much for myself as for those respectable parents whose name I bear, and who must suffer in my fate. I ask it for the sake of that home which will be rendered cheerless and desolate by my death. Gentlemen, I am incapable of any dishonourable action. Those who know me best know that I am utterly incapable of an unjust and dishonourable action, much less of the horrid crime with which I am now charged.

There is not, I think, one in this court who does not think me innocent of the charge. If there be, to him or them I say in the language of the apostle, 'Would to God ye were altogether such as I am, excepting these bonds.' Gentlemen, I have now done. I look with confidence to your decision, I hope your verdict this day will be such as you may ever be able to think upon with a composed conscience; and that you will also reflect upon the solemn declaration which I now make— So help me God, I am innocent.

This last sentence Thurtell pronounced in a manner most forcible and touching; and after pressing his hands closely to his heart, he raised his eyes to heaven in a most devout and imploring manner, bowed to the judge and jury, and respectfully resumed his seat. This affecting behaviour appeared to have excited a considerable degree of sympathy in his favour.

The judge then addressing himself to the prisoner Hunt, said, Joseph Hunt, it is now your time, as your counsel cannot address the jury on your behalf, to say what you think proper in your defence; but before you begin, the purposes of justice require that the witnesses for the other prisoner should be heard first.

The witnesses having been examined, Mr. Justice Park said, he would now hear Hunt's defence.

Hunt said, I have a defence, which from the extreme anxiety of mind under which I labour, I think I shall not be able to read through myself.

Mr. Justice Park. You had better hand it to the officer of the court, and allow him to read it.

Hunt accordingly gave a paper one of the sheriff's officers, who put it into the hands of Mr. Knapp, the clerk of arraigns. That gentleman proceeded immediately to read it. It was as follows:

My Lord,—Having, under a positive assurance that I should be admitted a witness for the crown, made a full and true confession of all the facts within my knowledge respecting this horrible and melancholy event, and having implicitly relied on the good faith of magistrates for the due performance of their solemn promises, made subsequently to my disclosure, I forebore to make the slightest preparation for my defence; and after your lordship shall be made acquainted with the circumstances under which that confession was drawn from me, your lordship's feelings and compassionate heart will be able to appreciate, although I am unable to describe, the painful emotions of surprise and disappointment by which I was overwhelmed, when, only a few days before the assizes, it was notified to me, for the first time, that I was to be placed in my present perilous and awful situation. You lordship will perceive that the very circumstance which I was told would procure me forgiveness, and ensure my safety, has alone rendered me amenable to the laws—namely, my own disclosure and declaration; for, although the prosecutors may not offer my confession in evidence, yet, as that confession has been published in every newspaper in the kingdom, and has been circulated in many a thousand pamphlets, and been the subject of universal conversation, is it probable or even possible, that any of the gentlemen who are now sitting in judgement on my case can be ignorant that such a confession has been made? How futile, then, and unavailing would be any observations or arguments to raise a presumption of the innocence of a man, who already to a certain extent, stands self-condemned. Feeling myself in this dilemma, I shall abstain from troubling your lordship with any detail of facts or observations upon the main question involved in the indictment, but merely assert, that I was not present when the unfortunate deceased lost his life, and that I was ignorant of any premeditated plan or intention to destroy him; I never knew of the murder until after it was committed, my crime consists solely in concealment; and my discovery could not bring the dead to life; my error arises, not from any guilt of my own, but from my concealment of the guilt of others. I

am now on my trial for having been privy to t
previous design—I never was; I certainly co
cealed it afterwards, sooner than betray the m
fortune which had been confided to me. Yo
lordship, however, will, I am sure, tell the gentl
men of the jury that no concealment or condu
of mine after the death will make out the pr
sent charge, and I hope both your lordsh
and these gentlemen are too just and me
ciful to convict me from prejudice, and not fro
proof.

I now, my lord, most respectfully solicit yo
humane attention to the following statement:—

On the morning of Wednesday the 29th of O
tober, I was apprehended in London, and direc
conveyed to Watford, where an investigation w
going on respecting the then supposed murder
Mr. Weare. On my arrival I found several m
gistrates assembled, and Mr. Noel, who was a
parently conducting the prosecution, address
me as follows:—Mr, Hunt, for God's sake, t
the magistrates whatever you know of this murd
and in all probability you will be admitted as
evidence. It is clear that Mr. Weare has be
murdered, and we only want to find where t
body is, and if you know, for God's sake tell
I repeatedly denied all knowledge of the circu
stance, and Mr. Noel as frequently importun
and urged me to confess. At last the magistra
said, Mr. Hunt, you had better retire and consid
the offer made you, and recollect your perilo
situation. I was then conveyed into another roo

and was presently followed by Mr. Noel, who in the presence of Ruthven and Upson, repeatedly told me that if I would tell where the body was, provided I did not actually commit the murder,) that I should be admitted as an evidence, and my life would be spared ; and added, that the magistrates had authorised him to make a pledge to this effect. Still, however, I was firm in my denial, and continued so until Upson the officer tortured my feelings by the mention of my family. He said to me, Hunt, you have a mother? I answered, Yes, I have. And a wife also? I said, Yes. And you love them dearly? Then said he, For their sakes do not risk an ignominious death, but tell where the body is, and give your evidence immediately, or you may be too late, for Probert or the other will disclose, and then nothing can save you.

This address had a great effect upon me, and Noel perceiving it, again pressed me to confess what I knew, saying, Do not hesitate, for you have now a chance, consider the situation you are in, and avail yourself of the offer now made to you, for I am authorised by the magistrates to say, that you will be admitted as an evidence for the crown, and not be treated as the others. You will merely be confined until the trial, to give evidence, and then be discharged. On receiving this assurance, I consented to become a witness, and Mr. Noel then asked if I knew where the body was? I told him yes, that I could not describe the place by name, but I could point it out: on which Mr. Noel struck his hand on the table, and exclaimed, that's all we want, and shaking me by the hand, said, Hunt, I am very glad you have saved your own life.

" We now returned into the room where the magistrates were, and Mr. Noel told them I was ready to make a disclosure, and said, I have made known to him, through your orders, that if he discovers where the body is, he is to be admitted as evidence ; but, before he says any thing, I wish him to have that assurance in your presence, that he may be satisfied from yourselves that I was authorised to make the promise. The magistrates, Mr. Clutterbuck and Mr. Mason, replied, that Mr. Noel had their authority for what he had done ; and then Mr. Noel said, Now, Mr. Hunt, having heard the magistrates' decision as to your being a witness, I hope you are satisfied, and I beg you will take a seat, and tell us all you know. I then detailed every thing that occurred to my recollection, but having been apprehended early the preceding day, conveyed into the country and harrassed and importuned throughout the night, it could hardly be expected that I should, at four or five o'clock in the morning, in making a very long statement, recollect every circumstance ; indeed, the magistrates were aware that such could not be the case, and they told me, that as in the hurry and confusion of the moment, I had no doubt omitted many facts that I should afterwards on reflection recollect, and if such were the case, I had only to address a letter to the magistrates, and they would immediately attend to it. Shortly after quitting the room, several particulars came to my recollection which I had not named, and I directly sent for Mr. Noel and mentioned them to him. At nine o'clock the same morning, I went with the officers and pointed out the spot where the body had been deposited; I was then taken back to the magistrates to sign my statement, and previous to my being taken to prison, Mr. Clutterbuck desired that I should be treated with kindness, and not put under any unnecessary restraint. I was accordingly conveyed to St. Albans without being ironed or handcuffed, and was there treated with every possible indulgence.

It is perfectly true, than when before the coroner, I was admonished to make no farther confession; but the admonition was a mockery. I had already, under a solemn promise, confessed every thing material: and the coroner himself, when he thus affected to forewarn me, well knew that he and his jury were at that instant sitting in inquest on the body solely in consequence of my disclosure: no jury could have sat—no death could have been proved—no body could have been found—no trial could have been had, but for my instrumentality. I was trepanned into a confession by the plighted faith of the magistracy of this county. If they break it now, they will not merely make me the victim of its violation, but they will be answerable to society for every future crime against the discovery of which their conduct will be an eternal admonition. Who can rest his life on magisterial assurance? To no human being can they ever pledge themselves more sacredly than to me, yet here I stand to-day a proof of their sincerity; nay, more than this—

P

not only have they broken faith and violated honour, but while the press was unceasing in the excitement of prejudice—while the theatre and the painter were employed in poisoning the public mind—while every engine was at work to diminish the chances of an impartial trial, these very men, who had thus ensnared me by perfidious declarations, closed their prison door against friends and legal advisers, and opened them only to the mandate of the King's Bench. Thus was I first ensnared, and afterwards sought to be sacrificed. Seduced into a confession which was trumpeted through the world, and then cruelly secluded until the time arrived when I was to suffer—not for my crime, but my credulity; not because I erred, but because I trusted: not because I violated the law, but because I confided in the conscience of its ministers. It is in vain to say that my confession was not complete: it was as ample as could have been expected at the moment, from an exhausted frame and an agitated mind. It was subsequently amended, where it was at first deficient; and no sophistry can evade the fact, that through that confession alone the body was discovered. Thus, then, the main circumstance—that on which every thing turned, was disclosed at once: and it is absurd to attribute to ought but momentary confusion, any minor concealment, when the great essential, and indispensable developement had taken place.

The prosecutors, my lord, may affect to say that as they refuse to grant the boon promised for the disclosure, they will decline using, or taking any advantage of the confession, and I humbly submit that such a line of conduct would be alone inconsistent with justice and fair dealing; for if they retract their engagement, they ought not to place me in a worse situation than I was at the moment when, confiding in their integrity I unbosomed the secret. If the prosecutors act with liberality and forbear to offer a title of evidence respecting the body, and, in conducting the case, consider it as still undiscovered, I can have no cause to complain of plighted faith and broken promises, because your lordship need not be reminded that it has been laid down as a principle, that no death can be considered as proved, unless the body be found, and consequently in this case no conviction can take place. But if witnesses are produced to prove the finding of the body, can it be said that my confession is not taken advantage of? and will not the prosecutors be taunting me by an affectation of candour, if they take credit for not giving in evidence any declaration made by me, while they avail themselves of the very essence and substance of the communication.

In addition to this statement, Mr. Noel inserts a letter from Mr. Clutterbuck, to himself, in which the magistrate observes, that as my case was then gone out of the hands of the magistrates all that could be done for me was to ask of the court whether they would allow me to be evidence for the crown.

Having now, my lord, faithfully stated the inducements by which I was led to make that disclosure which alone rendered myself and my fellow prisoners amenable to justice, I respectfully submit to your lordship, whether, in being now put upon my trial, and made the victim of my own credulity, I have been fairly and candidly dealt with? I will not, my lord, attempt to point out or discuss the mischiefs likely to arise if such engagements as were entered into with me are to be cancelled at pleasure, because they will occur much more forcibly to your lordship's enlightened mind: indeed, so far as I am individually concerned, my fate is a subject of trifling importance. I have no desire to prolong a wretched existence, unless it be to afford the opportunity of endeavouring, by prayer and penitence, to obtain mercy and forgiveness of the Almighty, for the sins and transgressions I have committed. But in pity to the feelings of an aged and respectable mother, a virtuous and amiable wife, and my dearly beloved brother and sister, I do feel most anxious to avoid an ignominious death; and it is therefore for their sakes, more than my own, that I fervently and earnestly entreat the performance of the solemn pledge made to me of sparing my life.

I have nothing further to add, but most humbly repose my fate in the justice and humanity of your lordship,

Mr. Justice Park summed up the evidence to the jury at great length, and the jury retired at half past three. At four o'clock they returned, and pronounced their verdict, finding Thurtell guilty of murder; and Hunt also guilty as an accessory before the fact.

The Clerk of the arraigns now asked the prisoners if they had any thing to urge why sentence of death should not be pronounced upon them? Thurtell then, leaning over the bar, said, I implore your lordship to take what I have to say into your most serious consideration. I now for the last time assert my innocence. I repeat, I hope your lordship will take my request into your serious consideration, when I beseech you to postpone the execution until Monday next. My reason for asking this is, that my friends are at a considerable distance, and many of them wish to see me. For myself alone I do not ask this delay: for if the sentence were to be executed now, I am ready: but I ask it for the sake of those whose feelings on this occasion are of more interest to me than my own. Between me and some members of my family there are some matters to be arranged which will require the delay for which I ask.

The prisoner Hunt declined to address the court.

Mr. Justice Park, having put on the black coif, passed sentence upon the prisoners: and Thurtell was executed on the 9th of January, Hunt, however, escaped, and was sent to New South Wales for life.

LAMBERT READING.

Executed at Chelmsford, August 10, 1775, for Burglary.

THE only circumstance which we can trace in this robber's case, worthy of naming, is the detection of his crime through a hackney coachman, his confederate.

There are no greater set of villains infesting London and its environs than hackney-coachmen, and were it not for the strict regulations under which they are kept, no gangs would be more to be dreaded.

Lambert Reading was the principal of a desperate gang who robbed Copped-hall, in Essex, near London. He had a hackney-coachman in confederacy, who waited for him at Stratford.

A magistrate of the county happening to pass by the coach, was struck at its being there at an unusual hour of the night, and from which circumstance, he was induced to observe its number.

Hearing the next day of the robbery at Copped-hall, he wrote to Sir John Fielding his suspicions, and named the number of the coach.

From this information the thief-takers traced Reading to a house in Brick-lane, where they found him in bed with a woman who passed for his wife.

He was surrounded with pistols, hangers, picklock keys, dark lanterns, and other apparatus of a house breaker. He had an opportunity of using some of these arms in his defence, but he was so greatly intimidated, that he quietly surrendered himself.

The most material result of the search was, the whole of the plate stolen from Copped-hall, which was found hid in Reading's apartment, in three sacks.

On evidence to this effect, added to other corroborating circumstances, he was convicted and executed.

The hackney-coachman, whose name was Chapman, and who drove for one Conyers, the owner, was taken on the day of Reading's trial; and being found guilty as an accessary, received also sentence of death, which was afterwards commuted to transportation.

HENRY FAUNTLEROY,

Executed for forgery.

No act of the British Parliament in our day has given greater satisfaction than that which abolished the punishment of death for the crime of forgery. There is something truly revolting to human nature in the execution of a criminal, and it was peculiarly distressing in the case we are now about to record. Fauntleroy was in the prime of life, of superior talents and education, and moved in the first circles of society. It was generally believed, that he committed the fatal act with the intention of enabling the bank, with which he was connected, to surmount some pecuniary difficulties which by an unfortunate speculation of his were then pressing upon it. When he appeared in court, he seemed to feel deeply the position in which he was placed, his face became pale, his limbs shook, and his step faltered.

Seven different indictments for forgery were laid against him, to each of which he pleaded not guilty.

First—that on the 1st of June, in the 55th year of the late king, in the parish of St. Mary-le-bone he did feloniously and falsely make and forge, and counterfeit a certain deed, purporting to bear the name of Frances Young, for the transfer of £5450 long annuities of her monies in the stocks established by the act of 5th of the late king George II., with intent to defraud the said Frances Young of the said stock.

The second, for that he, on the 3rd of June, in the 55th year of the late king, falsely forge and counterfeit a certain transfer, purporting to be that of Frances Young, for £5000 of her annuities, with intent to defraud her. The forgery and fraud were also laid as in the first indictment, as with intent to defraud the governor and company of the bank of England.

The third indictment, was for forging a transfer of the stock held in the name of T. Lister, Esq., of Wexford, in Ireland, and uttering the same.

The fourth indictment, was for forging a transfer for £3000. stock, also uttered in the same name, on the 16th of December, in the 60th year of the late king's reign.

The fifth indictment, was for forging a transfer of £435. stock, with intent to defraud the bank and John Griffiths.

The sixth indictment was for, on the same date, forging and putting away a transfer of £500. stock, held in the same name.—And the seventh indictment was, for forging and uttering a power of attorney to transfer £300. annuities entered in the name of Jacob Tubbs.

The attorney-general stated the case for the prosecution as follows:—May it please you, my lords and gentlemen of the jury,—you have heard during the reading of this indictment, that the prisoner at the bar stands charged with fraudulently forging and uttering a certain power of attorney for the transfer of certain stock, entered in the Bank of England in the name of Miss Frances Young. It is my duty on the part of the prosecution, to state to you the circumstances out of which, according to my instructions, the present prosecution has originated; and afterwards to lay before you the evidence which I have to offer in support of this indictment.

The prisoner at the bar, gentlemen, was well known as a partner in the banking-house of Marsh, Sibbald, and Co., of Berners-street, which was established about thirty years ago. His father was a partner in the original firm—he had previously been an active clerk in a banking house in the city, and the partners who established the firm, not being equally men of business themselves, gave him a share to avail themselves of his practical information in the management of their affairs. The elder Mr. Fauntleroy died in the year 1807, and his situation was immediately occupied by his son, the prisoner at the bar, upon whom, also, for his practical knowledge of business, and the comparative superiority which he had in this respect over his co-partners, nearly the whole of the actual business devolved. In the year 1815, Miss Frances Young, of Chichester, became a customer to the firm, and had then entered in her name at the bank a sum of £5430., in what were called the three per cent. consols. She gave the firm of Marsh and Co., a power to receive the dividends in her name, but gave them no power to sell or otherwise dispose of the principal. In May, 1815, however, an application was made at the bank, and represented as having been so made in behalf of this lady, to sell, by her power of attorney, £500. of this stock.

You are probably aware of the forms prescribed by the Bank of England in transacting the business of these transfers. The applicant goes to the bank, and obtains a slip of paper, which he fills up with the names of the party in whose behalf he applies, he describes the stock in the bank, the amount and particulars required to be transferred, and the name and address of the person to whom the transfer is to be made. Upon receiving these instructions in the form inserted upon a slip of paper, the bank clerk, to whom it is delivered, hands over a power of attorney which is to be transmitted to the person who is to make the transfer, for the purpose of receiving the requisite signature. It is customary at the bank to preserve these slips of paper, but in this instance the particular slip has been lost, and it cannot therefore be said to whom it was delivered, it being usual to endorse the name of the party on the slip. But the power of attorney, which was prepared according to the slip so made is referred, with the necessary attestations of the witnesses. There must be to these powers of attorney two attesting witnesses, and the description of their respective names and addresses. This power of attorney purported to be signed by Frances Young, and that signature would be proved to be a forgery. The attesting witnesses were John Watson and James Tyson, clerks in the bank of Marsh and Co., and their signatures were also forgeries—for they never transacted any business with Miss Frances Young, and never executed any transfer of stock for her. In all these documents it is required by the bank that the date shall be set forth in words at length. This is so done in this forged transfer, and it will be proved to be the hand writing of the prisoner at the bar, in all its parts.

It must be quite clear, therefore, that the forgery has been committed by the prisoner, or with his knowledge. The attesting witnesses are his clerks, men whose hand writing must have been known to him, and a forgery he must at once have detected if brought to him by a third party. The practice at the Bank of England was, that when these transfers, after being duly filled, were executed, they must be deposited for twenty-four hours with the clerk, for the purpose of being compared with the books, and for such other in-

spections as were deemed necessary on these o
casions for the security of property, so far as ti
and circumstances allowed.   After all these p
liminary steps the applicant was further cal
upon, before the instrument was completed,
write at the bottom these words : I demand t
power to be executed in my name, signed by t
party.   On the 31st of May, or the 1st of Ju
the prisoner at the bar attended in person at t
bank, and demanded in due form the execution
the said power of attorney.   So that here you w
have before you a power of attorney prepared
the prisoner's hand writing, purporting to be e
cuted by Frances Young, purporting to be att
ed by two of his clerks, with whose hand writi
I repeat, he must have been necessarily acqua
ed ; and he himself presenting the instrume
and demanding that it be executed in the us
manner.   But sufficient as this would be to pr
the case, it is not all, for I am about to state
you that we have besides a document of a chara
so extraordinary, so singularly complete in all
parts, as to leave no possible doubt that the
soner at the bar was the party who had commi
the offence.   When the prisoner was taken
custody in his own house, he, in the presen
the officer, locked his private desk, with a
which was then attached to his watch—that
was afterwards taken from him by the offi
and when the respectable solicitor for the b
who conducts this prosecution, went to search
house in Berners-street for the prisoner's pap
to ascertain whatever particulars he could the
find respecting these transactions, he found in

the rooms of Messrs. Marsh and Co's Bank, in which tin cases, containing title deeds of their customers were deposited, and on which the name the owners were inscribed, one tin box without name. This led him to examine it. The key found in the prisoner's private desk, which had himself locked in the presence of the officer, on opening the box he found a number of private papers belonging to the prisoner, and among them the extraordinary document of which have apprised you, and which ran thus, all in hand writing of the prisoner.

Consols, 11.1511. standing in the name of my trusteeship : 3000. E. W. Young ; £6000. consols, general Young ; £5000 in Long Annuities, Frances Young ; another £6000. ; Lady Nelson. 594 ; Mrs. Ferrer, £20,000. 4 per cent. ; Earl Ossory, £7000. ; T. W. Owen, 6400 ; J. W, kins, 4000 ; Lord Aboyne, £6000. ; P. Moore d John Marsh, £21,000. This paper, containing a total of sums considerably exceeding £100,000. is all written in the prisoner's hand-writing, and these words, in the same hand followed, and concluded the facts of the prisoner's guilt—In order keep up the credit of our house, I have forged powers of attorney, and have thereupon sold out these sums, without the knowledge of any of my partners. I have given credit in the accounts the interests when it became due.

May 7th, 1816. (Signed) Henry Fauntleroy.

These words followed :—

The bank began first to refuse our acceptances, d thereby to destroy the credit of our house, y shall therefore smart for it.

This is the extraordinary document to which I allude, and was there ever a record of fraud more intelligible, and yet more negligently kept? There is no doubt, I think, that when the prisoner at the bar drew up this singular and conclusive document, that he contemplated some intention for which it was applicable, perhaps to abscond, and protect his partners from any suspicion of participation in his acts. Be the intention, however, what it may, if to abscond, it was clear the prisoner had subsequently altered his intention, and at all events, nothing but unaccountable negligence could have prevented him from afterwards destroying a document of such a nature, and so fatal to his character. The Bank of England, in consequence of this information, proceeded to examine the private accounts kept by the prisoner with his firm, and there they found that the accounts of the parties whose monies were fraudulently transferred, were regularly kept up, and the dividends as regularly carried to them every half year, as if the original stock remained in being. In the particular case before you, the broker, (Mr. Spurling) employed by the prisoner at the bar, sold out the stock in question to the amount of £2950. 2s. 6d. that is exclusive of the commission for sale, which, according to practice, the broker divided with the firm. This amount was paid over by the broker to the banking house of Messrs. Martin and Co., in the city, and is regularly noted in the day book of the latter, by a clerk, by whom the entry was made at the dictation of the prisoner. But in further management of the accounts in passing from the day book to the private ledger, this sum appeared to have been carried to Mr. Fauntleroy's private account. The general produce was, however, afterwards posted, so as to keep up the accounts according to the original amount entrusted to the bank by the respective customers.

You will, gentlemen of the jury, naturally ask yourselves, as this occurred so far back as the year 1815, how it happened that during the successive years which have intervened, the dividends could have been so managed by the prisoner in his accounts, as to escape the detection of his partners? The fact however, was, that the prisoner had the entire management for the firm of their stock market business. When the dividends became payable, it was the practice to make out a list for one of the partners to go to the Bank of England and receive payment. These lists were always prepared by the prisoner himself, and he always continued so to manage the entry in the books as to correspond with the nominal amount of stock entrusted to the firm by their customers. The list was of course so made out as to represent every thing entered in the manner the entries would have stood had the stock still existed; the sums were always carried on to the accounts, so as to keep up the delusion. It used to be the custom of Mr. Marsh to go to the bank and receive the dividends for the firm; he lived in the country, and only came to town to perform this part of the business: he was, therefore, as to all the other parts of the arrangement, entirely ignorant, and incapable of detecting the fraud. There is another fact which I think it my duty to ex-

plain to you ; the note of the broker for the sa
of this particular stock, which Mr. Fauntler
ought, were the transaction a *bona fide* one, 1
have transmitted to the owner, was found again
his other papers in the private tin box, which co
tained the extraordinary document I have alread
read to you.

These, gentlemen, are the whole of the fac
which I undertake to establish by evidence befor
you, against the prisoner at the bar. I shall fir
prove the forgery, by producing the instrumen
and proving, by the parties whose names are sai
to be affixed to it, that the signatures are n
theirs. I shall next prove that the hand writin
in the body of the instrument is that of the pr
soner himself. I shall then, by the production
the extraordinary document to which I have a
luded, prove that he recorded the act as his, an
from the accounts it will be clear that they we
so continued by him, with great activity and ca
tion, as to evade the detection of the forgerie
which he alone could have committed.

Several witnesses were examined on the part
the prosecution, and on the prisoner being call
upon for his defence, he read the following a
dress :—

My lords and gentlemen of the jury, overwheln
ed as I am by the situation in which I am place
and being uninformed in what manner I shou
answer the charges which have been alleg
against me, I will endeavour to explain, so w
as the poignancy of my feelings will enable m
the embarrassments of the banking-house in whi
I have been for many years the active and on

responsible partner, and which have alone led to the present investigation. And although I am aware I cannot expect to free myself from the obloquy brought upon me by my anxiety to preserve the credit and respectability of the firm, still I trust that an impartial narrative of the occurrence will obtain for me the commiseration of the well disposed part of the community.

Anticipating the court will extend its indulgence to me, I will respectfully submit such observations as I think will tend to remove from influenced minds, those impressions, which with sorrow I say must have been made upon them by the cruel and illiberal manner in which the public prints have falsely detailed a history of my life and conduct, hoping therefrom I may deserve your compassion, although I may be unable to justify my proceedings and secure my liberation, by a verdict of the jury; yet they may be considered, in the mercy of the court and a discerning public, as some extenuation of the crimes with which I stand arraigned.

With this object it is necessary that I should first state, shortly, the circumstances under which I have been placed under my connection with Marsh and Co.

My father established the banking-house in 1792, in conjunction with Mr. Marsh and other gentlemen. Some of the parties retired in 1794, about which time a loss of £20,000 was sustained. Here commenced the difficulties of the house. In 1796, Mr. Stracey and another gentleman came into the firm, with little or no augmentation of capital.

In 1800, I became a clerk in the house, and continued so six years, and although during that time I received no salary, the firm were so well satisfied with my attention and zeal for the interest and welfare of the establishment, that I was handsomely rewarded by them. In 1807 my father died; I then succeeded him; at this time I was only twenty-two years of age, and the whole weight of an extensive but needy banking establishment devolved upon me, and I found the concern deeply involved in advances to builders and others, which had rendered a system of discounting necessary, and which we were obliged to continue in consequence of the scarcity of money at that time, and the necessity of making further advances to those persons to secure the sums in which they stood indebted.

In this perplexed state the house continued until 1810, when its embarrassments were greatly increased, owing to the bankruptcies of Brickwood and others, which brought upon it a sudden demand for no less a sum than £170,000, the greater part being for the amount of bills which our house had accepted and discounted for these parties, since become bankrupts.

About 1814, 1815, and 1816, from the speculations with builders, brickmakers, &c., in which the house was engaged, it was called upon to provide funds to nearly £100,000, to avert the losses which would otherwise have visited it from those speculations.

In 1819, the most responsible of our partners died, and we were called upon to pay over the amount of capital, although the substantial re sources of the house were wholly inadequate to meet so large a demand.

During these numerous and trying difficulties the house was nearly without resources, and the whole burthen of management falling upon me, I was driven to a state of distraction, in which I could meet with no relief from my partners, and almost broken-hearted, I sought resources where I could, and so long as they were provided, and the credit of the house supported, no enquiries were made, either as to the manner in which they were procured, or as to the sources from whence they were derived.

In the midst of these calamities, not unknown to Mr. Stracy, he quitted England, and continued in France, on his own private business, for two years, leaving me to struggle as well as I could with difficulties almost insurmountable.

Having thus exposed all the necessities of the house, I declare that all the monies temporarily raised by me were applied, not in one instance, for my own separate purpose or expenses, but in every case they were immediately placed to the credit of the house in Berners street, and applied to the payment of the pressing demands upon it. This fact does not rest upon my assertion, as the transactions referred to are entered in the books now in the possession of the assignees, and to which I have had no access since my apprehension. These books, I understand, are now in court, and will confirm the truth of my statement; and to whatever accounts all the sums may be entered, whether to that of stock, of exchequer bills, or to any private account, the whole went to the general funds of the banking house.

I alone have been doomed to suffer the stigma of all the transactions ; but, tortured as I have been, it now becomes an imperative duty to explain to you, gentlemen, and through you to the world at large, that the vile accusations heaped upon me, are known to be utterly false, by all those who are best acquainted with my private life and habits, and have been heaped upon me for the purpose of loading me with the whole of the obloquy of those transactions, from which, and from which alone, my partners were preserved from bankruptcy. I have been accused of crimes I never even contemplated, and of acts of profligacy I never committed, and I appear at this bar with every prejudice against me, and almost prejudged. To suit the purposes of the persons to whom I allude, I have been represented as a man of prodigal extravagance ; prodigal indeed I must have been, had I expended those large sums which will hereafter be proved to have gone exclusively to support the credit of a tottering firm, the miseries of which were greatly accelerated by the drafts of two of its members to the amount of nearly £100,000.

I maintained but two establishmente, one at Brighton, where my mother and sister resided in the season—the expenses of which to me, exclusive of my wine, were within £400. per annum. One at Lambeth, where my two children lived, from its very nature, private and inexpensive, to which I resorted for retirement after many a day passed in devising means to

avert the embarrassment of the banking house.
The dwelling house in Berners-street, belonging
solely to my mother, with the exception of a
library and a single bed-room. This was the extent of my expenditure, as far as domestic expenditure is concerned. I am next accused of being
an habitual gambler, an accusation which, if true,
might easily account for the diffusion of the property. I am, indeed, a member of two clubs, the
Albion, and the Stratford, but never in my life did
I play at either, at cards or dice, or any game of
chance this is well known to the gentlemen of the
clubs: and my private friends with whom I am
more intimately associated, can equally assert my
freedom from all habit or disposition to play. It
has been as cruelly asserted, that I fraudulently in-
vested money in the funds to answer the payment
of annuities, amounting to 2200l. settled upon
females. I never did make any such investment;
neither at home nor abroad, in any funds whatever, have I any investment; nor is there one
shilling secretly deposited by me in the hands of
any human being. Equally ungenerous, and
equally untrue it is, to charge me with having
lent to loose and disorderly persons large sums
which never have, nor ever will be repaid. I lent
no sums, but to a very trifling amount, and those
were advanced to valued friends. I can, therefore, at this solemn moment, declare most fervently, that I never had any advantage beyond that in
which all my partners participated, in any of the
transactions which are now questioned. They,
indeed, have considered themselves partners only
in the profits, and I am to be burthened with the

whole of the opprobrium that others may consider them as the victims of my extravagance. I make this statement, not with a view to criminate others, or to exculpate myself; but borne down as I am by calumny, I will not consent to be held out to the world as a cold blooded and abandoned profligate. ruining all around me for the selfish gratification of vice and sensuality, and involving even my confiding partners in the general destruction.

Gentlemen, I have frailties and errors enough to account for. I have sufferings enough, past, present, and in prospect; and if my life was all that was required of me, I might endure the odium on my memory, of having sinned to pamper delinquences to which I never was addicted. Thus much has been extorted from me by the fabrications which have been cruelly spread among the public, that very public from whom the arbiters of my fate were to be selected. Perhaps, however, I ought to thank the enemy who besieged the prison with his slanders—that he did so while my life was spared to refute them, and that he waited not until the grave, to which he would hurry me, had closed at once on my answer and forgiveness. There is one subject more connected with the charges to which I am compelled to advert, and I do so with great reluctance. It has been added to other charges made against me, lest the world should think there was any vice in which I was not an adept. I have been accused of acting treacherously towards the female who now bears my name, having refused to make reparation until threatened by her brother, and of having deserted her at a moment when she had the greatest claim on my protection. Delicacy forbids me entering into an explanation on this object further than to declare, that the conduct I adopted on that occasion was uninfluenced by the interference of any individual, and arose as I then considered, and do still consider, from a laudable and honourable feeling on my part, and the lady's brother, so far from coming forward at the time alluded to, was on service in the West Indies. Could all the circumstances be exposed, I feel convinced that every liberal minded man would applaud my determination, and I feel satisfaction in stating, that the lady in question has always been, and still is actuated by the best of feelings towards me.

I have only now to apologize to the court for having entered so much at length into the statement of my unfortunate case, and in conclusion I have to express my perfect confidence, that it will receive every favourable consideration at your hands: and I will fully rely that you, gentlemen of the jury, will give an impartial and merciful decision.

After this extenuating address, the prisoner bowed to the court, and sat down evidently very much overcome by the effort he had made to deliver it in an audible manner. Proof was now adduced as to the prisoner's character, and several highly respectable gentlemen spoke most favourably of him.

Mr. Justice Park having summed up the case very minutely, the jury retired to deliberate on their verdict, and after an absence of twenty minutes, they returned a verdict of ' *Guilty of uttering the forged instrument, knowing it to be forged.'*

On November 2nd, Mr. Fauntleroy was brought up to receive his sentence, when the recorder passed sentence of death in the usual terms.

Perhaps in no case were the petitions for a commutation of sentence, so numerous, and so respectably signed ; but all efforts were unavailing, and the last sentence of the law was executed upon him on the 20th of November.

ANTHONY DRURY,

Executed at Tyburn on the 3rd of November, 1726, for Highway Robbery.

THIS offender was a native of Norfolk, and the son of parents in reputable circumstances, who imprudently neglected to bring him up to any business ; so that when he arrived at years of maturity, he wandered about the country curing smoky chimnies, which procured him the appellation of the smoky doctor, among those who knew his profession.

At length he married a woman, who was said to possess a large fortune ; but whatever this fortune was, Drury never received more of it than £500. He now lived some years with his wife at Andover ; but occasionally ranged the country in search of that business in which he seemed to take his chief delight. His wife used every argument to prevail with him to remain at home; but her solicitations were without effect.

Sometimes he would stroll to London; and bring with him valuable articles for his support: and on these occasions he pawned some plate for twenty pounds, and dissipated the money in company with women of abandoned character.

By degrees he stripped his wife of great part of what should have supported her, so that she was obliged to the friendship of her relations for a maintenance. By a continued course of extravagance he grew daily more and more vicious, and at length determined to commence highwayman.

In London he made an acquaintance with Robert King, the driver of the Bicester waggon.— This King was a fellow of the most execrable character, whose practice was to inform the highwaymen when he had any persons to travel in his waggon, who possessed any considerable sum of money or valuable effects, that they might be robbed on the road; on which occasions a share was always given to the driver.

Drury being in company with King, the latter told him that a gentleman named Eldridge would travel in the waggon on the following day, and that it would be prudent to rob him before he got far from town, as he would have with him a considerable booty.

Our adventurer listened eagerly to this tale, and the next day robbed Mr. Eldridge of two hundred and fourteen guineas. As he took money only, he had very little apprehension of detection; but another traveller in the waggon, happening to know him, repaired to London, and gave information against him ; whereupon he was taken into custody, and being brought to trial, was convicted on clear evidence.

After he received sentence of death, his behaviour was consistent with his unhappy situation. He was a regular attendant on divine worship, and a constant peruser of books of religion ; but at the same time he did every thing in his power to procure a respite of the fatal sentence. Some people of consequence exerted themselves to obtain the royal mercy for Drury, but in vain : his character and crime militated too forcibly against him.

After conviction he repeatedly wrote to his wife, desiring her to come to London : and among other motives to prevail on her, told her that she might redeem the plate which he had pawned; but all he could say had no effect ; she lent a deaf ear to all his entreaties. He appeared to be greatly disturbed in mind at this unfeeling indifference of his wife, which prevented that calmness of disposition which was requisite for his proper preparation for his approaching exit. Two days before his death he received the sacrament with every mark of real contrition. On the evening preceding his execution, a gentleman sent a woman to enquire what declaration he would make respecting the waggoner ; to whom he answered that he had no idea of committing the crime till King proposed it to him ; and that his life was sacrificed in consequence of his taking that advice.

When at the place of execution, he appeared to possess more courage than he had done some time before, and again declared that the waggoner had seduced him to commit the robbery. He earnestly exhorted young people to avoid bad company, as what would most infallibly bring them to destruction.

This malefactor suffered at Tyburn, on the 3rd of November, 1726, at the age of twenty-eight years.

WILLIAM GATESBY,

For Robbery.

THE following narrative, written by this unhappy individual, exhibits such a continued train of crimes. as can scarcely be credited. It is taken from his own handwriting, with mere verbal corrections.

I was born in the city of Litchfield, in the county of Stafford, of honest and creditable parents, who gave me education as far as their circumstances would allow. But being of a wild disposition, I gave little attention to my education. My uncle, who is a farmer in that county, took me under his charge at the age of fourteen : and having no child of his own, gave me great indulgence, till I became master of him, and then he sent me back to my father. I remained at home some time before I committed any act of theft. The first that I remember, was a pocket-book from a stationer's shop, which theft having reached my father's ears, I was severely beaten for the crime.

At the age of sixteen my father bound me apprentice to a blacksmith at Birmingham, and I behaved myself very well for a considerable time. But getting acquainted with a gang of thieves proved my ruin. I was well skilled in making locks and keys, and I made many false keys, and picklocks for them. With the assistance of these they robbed many capital shops, and I got an equal share of their booty. My master getting intelligence of my connection with these people, turned me off at the age of eighteen. I some time after got the place of boots to a great inn in Birmingham ; and being a clever lad, I was engaged by one Jenkins, a player, and was to receive ten shillings a week. I continued in this way five months, when my extravagance rendered the wages insufficient. I then engaged with a gentleman who was going to travel, and went with him to France. My master finding the inconvenience of my not understanding the language, was for parting with me, but delayed for some time, till he could find one who would carry me back to England. My master being of a gay and dissipated disposition, and being desirous of being acquainted with the manners of the country, frequently left me the charge of his clothes and money; and particularly when he went out at one time with some companions on a party of pleasure. I knowing that I was to leave him very soon, thought it was high time to make my market. I therefore immediately went off with his clothes and money—which last amounted to 307 guineas, and I arrived safe at London, and then at London. My unsettled mind and fear of detection would not allow me to stop there, and I therefore took a passage in a vessel to Dublin. I there passed for a gentleman's son. I got acquainted with a young gentleman, and being very intimate in the family, in the course of three months I became the lover of his sister. All this scene I went through in the course of a year. But my money becoming low, I was obliged again to take to my shifts; either to steal, or do what I could, for money. I began to be a thief again, and to save my credit, I wrote and forged letters to my mistress, on pretence that I had received money from my friends to visit my father. But being detected in the act of theft, I durst no more write nor approach the dwelling house of my mistress, whose father threatened my life if I presumed to come near his house. I then tried my fortune through some parts of Ireland, but nothing remarkable happened.

I left Ireland in the twentieth year of my age, and came to England to the town I was born in. My parents knew my bad character, and gave me little countenance. I therefore had my fortune to seek once more. On a Friday, being market day, I began to try my hand on picking pockets, and got a good booty off a gentleman that I was well acquainted with. I then left the place, and soon got a companion of the same profession. We went together through the country, and committed numerous acts of theft. I was apprehended at Stafford for picking a man's pocket of nine guineas and stood my trial, but did not get off without being publicly whipped. Five weeks after I got my liberty, I was apprehended again for robbing a man of fifteen guineas and stood my trial before Judge Buller but got clear. I got a companion, and we then went to London together. There we committed many daring acts of theft and robbery, particularly one on a gentleman's carriage at ten o'clock. By mistake in the dusk my companion's pistol went off, and wounded me in the left hip. Finding London too sharp for men of our trade, we determined to leave it. I was discovered, however, picking a gentleman's pocket of his purse, which contained seventy guineas, and after some time, finding I was pursued and would be taken, I threw it away; but when I was taken I was sent to Tothill-fields Bridewell for three months. I sent for my companion, and he gave the jailor some money; and in less than fourteen days my liberation was obtained on the footing of bad health. I left London four days after this, and went the direct road to Oxford; and I robbed two men on the road, but got very little from them. I became by this time very well known to the greatest part of the thieves in England, and was noted amongst them for picking both locks and pockets, and there were few that could surpass me.

I began to think it high time to alter my name I therefore went under the name of John Smith and made much booty in Oxford; but I left that city to go to a fair, to see what I could get. The place was called Banbury, about twelve miles from Oxford; I had not been there long before I joined a companion in the trade, and going together, we got some trifles from the multitude, but not sufficient to supply our greedy minds.

We were determined to have more before we left the place. We dined at an inn that day, and supped there likewise, and left the place at night determined to rob some person. We lighted ou a gentleman and lady in a carriage, and got between sixty and seventy guineas, with a gold and silver watch. We then took the direct road for Birmingham, but nothing happened extraordinary on our travels; only that I stole two silver tankards at an inn, in Coventry. When we came to Birmingham, we got ready sale for the watches and plate.

Being too well known at Birmingham, I remained there but four weeks during which time I drew up with a woman, and we cohabited as man and wife. I left her, and took the road to Bath. At Gloucester I took a booty to the value of eighty guineas from a silversmith, and then altered my route, taking the stage coach to Newmarket, where I had learned the races were to begin the next week. Arriving there two days before the races, I went to the play, and got that night eighty guineas.

I passed my time here among the girls of the place, and for a month appeared in the habit of a gentleman, but got many a good beating. When I left this place I had still remaining between seventy and eighty pounds, and was determined to see Bath. I went first to Bristol, and the night that I arrived there, I fell into company with three seafaring people, and won from them about £100, at cribbage. The next day I went in the

fly coach to Bath. Here I began to think of a
wife, as Bath was a place for a gentleman to make
his fortune in that way, and I thought I would
try mine. I did all that lay in my power to get
acquainted with the gentlewomen in the place,
and got acquainted with Mr. ———— a great merchant's son, who introduced me to a great deal
of company. Being one night at a card-room, I
had a great run of luck, and won near
three hundred guineas from a young gentleman,
but I being of a good natured temper, besides
thinking it might serve other good purposes, made
him a present of a hundred pounds af the money.
He was very grateful to me for my generosity,
and invited me to his father's house. This invi-
tation I accepted of, and got good entertainment
from his parents. My first introduction was to
tea, and I stayed supper. In the course of conversation I gave them a description of Ireland, as
at this time I passed for an Irish gentleman, under the name of Mr. John Burke, from the city
of Dublin. I visited the family very often, became very familiar in it, and attached myself to
the young lady. I made many valuable presents
to ingratiate myself in her favour.

I committed few acts of theft this winter, for I
had such luck at cards that I had no occasion to
employ other means for supplying myself with
money ; one exploit, however, is worthy of mentioning, viz. the robbery of the stage coach between Cricklade and Bath. There were six passengers in all, and I got from them a sum of very
near sixty guineas. Being thus at perfect liberty,
and unsuspected, I used every endeavour to gain

the favour and affection of the young lady above mentioned ; and I succeeded so well that she was always obliging and remarkably civil to me. We frequently walked together in the country: but one day, unluckily happening to drop a letter out of my pocket from a man of my own profession, who was then a prisoner in Exeter jail ; and I not missing it, she had an opportunity of perusing it, which made her acquainted with my true character. I did not fail to invent a number of stories, such as that it was a letter I had found, &c. but all these were to no purpose, when she remarked that the directions was to me at my lodgings. This was the occasion of the match between us being broken off. I then thought my character would be blasted at Bath, and I resolved to leave it; but before I did leave it, I committed the vilest action of my life, which I think the greatest sin I have to answer for to God, and for which I feel the greatest affliction.—Having settled all my affairs, and paid for my lodging, &c, I contrived to send a letter to the young lady, requesting her to meet me that evening near a certain gate at nine o'clock, that I might explain what had happened. This she complied with, I tied my horse to the gate, and talked with her for some time : and endeavoured to reconcile matters, but to no purpose. I then treated her very ill, mounted my horse, took the road for Birmingham, and never after heard of, or saw her.

I went on the Marlborough road and that night robbed the post, but got nothing of value. At Birmingham I went under the name of John

R

Brown, and got intimate with a woman who kept
a house of bad fame. She supplied me plentifully with money, and paid half a guinea a week for
my horse at the livery stables. I went to Litchfield races, where I lost all my money, and was
again obliged to try my hand at my old trade.
With a companion I there met, we robbed a
gentleman of his purse containing thirty guineas.
I returned again to Birmingham and lived with
the woman above-mentioned for four months,
during which time I committed many thefts. I
was apprehended on suspicion of a robbery, and
lay in jail eight days, but no proof coming out, I
got clear. I then began to see, that if I did not
alter my course of life, I should soon be brought
to the gallows. I now went northward, but without committing any great acts of theft for some
time. At Carlisle I picked a gentleman's pocket
of Scots notes and cash to the amount of £46. I
then began to think of settling and returning to
my own country. I engaged with a smith in
Derbyshire, and worked with him soberly and
diligently for some months; till having seduced a
servant-girl, her situation obliged to marry her
or leave the country. I therefore left my master,
which I was very sorry to do, as he was making
me a capital workman, and went to the place
where I was born. I there committed some small
thefts which obliged me to list as a soldier. I
enlisted in the 7th regiment, or royal English
Fusileers, then recruiting in Litchfield, March
1784. I joined the regiment at Gloucester, and
behaved myself very well for some months. Having been on a recruiting party at Leicester, and

returning with the recruits through Birmingham, I fell in with some of my old companions; and on the last of the three nights we halted there, I was concerned in taking a trunk from behind a carriage. It contained wearing apparel of great value. I received my share of the booty, and proceeded on our march with the recruits the next day. After I had again joined the regiment, I began to dislike the military life, and I therefore deserted in February, 1786, as I well remember, on the 5th day of the month. I went directly to find out my old companions at Birmingham; but I soon learned they were all in prison. I was therefore obliged to try my fortune in some other place. I then went to my parents, and imposed on them, by telling them that I was behaving myself well. They did not know that I was a deserter; so that they furnished me with both money and clothes. I soon left them, being determined to begin my old trade of thieving. I went direct for Derby, and on the night of my arrival there, I stole from a shopkeeper near six dozen of silk handkerchiefs, and then travelled the country as a hawker, selling them. In this progress I got acquainted with a northern traveller, and soon after I was taken up at Nottingham for passing bad money, which I and my companion had made and was sent to jail. Not knowing me to be a deserter, the magistrates allowed me to enlist. I accordingly enlisted in the dragoons under the name of John Boodle, and got three guineas bounty-money. I joined the regiment at Stamford, and behaved myself well for some weeks. Being at drill one day with my horse, I received a hurt

which disabled me from my duty, and occasioned
my being sent on a recruiting party only nine
miles from the place in which I was born. This
made me think that if I stopped here I should be
very soon apprehended. In the house where I
was billetted, I picked the lock of my landlord's
trunk, and took a suit of black clothes, and then
deserted in July, 1786. I left my quarters at
twelve o'clock at night, leaving my regimentals in
place of my landlord's black suit, thinking an exchange no robbery. I was determined to go to
Birmingham again: but finding I could not reach
it soon on foot, I took a horse from a stable about
six miles from the place I left, and rode him many
miles, and then turned him to grass; but whether
his owner ever got him again I cannot tell. I got
safe to Birmingham in the evening. Having little
money, I began to try my hand at thieving again.
Next morning I enquired for my old mistress, but
she had left her former house. I found, however, one of my old companions, with whom I had
done a deal of business. He got my clothes
changed as they were very remarkable. We then
determined to travel together. But making further enquiry after my late mistress, I found that
she was doing extremely well: and he took me
to her new house. When she saw me she faint-
ed; for, as she afterwards said, she had heard
that I had been hanged at Nottingham for coining. I stopped here all night, and when in bed,
she begged me to give her the history of my last
travels, which I faithfully did. She pitied my
situation very much, and begged me to stay with
her and travel no more. I promised to do so,

and next day she clothed me extremely well, and gave me a good watch. She never wanted money, for she had ten of the finest girls in the place in her house. I went about more like a gentleman than the bully of a bawdy house, and was known at this time by the name of John Brown, Esq. I staid two months with this woman, after which she was seized with a sudden fit of illness, and died. I gave her a decent burial, and ordered the girls to leave the house. I sold all the goods, and paid the landlord the house-rent, after which I had about £12.

I sent for my last companion, and met him at the sign of the Red Lion at Digbeth. We then concerted what was to be done, and we agreed that the roads would be best place to go to. That same night we got three watches, and near forty guineas. We sold the watches, but at astonishing low prices. If I had the king's crown of gold I could sell it in Birmingham. We left Birmingham, and went to Warwick, and there I altered my name again, calling myself John Booth, as that was my mother's maiden name. We committed here some few crimes, but not worth mentioning. We went from Warwick to Ipswich in Suffolk, where I contrived to pick a man's pocket of near a hundred and fifty pounds. We left the place that same night, and took the road to Cambridge. When we came there, I found that my companion was too well known, and we were obliged to take some other quarter. I was desirous to go to Scotland, as I told him it was a very *flat place*. He said he did not wish to go there, as he had been twice banished from that country already. We therefore agreed to go to the north of England, and first took the coach to Nottingham. Here I learned that William Cook, an old companion of mine, lay under sentence of death. I went to see him, next day, and finding him in a bad situation, I made him a present of two guineas. He begged of me that I would leave my way of life, and I promised to do so the first good booty that I made. I left him, but his situation and advice made no impression on me.

I left Nottingham, and then my companion and I went to Leeds fair. Here I picked a farmer's pocket of sixty guineas. We stopped four days, and returned on our road to Birmingham. We went by the way of Sheffield, and there I picked several pockets, but of no value. We went from thence in the coach to Leicester, and there we committed many robberies during our stay of seven weeks. The many robberies committed at Leicester, occasioned a strict enquiry to be made and every stranger was apprehended, and I among others. My companion, however, got fortunately out of the way, otherwise it might have been very bad for us both. I was examined, and a silver watch being found upon me; the maker's name and number of which being erased, and twenty-six guineas found in my pockets, occasioned great suspicion against me. But no clear evidence coming out, I escaped punishment. I was, however, sworn to, as a deserter from the 7th regiment, and I lay eight weeks and four days in prison, and then I was sent to join the regiment at Plymouth, near the Land's End of England. On the march from Gloucester to Exeter, at a place called Wellington, the money of our party ran low. I prevailed by my address in having my handcuffs taken off, as I could procure money, others could not. It was market day, and I went to the marketplace amongst the farmers. I picked a farmer's pocket of eighteen guineas and seventeen shillings. There were three soldiers and a corporal with me. I gave them eight guineas, and kept the rest to myself. Besides I treated them that evening with six crown bowls of punch, and we were all very merry. We then proceeded the next day for Exeter, and there I was prisoner under the 40th regiment. Nothing particular happened between Exeter, and Plymouth barracks, where I arrived the first of November, 1715, and I think it was on a Sunday. I was committed to the black-hole, and was afterwards tried by a court martial. Being a likely young man the major was not for punishing me, and I was only confined to the black-hole for five days. After this I behaved myself well, and was always reckoned a good clean soldier, and gained the good opinion both of soldiers and officers of the regiment. I took up with a woman here, and lived with her as my wife, and she kept me in pocket money and every thing I wanted. In the latter end of February, I was ordered on a party, viz. twenty five of our regiment, and twenty five of the 23rd regiment, to do duty on board a Dutch vessel that had got ashore, the ship being loaded with valuable goods, the country people were eager to plunder her. The name of the place where this happened is Padstow, and a good quarter it is for soldiers. The captain of the

stranded vessel paid a shilling a day for each soldier. When I was on duty, I sold many of the
things put under my charge; and the sailors
knowing nothing of the language or manners of
our country, it was easy to take them in. There
were only two men on board that could speak any
English at all. We remained here seventeen days,
and when I marched to join the regiment again, I
had in money twenty four guineas and eleven dol-
lars, besides some valuable goods. When we arrived at Plymouth dock barracks, I went to my
fair doxy, and she was very happy at my return
and success. I now kept up the drinking scheme,
and in four weeks I had not a penny left. As my
pretended wife had at that time a house well furnished, I got her persuaded to sell all off as I told
her, it was impossible to carry household goods or
furniture on the march. She accordingly did as
wished, and after paying off every thing, she had
fourteen pounds. This kept me in drink for a
considerable time: but when it was all gone I
made her sell her best clothes. When I found I
had got all that she had, and there was nothing
more to expect, I turned her off, when we marched from Plymouth on the twentyfifth of April,
1786. Our route was for Scotland. Nothing remarkable happened till we came to Exeter, and
there I picked the lock of one of my landlord's
trunks, and took out of it half a guinea and some
small silver. We marched next morning, and I
heard nothing of the theft, as I suppose it would be
some time before the money was missed. We arrived at Bath upon a Saturday, and there halted
all next day. In the house where I was billeted,

I made a conquest of the maid-servant, and we slept together. She was determined to go with me, and be married, but her friends interposed. Indeed I only intended to have carried her as long as her money and clothes lasted. We proceeded from Bath to Gloucester, and there the regiment was reviewed.

When we left Gloucester, I carried two of my landlord's tea spoons with me. At Worcester, however, I stole three dozen of women's gloves, some blue, some green, from a glover who lived in my landlord's entry. When we arrived at Birmingham I met with some of my old companions, and being offered some handsome presents, I chose a silver watch. They did every thing in their power to induce me to desert, but at that time I was bent upon Scotland. The regiment halted two days at Birmingham, and I did not pass that time without some acts of theft. In particular, my landlord being an engraver, I stole a large quantity of coat and waist coat buttons. We came next day to my native place, and my parents were happy to see me. They got leave from the major for me to stop a day with them and to join the regiment the next, but I staid four days. I was now determined to desert, but my schemes came to my father's ears, and he threatened to have me taken up. But on giving me some guineas I promised to join the regiment, and accordingly I overtook them at Matlock. The major with whom I was a favourite, did not confine me, but gave me a severe reprimand. The regiment went forwards, and I was never sober, till I had spent all my money. I was perfectly honest till we came to Leeds. There I stole from an inn a horn cup tipped with silver on the top and bottom, and also two silver spoons. I sold them the same evening to a person that I knew was accustomed to buy suspicious goods. At Darlington I met with one of my old companions, and he gave me two guineas. He is well known in Scotland, and is at the time I am writing this, a convict for Botany-bay.

I left Darlington next morning, and parted with my companion, but not without plenty of liquor. At Bedford I was quartered in a shoemaker's house, and I stole from him in the morning of our departure, a quantity of leather, which I sold at Berwick for twelve shillings. During our stop of some days at Berwick, I stole two silver cups, and sold them for two guineas. From thence we marched to Musselburgh to remain some time. I was sent to Edinburgh for three days on a recruiting party, and there I got intimate in a public house in the Grass market, with a gentleman who suffered about two years ago.

When the party went back to Musselburgh I sold a pair of new shoes to a country fellow, and while he was trying them on, I picked his pocket of eight shillings. But he missing the money, it was with difficulty I persuaded him that he had left it at home. I then got three shillings for my shoes, which I thought were well sold. I was exceedingly sorry that I could not get at his pocket-book for there were a good many notes in it.

I was soon after this sent with a working party to the north of Scotland. We left Musselburgh in July, and were to go to Dunkeld. We went

through Edinburgh, and while we stopped, I stole
a shirt, a pair of women's black stockings and a
worsted night cap, from a house in the Canongate.
We went that night to Inverkeithing, after crossing the ferry. Here I sold the shirt for three
shillings, and I stole a silk handkerchief from the
house where we were drinking. We marched
next morning, and reached Kinross, where I stole
from my quarters a white stock and silver stock
buckle. The next day we arrived at Perth on the
market day, and there being a stage doctor, I
thought of trying my hand in the crowd as I was
short of money. The first thing I got my hand on
was a woman's Bible, but it being covered, I took
it for a pocket-book. Finding my mistake, I was
resolved to try for something else and got six
pocket handkerchiefs, and at last a pocket-book,
which contained some bills and two twenty shilling
notes. Before I left the place I heard some persons say that there were some pick-pockets about,
and then I made off directly.

I went to my quarters, and gave my companion
one of the notes to get silver, and I took the other
myself for the same purpose. The woman of the
house where I changed my note, asked if I would
take five shillings of halfpence, which I agreed to.
She left me in a small room while she went to
fetch the change, and I stole from a cupboard a
quantity of halfpence I saw there. I then went
to my companion, and found that he had got
change, and gave him five shillings for his trouble.
I also sold the Bible to my landlady for a pint of
whisky. Not being contented with what I had
gotten, I went back to the stage-doctors, but

found the multitude mostly gone. I went to the flesh-market, and took a purse from a woman which had twelve shillings in it. My companion and I then went to a publichouse, where we drank very heartily. We wanted to go to a house of bad fame, and I gave a barber half a crown to conduct us, and we staid till near three o'clock in the morning in the monster's. When coming home I broke the window-shutter of a shop, and got several things, particularly about thirty pieces of ribbons. We then went directly to our quarters, and left the place next morning for Dunkeld. We came to a river, close by that place, and I being much in liquor, I would not pay the ferry, and was determined to ford the river. In attempting this, I was carried off my feet and with the weight of my knapsack I certainly would have lost my life, if the boatman had not come to my relief, and taken me up. I had at this time near two guineas in my pocket. When I recovered, I gave the boatmen who had saved me one shilling a piece, and a shillings worth of whisky. I was quartered at a public house near the cross at Dunkeld, and met with very civil usage. We halted here on Sunday, and next day went to a place called Strathbrand.

At a place called Amulree we got our meal, viz; a peck a week for each man.—While they were busy serving out the meal there, I slipped into another room, and stole a pair of woman's shoes, with silver buckles, and a large mutton ham. I gave the ham to my companion to carry to quarters. We went into another room, and there we found under the bed a small barrel, which being examined proved to be whisky. I searched about, and found some empty bottles in a corner; and afterwards got a cock, and we tapped the barrel, and carried off five bottles each which we concealed in the bag with our meal. It was not missed for some time; but, shame to our party, one of them told the truth concerning this theft. But the whole, except this one, paid a shilling each, rather than see me sent off a prisoner; and I promised to pay them again.

I stopped here for ten days before I committed any other theft, only a single bottle of whisky from a public house. I then with my companion stole from a green, twelve shirts, two velvet waistcoats, and some stockings, and we hid them in a heap of stones. We were four weeks in this quarter; and in the course of that time we broke into the house of one Catherine Gordon, and got some women's wearing apparel. I got them sold easily to a travelling man who went through the country.

I now got acquainted with a maid servant of the name of M'Leod, and was a great favourite with her. When we had got the goods which were concealed in a heap of stones made clean and ready by means of the soldiers' wives, we were ordered to Blair of Athol; but we carried the goods with us. We sold them afterwards to one F———, a change keeper.

We stopped at a place about nine miles from Dunkeld, and there my companions and I stole a number of yards of linen then bleaching; with shirts, handkerchiefs, stockings, &c. But the shirts being given to one of the soldiers' wives to pick the marks out, she was discovered by the landlord of our quarters; and a warrant being obtained for searching, the whole of the goods were found. We were taken prisoners that evening, and the next morning were carried before a justice of the peace. The justice having been a late captain in the army, took the soldier's part, and told the people who had lost the goods, that they might be very well satisfied with having recovered them. He then desired us to go with our party; but, before we went, he ordered us all four, a dinner in the kitchen; and a very good one it was. Having some time to consider, we determined upon having something more from his worship, and accordingly brought off two hams with us.

The Sunday following, we went over a river to a small pretty village. We went to a change house, and I picked the lock of a trunk, and got some shirts, and near forty shillings in silver. I gave two of my companions the shirts and sent them off. I and another staid behind to pay the reckoning, and we came off without being discovered.

We attended to our work all the following week, but our money was spent all on Saturday night. We were therefore determined to try our hands again, and we went four miles into the country, and there broke into a barn, and in a chest got four very good country blankets, and some sheets. We sold them the next day, which was Sunday, to F————. I went to my quarters that evening a little worse for liquor, and my landlady told me that my wife was come. I told her

I had a wife, but had left her to finish the harvest and on going into the cow house (or byre) I found Kate assisting my landlady's daughter in milking the cows. We were very happy at meeting, and the people behaved to her extremely well. One night, however, I came home in liquor, and took all her clothes, and sold them for three pounds to F——, and she had an excellent gold ring. The next day I got my landlady to turn her out of quarters, as I told her she was a very bad woman ; and accordingly that day we got her mobbed out of the place. She went off, and I never saw her again. I continued to drink till all this money was spent.

We were sent to a place called Dalnecarnoch, to work on the roads ; but I and eleven more went with the engineer forwards to Dalwhinnie, where we halted. There was a packman or pedlar in the house selling goods, and I thought of trying my hand upon him. Accordingly, I contrived to steal from him six yards of printed cotton, some ribbons, lace, and three handkerchiefs. But one of our party finding out this theft, I was obliged to give him a large share to stop his mouth. The next day we advanced to where we were to work, and on the road stole a sheep from a sheeling, and brought it to our quarters, where it was cooked. The packman, however, missing the lace and some of the other things, followed us, and to prevent my going to gaol, I gave up to him all that I had. We left our work the latter end of the year, and when we returned to Dunkeld, we got a good dinner from the Duke of Athole. That same night I was concerned in stealing some linen from the commissary. Next day we went to Cupar Angus, on our road to Dundee, to join the regiment. On this march I picked up some small things, and brought them safe to Dundee. I did no business there for some time, but about a month after we arrived, I was stopped for stealing some wearing apparel; and being tried by a court martial, I was sentenced to receive 800 lashes, but got only 250, and was kept in the black hole for ten weeks. But this punishment did not cure me of my disposition for thieving, for I picked a gentleman's pocket after this at Dundee. When I got my liberty, I paid my addresses to a very decent servant girl: but when she knew of my character, and the punishment I had received, she left me, and it was well for her, for I would have been her ruin. I lived, however, with another woman as my wife, and left her when the regiment marched for Fort George. I behaved myself well there for twenty weeks. But one night I went to Campbolton, stole some ducks, for which I received no payment but 200 lashes; and I was very ill after this punishment.

On our march southward by Banff, Aberdeen, and Montrose, I committed several thefts. We came again to Dundee, where we halted ten days, and during that time I committed several crimes. In particular, a brewery, where we had intelligence that there was a good deal of money in the counting house. But after breaking the place we only got ten shillings. We had information that there were four hundred pounds there the night before. This was a great disappointment. When

we came to Edinburgh castle I behaved myself
well for some time. I do not choose to write any
thing concerning my transactions at Edinburgh,
in my present situation. I came to the castle May
15th, 1786. The regiment was reviewed the 17th
of June, on Bruntsfield links, and on the 25th I
got acquainted with Margaret Hamilton, whom
I afterwards married, and constantly adhered to
since. I lived a sober life while in Edinburgh
castle, but not without committing some petty
crimes, such as shoplifting.

We left Edinburgh to go to Glasgow, where we
arrived some time in April 1787. I behaved
well for a long time, and getting employment at
Anderstone, I could earn sometimes ten and fifteen
shillings a week. In Glasgow I got acquainted
with a gang of thieves, as we all know one another by our language. My wife and I having
once harboured them in our house, we were very
uneasy that we could not afterwards keep them
away. My wife bought a gown from one of them,
and he being apprehended, told to whom he had
sold the gown; she was confined for this ten
weeks.

During this time I began my old trade again
with some town blackguards. I don't think I
would have done this, if my wife had had her
liberty. The first night we went out we stole
some whisky from a cellar: and the same night
broke into a gentleman's house at Little Govan,
and from thence got some wearing apparel, some
ducks, and fowls. On Saturday night that same
week, I and a townsman broke into a house in St.

Andrew's Churchyard, and got some silver plate, and two hats. We sold them all the next day, as I was well acquainted where to dispose of them. I never was in a town three days before I found out a place of that kind.

The next week I and two of my fellow soldiers broke the poor's house, and stole some clothes and shoes, and a plated tankard, which we thought was silver. The night following we went into the country, and broke into a house ; and going in, were obliged to return, on account of the intolerable smell. On making enquiry afterwards, we found it was the *unknown work.* We got nothing there, but we desired to have something before we slept. We went half a mile further, and robbed a bleach green of holland, dimity, and stockings.— We hid part in a hay stack, where it was discovered next day, and the people got their own again. On Saturday night we went to the country again, and got a number of fowls ; some we sold, and used the rest.

A few nights after, I and two of my fellow soldiers, broke into a cellar, and got a quantity of salted beef, bottled porter. and some whisky. Not satisfied with that, we broke another, and got a quantity of salt herrings. The next week we broke into a cellar in the Calton, and got some bottled porter. The serjeant hearing of the bad way I was going on, and frequently seeing me in liquor, spoke to the officer, and I was ordered to join the party at Port Glasgow.

I left my wife in prison, after giving her what money I had, and marched with the party on Friday. On Monday I went to work in the dry-dock at Port Glasgow, and got five shillings for two days. The next day I got nine shillings for nine hours heaving ballast into the ship British Queen. I sent my wife two shillings to get her tea and sugar.

Having spent all my money, I resolved to try the country houses; and I and my comrades committed several depredations in the neighbourhood.

We had formed a scheme for robbing a silver-smith's shop, but were prevented in the execution by some tailors. We afterwards broke a hardware shop, but what we got was of little value.

We were soon after this sent across the Clyde to work, but had to return every Saturday evening to show ourselves to the officer of the party on Sunday. My wife had now got her liberation, and had come to Port Glasgow; and I carried her with me across the river on the Monday morning.

I worked very hard for a fortnight, when we were ordered to join the regiment at Glasgow. When the party left Port Glasgow, I was much the worse for liquor, and could not keep up. My wife and me took twenty hours to travel twenty miles, but I joined on Sunday evening.

I now hired a room in the Gorbals, and continued there till I was sent to gaol. One night when I was on guard, my comrade and I broke open the window of a ware-room, which we left, being afraid of being missed in the guard room.

What had been done, being observed by some passengers, created an alarm, and information was sent to the guard room. My comrade and I among others, were appointed to the duty of guarding the broken shop. While we were stationed in the place, I picked one of the gentlemen's pockets of a pair of new buckles and a pack of cards. When my comrade and I were relieved from this duty, we contrived to break another warehouse in a different quarter, and got a great quantity of shawls. We could have done a great deal more if it had not been so late in the morning, and a stir in the streets beginning at six o'clock.

After this we broke a warehouse in Stockwell street, and got a quantity of wine and rum in bottles. We got sale for the rum and the shawls but we drank the wine. My wife was very angry with me, and after this would not let me go out at night: so that what I did for some time afterwards, was done the nights I was on guard. Accordingly, the next guard we were on, we stole some salt beef, and a quantity of bottled porter, and sold them next day for ten shillings. Another guard I was on, my comrade and I opened a window, and took out of a house, a man's coat, waistcoat, and breeches. which we sold the next day. I now got my wife's mind reconciled to my going out at night. I went one night with two more, but we got nothing. The next night, however, that we went out we were more successful, and robbed a house about four or five miles from the town. There were four of us, and we brought away a quantity of wearing apparel, and some table cloths, sheets, and blankets, &c.; part o. which we hid in a hay-stack, others we sold. Those left in the hay stack were discovered, and returned to the owners, as we heard.

About four days after this, one of my compa-

nions came to my room, and desired me to go
along with him to a place where there were plenty
of geese.

We went and broke open the door, but he
found no geese, but said there was a sow. I desired him to bring it out, but on kicking it, he
heard the rattling of a large chain, and ran off.
A few days afterwards we understood that it was
a bear in the yard.

I and one of my companions went out another
night, and met a gentleman who gave us half-a-
crown to convey him home, as he was afraid from
the numerous robberies that had lately happened.
When we arrived at his house he made us drunk,
and then we determined to break open some house.
Accordingly, we forced open a window, and my
companion going in, found it was a chapel or
church, and nothing to be got but some candles
or candlesticks..

The next week I and two more went out on
the Kirkintilloch road, and we robbed a house of
some linens and wearing apparel, and some fowls.
We had some difficulty in carrying this booty so
far, but we got all safe, and had ready sale the next
day. This kept us drinking for some days.

On going along the street one day, a soldier told
me that one Dallas had been enquiring for me at
the guard house, and he informed me where he
was quartered. I found him, and brought him to
my room, and gave him the best I had, to eat
and drink. He told me that Tennant was to be
hanged, and I was very sorry for it,—I got acquainted with these men when I was with the
regiment in Edinburgh castle.

The night Dallas was in Glasgow, I and one of my companions stole a pocket-book from a merchant's counter, but we found only one twenty shilling note in it. Dallas called the next morning at my room, before he marched, and I gave him plenty of drink, and a shilling to put in his pocket. He went to join his regiment, and I never saw him again in Edinburgh.

One night in the Calton of Glasgow, I broke open a shop, and got ten shillings and sixpence in the drawer, and brought away two cheeses, and some tea and sugar. There was a woman in the back room, in bed, and I went and lighted a candle; but she was either so afraid, or so fast asleep, that I met with no disturbance.

A few nights after this, being on guard, a companion and I broke a hen-house in Gibson's wynd, and got three hens —I would advise all officers on guard to call the roll every hour, for we had plenty of liberty.

One evening two of my companions came to my room, and asked if I would go and try some of the shops. Accordingly we went, and from a shop in the Gallowgate got a dozen of silk handkerchiefs.

I was afterwards detected in stealing some ready made shoes, and was sent to the guard house; and I expected to be tried by a court-martial, but the man failing to prosecute, I got free.

The same night that I was released, I and one of my fellow-soldiers set out at ten o'clock for the country, and on our road we stopped a man. He had only a shilling and a few half pence; and, telling a lamentable story, I gave him back his money, and with a kick I bade him go home to his wife and family. We went forward to Aderstone, but got nothing there. On the road to Woodside we got some fowls; but not contented with this, we broke into another house. I entered through the window of a washing house, but we got nothing in it, except some bread and cheese: and there being a good fire, we sat down, and enjoyed ourselves for some time. We opened a door that led to the garden and from thence we opened a back window, and got some women's and children's wearing apparel, as stockings, gowns, petticoats, &c., and the next day we sold the greatest part of them.

The next day I was on guard, I and one of my companions broke open two windows, but got nothing worth mentioning. The same night we broke a cellar near the guard house, and got some liquor. We could have got a great deal more, but the people being alarmed, we made off. We then went down a close, and opened the window of a house belonging to one M'Alpin, a baker. The first thing I got was a great coat, and some blue cotton yarn. But while I was busied picking the locks of a chest of drawers, my companion begged me to come out, as the people he said were getting up. We committed several other robberies both in town and country.

One night that I was on guard, I and two of my fellow-soldiers broke into a cellar, and got out of it a parcel of smoothing irons, a salt tongue, and some bottles of ale, and three of vinegar.—A few nights after we tried the country again, but got nothing but some fowls.

On the 8th day of March, 1790, when I had come off guard, the town officers came to my room to search for goods. They asked if I had ever sold any thing to serjeant Crabb? I denied that I had :—but they searched, and found some shirts and linens, the marks of which had been taken out. Crabbe's wife swore, that those found in her possession she bought from me : but I had only sold her two; the rest she had bought from my companions. The officers making a further search, found some table cloths, which had been left at my house in order to be sold, at a time when I was on guard.

I was committed to prison to take my trial at the next assizes.

But the war beginning, I was relieved to go abroad with the regiment for Gibraltar. When we marched from Glasgow, our route was for Linlithgow. I was ordered to be confined in the guard-house at every place till the regiment embarked at Leith But understanding that my wife would not be allowed to go with me, I was determined to desert, if a fit opportunity offered. I was under the charge of a sergeant and twelve men, but I made my escape at night from them at Linlithgow, without either coat or hat I took the direct road to Edinburgh, as at that time my wife was there with her father, who is a cowfeeder in Fountain-bridge. I ran about three or four miles, and then got the coulter of a plough, with which I opened a stable door, and took a horse with which I rode a considerable way, and thereby prevented the party from overtaking me. I reached Edinburgh about five o'clock in the morning and went straight to my father-in-law's house. My wife instantly got up, and I was soon provided with a coat and hat. We then went together to Warrander's park, adjoining to Bruntsfield links. Here we sat down a long time to consider what was to be done. My wife went to her father's to fetch me some breakfast, but when she went there she found a party in search of me. They not being able to get any intelligence from her, took her into custody, and kept her till evening. When she was dismissed she came to me, and I was very impatient to learn what had transpired.

We got a lodging the two following nights in Richmond-street, and then took a room near the Gibbet toll; where we lived till the regiment was embarked, and had sailed from Leith to Gibraltar.

[Gadesby's manuscript ends here.]

Some time after the embarkation of the regiment, several house-breakings and shop-robberies happened at Edinburgh; and search being made, nineteen suspicious persons were committed, and among others William Gadesby.

He was indicted for three robberies, one theft, and a house breaking, viz: 1st, for assaulting and robbing William Procter, on the 31st of July, at the back of the castle, or the castle walk. 2nd, Thomas Elliot, near the Scinnes, or near the Archers' Hall, on the 2nd of August. 3rd, James Logan on the Earthen Mound, on the 4th of August. 4th, of stealing a silver watch from Thomas Tait, in the Cowgate; and 6th, of breaking into the house of William Lyon, at Kirkbraehead, and stealing a number of articles.

The jury returned their verdict the next day unanimously finding William Gadesby guilty of the 4th and 5th charges in the indictment; but finding the 1st, 2nd, and 3rd charges not proven.

William Gadesby was then, with the usual awful solemnities conducted to be hanged on Wednesday the 2nd of February, 1791, but having given some hints that he would make discoveries of importance to the country before he died, the lords of justiciary were induced to suspend the execution till Wednesday the 23rd of February, to give time to enquire into the truth of some further confessions he had made.

Gadesby knew nothing of this respite being granted. The guard surrounded the place of execution at the usual hour, and an immense multitude of spectators attended. In about an hour after this, the respite was intimated to him, and he expressed dissatisfaction at it.

Mr. Williamson, king's messenger, was dispatched with a warrant to apprehend the persons named in Gadesby's information. There were four persons named as concerned in the robbery of the bank, two at Dundee, one at Arbroath, and Gadesby himself. Mr. Williamson reached Dundee at five in the morning, of the 3rd of February. The watchman showed him the house he wanted, and the man was found quietly sleeping in his house. He was conveyed to prison, and Mr. Williamson afterwards proceeded to Arbroath. There the person against whom he had the warrant was gone to sea. On his return to Dundee, the streets were immensely crowded. He conveyed his prisoner to Edinburgh the next day. The other person in Dundee, against whom he had a warrant, had left the place some time before. The suspected person apprehended by Mr. Williamson, was examined on the 4th of February. Gadesby was brought from prison, handcuffed, in a chair, and was desired to select out his accomplice, or accomplices, from about a dozen of people assembled, the person from Dundee making one of them.

He looked round and pitched upon one man, and this person being removed, he pitched upon another. He was also removed, and on being desired to see if there were any more : he looked round, and said, no more. The persons then selected belonged to Edinburgh, and his alleged accomplice from Dundee he did not know.

This at once proved most decisively, that all he had said was an artful invention to delay his execution : he never afterwards spoke on this subject.

On the 23rd of February, at two o'clock in the afternoon, the guard having surrounded the place of execution, the prisoner was brought on the platform, and having addressed the multitude in a long speech, he was launched into eternity.

WILLIAM BURRIDGE,

Executed at Tyburn on the 22nd of March, 1772, for Horse Stealing.

THIS offender was a native of Northamptonshire, and served his time with a carpenter : but giving

the proof of his knavish disposition, and havin
ruined several young women, his friends determin
ed to send him to sea, as the most probable metho
to prevent his coming to a fatal end.

In consequence thereof, they got him rated
midshipman, and he sailed to the coast of Spain
but soon quitting the naval service, he returne
to England, and commencing highwayman, com
mitted many robberies on the road to Hampstead
on Finchley-common, and in the neighbourhoo
of Hammersmith.

When he first began the practice of robbing
he formed a resolution to retire when he had ac
quired as much money as would support him
but this never arrived; for finding his success b
no means proportioned to his expectations, h
became one of the gang under Jonathan Wild, o
infamous memory; and was a considerable tim
screened from justice by that celebrated master o
thieves.

Burridge being confined in New Prison, for
capital offence, broke out of that gaol; and h
was repeatedly an evidence at the Old Bailey, b
which means his associate suffered the rigour o
the law. At length, having offended Wild, th
latter marked him down as one doomed to suffe
at the next execution after the ensuing seasons a
the Old Bailey; which was a common practic
with Wild, when he grew tired of his depend
ants, or thought they could be no longer service
able to him.

Alarmed at this circumstance, Burridge fled
into Lincolnshire, where he stole a horse; and
brought it to London, intending to sell it a

Smithfield for present support; but the gentleman who had lost the horse, having sent the
description of it to London, Burridge was seen
riding on it through the streets, and watched to
a livery stable.

Some persons going to take him, he produced
a brace of pistols, threatening destruction to any
one who came near him, by which he got off; but
being immediately pursued, he was taken in May-
Fair, and lodged in Newgate.

On his trial, a man and a woman swore that
they saw him purchase the horse; but as there
was a material difference in their stories, the
court was of opinion, that they had been hired
to swear, and the judge gave directions for
their being taken into custody for the perjury.

The jury did not hesitate to find Burridge
guilty; and after sentence was passed, his behaviour was extremely devout, and he encouraged
the devotion of others in the like unhappy circumstances.

He was executed at Tyburn on the 22nd of
March, 1722, in the 34th year of his age; having
first warned the spectators to be obedient to their
parents and masters, and beware of the crime of
debauching young women, which had first led
him from the path of duty, and finally ended in
his ruin.

NATHANIEL JACKSON,

Executed at Tyburn, the 18th of July, 1722, for Robbery.

THIS malefactor was a native of Doncaster, in Yorkshire, and his father dying while he was very young, left a sum of money for his use in the hands of a relation, who apprenticed him to a silk weaver in Norwich. He had frequent disputes with his master, with whom he lived three years, and then ran away from him.

At length his guardian found out his retreat, and sent to inform him, that, as he was averse to business, his friends wished that a place might be purchased for him with the money left by his father. But Jackson being of an unsettled disposition, enlisted in the army, and was sent to Ireland where he engaged in all those scenes of low debauchery by which the common soldiers are too much distinguished.

At length being disgusted with his low condition, he solicited his discharge, which having obtained, he procured some money of his friends, and gave fifteen guineas to be admitted into a troop of dragoons; but soon quarrelling with one of his comrades, a duel ensued, in which Jackson wounded the other in a most horrid manner, for which he was turned out of the regiment.

He now returned to England, and lived some time with his guardian in Yorkshire; but being averse to a life of soberity, he soon went to London where he spent, in the most extravagant manner, the little money he brought with him, and was reduced to the utmost distress, when he casually met John Murphey and Neal O'Brien, whom he had known in Ireland. After they had drank together, O'Brien produced a considerable sum of money, saying, You see how I live; I never want money, and if you have but courage, and dare walk with me towards Hampstead to night, I'll shew you how easy it is to get it.

As Jackson and Murphey were both of dissolute manners, and very poor, they were easily persuaded to be concerned in this dangerous enterprise. Between Tottenham Court Road and Hampstead they stopped a poor man named Dennis, from whom they took his coat, waistcoat, two shirts, thirteen pence in money, and some other trifling articles; and then bound him to a tree. No sooner were they gone, than he struggled hard and got loose, and meeting a person whom he knew, they pursued them to a night-house, in the Haymarket, where Murphey and Jackson were taken into custody, but O'Brien made his escape.

On their trial, as soon as Dennis had given his testimony they owned the act they had committed in consequence of which they received sentence of death; but Murphey obtained a reprieve. Jackson's brother exerted all his influence to save his life; but his endeavours proving ineffectual, he sent a letter to inform him of it, which was written in such an affecting manner as to overwhelm his mind with the most pungent affliction.

While under sentence of death, Jackson behaved in the most penitent manner; confessed the sins of his past life with the deepest signs of contrition; was earnest in his devotions, and made every preparation for his approaching end.

RICHARD TURPIN,

(HIGHWAYMAN, HORSE-STEALER, & MURDERER,)

Executed at York, April 10th, 1739.

THIS was another daring depredator, notorious as any of his day, and long the dread of travellers on the Essex road; but the finger of Providence we find continually pointed, in some direction, at sinners. How many murders have we to shew, where the perpetrators have been discovered by the most unexpected incidents; and how many murderers shall we find, as it were irresistibly drawn to discover themselves. Turpin was apprehended in consequence of wantonly shooting a fowl; and his conviction was in consequence of his brother refusing a single sixpence, for the postage of his letter!

Turpin was the son of John Turpin, a farmer at Thackstead in Essex, and having received a common school education, was apprenticed to a butcher in Whitechapel: but was distinguished from his early youth for the impropriety of his behaviour, and the brutality of his manners.

On the expiration of his apprenticeship, he married a young woman of East Ham in Essex, named Palmer : but he had not been long married before he took to the practice of stealing his neighbours' cattle, which he used to kill and cut up for sale.

Having stolen two oxen belonging to Mr. Giles, of Plaistow, he drove them to his own house : but two of Giles's servants suspecting who was the robber, went to Turpin's, where they saw two beasts of such size as had been lost : but as the hides were stripped from them, it was impossible to say that they were the same ; but learning that Turpin used to dispose of his hides at Waltham-Abbey, they went thither, and saw the hides of the individual beasts that had been stolen.

No doubt now remaining who was the robber, a warrant was procured for the apprehension of Turpin ; but learning that the peace officers were in search of him he made his escape from the back window of his house, at the very moment that the others were entering at the door.

Having retreated to a place of security, he found means to inform his wife where he was concealed ; on which she furnished him with money, with which he travelled into the hundreds of Essex, where he joined a gang of smugglers, with whom he was for some time successful ; till a set of custom house officers, by one successful stroke, deprived him of the whole of his ill-acquired gains.

Thrown out of this kind of business, he connected himself with a gang of deer-stealers, the principal part of whose depredations were committed on Epping Forest, and the parks in its neighbourhood ; but this business not succeeding to the expectations of the robbers, they commenced house breaking.

Their plan was to fix on houses that they presumed contained any valuable property ; and, while one of them knocked at the door, the others were to rush in, and seize whatever they might deem worthy of notice.

The first attack of this kind was at the house of Mr. Strype, an old man who kept a chandler's shop at Watford, whom they robbed of all the money in his possession, but did not offer him any personal abuse.

Turpin now acquainted his associates that there was an old woman at Loughton, was was in possession of seven or eight hundred pounds ; whereupon they agreed to rob her ; and when they came to the door one of them knocked, and the rest forcing their way into the house, tied handkerchiefs over the eyes of the old woman and her maid.

This being done, Turpin demanded what money was in the house ; and the owner hesitating to tell him, he threatened to set her on the fire if she did not make an immediate discovery. Still, however, she denied information ; on which the villains actually placed her on the fire, where she sat till the tormenting pains compelled her to discover her hidden treasure ; so that the robbers possessed themselves of above four hundred pounds, and decamped with the booty.

Some little time after this, they agreed to rob

the house of a farmer near Barking; and knocking at the door, the people declined to open it, on which they broke it open; and having bound the farmer, his wife, his son in law, and the servant maid, they robbed the house of above seven hundred pounds; which delighted Turpin so much that he exclaimed, Aye, this will do, if it would always be so! and the robbers retired with their prize, which amounted to above eighty pounds for each of them.

This desperate gang, now flushed with success, determined to attack the house of Mr. Mason, the keeper of Epping Forest; and the time was fixed when the plan was to be carried into execution; but Turpin having gone to London, to spend his share of the former bounty, intoxicated himself to such a degree, that he totally forgot the appointment.

Nevertheless, the remainder of the gang determined that the absence of their companion should not frustrate the proposed design; and having taken a solemn oath to break every article of furniture in Mr. Mason's house, they set out on their expedition.

Having gained admission, they beat and kicked the unhappy man with great severity. Finding an old man was sitting by the fire side, they permitted him to remain uninjured; and Mr. Mason's daughter escaped their fury, by running out of the house, and taking shelter in the hogstye.

After ransacking the lower part of the house, and doing much mischief, they went up stairs, where they broke every thing that fell in their way, and amongst the rest a china punch-bowl,

from which dropped one hundred and twenty
guineas, which they made a prey of and immediately effected their escape. They now went
to London in pursuit of Turpin, with whom they
shared the booty, though he had not taken an active part in the execution of the villainy.

On the 11th of January, 1735, Turpin and five
of his companions went to the house of Mr. Saunders, a rich farmer at Charlton in Kent, between
seven and eight in the evening, and having knocked at the door, asked if Mr. Saunders was at
home. Being answered in the affirmative, they
rushed into the house, and found Mr. Saunders,
with his wife and friends playing at cards in the
parlour. They told the company that they should
remain uninjured if they made no disturbance.
Having made prize of a silver snuff box which lay
on the table, a part of the gang stood guard over
the rest of the company. while the others attended Mr. Saunders through the house, and breaking
open his escrutoires and closets, took away above
a hundred pounds, exclusive of plate.

During these transactions the servant maid ran
up stairs, barred the door of her room, and called
out Thieves, with a view of alarming the neighbourhood; but the robbers broke open the door
of her room, secured her, and then robbed the
house of all the valuable property they had not
taken before. Finding some minced-pies, and
some bottles of wine, they sat down to regale
themselves; and meeting with a bottle of brandy,
they compelled each of the company to drink a
glass of it.

Mrs. Saunders fainting through terror, they ad-

ministered some drops in water to her, and recovered her to the use of her senses. Having
staid in the house a considerable time, they packed up their booty and departed, having first declared, that if any one of the family gave the least
alarm within two hours, or advertised the marks
of the stolen plate, they would return and murder
them at a future time.

Retiring to a public-house at Woolwich, where
they had concerted the robbery, they crossed the
Thames to an empty house in Radcliffe Highway,
where they deposited the stolen effects till they
found a purchaser for them.

The division of the plunder having taken place,
they, on the 18th of the same month, went to the
house of Mr. Sheldon, near Croydon, in Surrey,
where they arrived about seven in the evening.
Having got into the yard, they perceived a light
in the stable, and going into it, found the coachman attending his horses. Having immediately
bound him, they quitted the stable, and meeting
Mr. Sheldon in the yard, they seized him, and
compelled him to conduct them into the house,
they stole eleven guineas, with the jewels, plate,
and other things of value, to a large amount.
Having committed this robbery they returned Mr.
Sheldon two guineas, and apologized for their
conduct.

This being done, they hastened to the Black-
horse, in the Broad way, Westminster, where
they concerted the robbery of Mr. Lawrence, of
Edgware near Stanmore, in Middlesex, for which
place they set out on the 4th of February, and
arrived at a public-house in that village, about

five o'clock in the evening. From this place they
went to Mr. Lawrence's house, where they arrived about seven o'clock, just as he had discharged some people who had worked for him.

Having quitted their horses at the outer gate,
one of the robbers going forwards, found a boy
who had just returned from folding his sheep;
the rest of the gang following, a pistol was presented, and instant destruction was threatened if
he made any noise. They then took off his garters, and tied his hands, and told him to direct
them to the door, and when they knocked to
answer, and bid the servants open it, in which
case they would not hurt him; but when the
boy came to the door he was so terrified that he
could not speak; on which one of the gang
knocked, and a man servant, thinking it was
one of the neighbours, opened the door, whereupon they all marched in, armed with pistols.

Having seized Mr. Lawrence and his servant,
they threw a cloth over their faces, and taking
the boy into another room, demanded what fire
arms were in the house; to which he replied,
only an old gun, which they broke in pieces.
They then bound Mr. Lawrence and his men,
and made them sit by the boy; and Turpin
searching the gentleman, took from him a guinea,
a Portugal piece, and some silver; but not being
satisfied with this booty, they forced him to conduct them up stairs, where they broke open a
closet, and stole some money, and plate; but that
not being sufficient to satisfy them, they
threatened to murder Mr. Lawrence, each of
them destining him a different death, as the

savageness of his own nature prompted him. At length one of them took a kettle of water from the fire, and threw it over him ; but it providentially happened not to be sufficiently hot enough to scald him.

In the interim, the maid servant, who was churning butter in the dairy, hearing a noise in the house and apprehending some mischief, she blew out her candle to screen herself; but being found in the course of their search, one of the miscreants compelled her to go up stairs where he gratified his brutal passion by force. They then robbed the house of all the valuable effects they could find, locked the family into the garden, and took their ill gotten plunder to London.

The particulars of this atrocious robbery being represented to the king, a proclamation was issued for the apprehension of the offenders, promising a pardon to any one of them who would impeach his accomplices ; and a reward of fifty pounds was offered, to be paid on conviction. This, however, had no effect : the robbers continued their depredations as before ; and, flushed with the success they had met with, seemed to bid defiance to the laws.

On the 7th of February, six of them assembled at the White Bear Inn, in Drury Lane ; where they agreed to rob the house of Mr. Frances, a farmer near Mary le bone. Arriving at the place they found a servant in the cow house whom they bound fast, and threatened to murder him if he was not perfectly silent. This being done, they led him to the stable, where finding another of the servants, they bound him in the same manner.

In the interim, Mr. Frances happening to come home, they presented their pistols to his breast, and threatened instant destruction to him, if he made the least noise or opposition.

Having bound the master in the stable with his servants, they rushed into the house, tied Mrs. Francis, her daughter, and the maid servant, and beat them in a most cruel manner One of the thieves stood as a sentry, while they rifled the house, in which they found a silver tankard, a medal of Charles the First, a gold watch, several gold rings, a considerable sum of money and a variety of valuable linen and other effects, which they conveyed to London.

Hereupon a reward of one hundred pounds was offered for the apprehension of the offenders; in consequence of which two of them were taken into custody, tried, convicted on the evidence of an accomplice, and hanged in chains: and the whole gang dispersed. Turpin went into the country, to renew his depredations on the public.

On a journey towards Cambridge, he met a man genteelly dressed, and well mounted; and expecting a good booty, he presented a pistol to the supposed gentleman, and demanded his money. The party just stopped happened to be one King, a famous highwayman, who knew Turpin; and when the latter threatened instant destruction if he did not deliver his money, King burst into a fit of laughter, and said, " What, dog eat dog ?—Come, come, brother Turpin ; if you don't know me, I know you, and shall be glad of your company."

These brethren in iniquity soon struck the bargain, and immediately entered on business, and committed a number of robberies; till at length they were so well known, that no public house would receive them as guests. Thus situated, they fixed on a spot between the King's Oak, and Loughton Road, on Epping Forest, where they made a great cave, which was large enough to receive them and their horses.

This cave was inclosed within a sort of thicket of bushes and brambles, through which they could look and see passengers on the road, while themselves remained unobserved.

From this station they used to issue, and robbed such a number of persons, that at length the very pedlars on the road carried fire-arms for their defence; and, while they were in this retreat, Turpin's wife used to supply them with necessaries, and frequently remained in the cave during the night.

Having taken a ride as far as Bungay, in Suffolk, they observed two young women receive fourteen pounds for some corn, on which Turpin resolved to rob them of the money. King objected, saying it was a pity to rob such pretty girls: but Turpin was obstinate, and obtained the booty.

Upon their return home the following day, they stopped a Mr. Bradele of London, who was riding in his chariot with his children. The gentleman seeing only one robber, was preparing to make resistance, when King called to Turpin to hold the horses. They took from the gentleman his watch, money, and an old mourning ring; but returned the latter, as he declared its intrinsic value was trifling, yet he was unwilling to part with it.

Finding that they readily parted with the ring, he asked what he must give for the watch: on which King said to Turpin, "What say ye Jack? —Here seems to be a good honest fellow; shall we let him have the watch?'—Turpin replied, "Do as you please:" on which King said to the gentleman, "You must pay six guineas for it: we never sell for more, though the watch should be worth six and thirty." The gentleman promised that the money should be left at the Dial, in Birchin Lane.

On the 4th of May, 1737, Turpin was guilty of murder, which arose from the following circumstance: a reward of one hundred pounds having being offered for apprehending him, one Thomas Morris, a servant of Mr. Thomson, one of the keepers of Epping Forest, accompanied by a higgler, set off in order to apprehend him. Turpin seeing them approach near his dwelling, Thompson's man having a gun, he mistook them for poachers; on which he said, there were no hares near the thicket: "No," said Morris, "but I have found a Turpin:" and presenting his gun, required him to surrender.

Hereupon Turpin spoke to him as in a friendly manner, and gradually retreated at the same time, till having seized his own gun, he shot him dead on the spot, and the higgler ran off with the utmost precipitation.

This murder being represented to the secretary

of state, the following proclamation was issued by government, which we give place to, from its describing the person of this notorious depredator.

"It having been represented to the king, that Richard Turpin did, on Wednesday, the 4th of May last, barbarously murder Thomas Morris, servant to Henry Thompson, one of the keepers of Epping Forest, and commit other notorious felonies and robberies, near London, his Majesty is pleased to promise his most gracious pardon, to any of his acomplices, and a reward of two hundred pounds to any person or persons that shall discover him, so that he may be apprehended and convicted. Turpin was born at Thackstead, in Essex, is about thirty, by trade a butcher, about five feet nine inches high, much marked with the small pox, his cheek bones broad, his face thinner towards the bottom; his visage short, pretty upright, and broad about the shoulders."

Turpin in order to avoid the proclamation, went further into the country in search of his old companion King; and in the mean time sent a letter to his wife, to meet him at a public house at Hertford. The woman attended according to this direction; and her husband coming into the house soon after she arrived, a butcher, to whom he owed five pounds, happened to see him; on which he said, Come, Dick, I know you have money now: and if you will pay me, it will be of great service.

Turpin told him that his wife was in the next room; that she had money, and that he should be paid immediately: but while the butcher was hinting to some of his acquaintance, that the person was Turpin, and that they might take him into custody after he had received his debt, the highwayman made his escape through a window and rode off with great expedition.

Turpin having found King, and a man named Potter, who had lately connected himself with them, they set off towards London in the dusk of the evening; but when they came near the Green Man on Epping Forest, they overtook a Mr. Major, who riding on a very fine horse, and Turpin's beast being jaded, he obliged the rider to dismount, and exchanged horses.

The robbers now pursued their journey towards London, and Mr. Major going to the Green Man, gave an account of the affair; on which it was conjectured that Turpin had been the robber, and that the horse which he exchanged must have been stolen.

It was on Saturday evening that this robbery was committed; but Mr. Major being advised to print handbills immediately, notice was given to the landlord of the Green Man, that such a horse as Mr. Major had lost had been left at the Red Lion, in Whitechapel. The landlord going thither, determined to wait till some person came for it: and at about eleven at night, King's brother came to pay for the horse, and take him away: on which he was immediately seized, and conducted into the house.

Being asked what right he had to the horse, he said he had bought it; but the landlord examining a whip he had in his hand, found a button at the end of the handle half broken off, and the name of Major on the remaining half. Hereupon

he was given into the custody of a constable; but
as it was not supposed that he was the actual robber, he was told that he should have his liberty, if
he would discover to them his employer.

Hereupon he said, that a stout man in a white
duffil coat, was waiting for the horse in Red Lion-
street; on which the company going thither, saw
King, who drew a pistol, and attempted to fire it,
but it flashed in the pan; he then endeavoured to
pull out another pistol, but he could not, as it got
entangled in his pocket.

At this time Turpin was watching at a short
distance, and riding towards the spot, King cried
out, Shoot him, or we are taken; on which Turpin fired, and shot his companion, who called out,
Dick you have killed me; which the other hearing, rode off at full speed.

King lived a week after this affair, and gave information that Turpin might be found at a house
near Hackney marsh; and, on enquiry, it was
discovered that Turpin had been there on the
night that he rode off, lamenting that he had killed King, who was his most faithful associate.

For a considerable time did Turpin skulk about
the forest, having been deprived of his retreat in
the cave since he shot the servant of Mr. Thompson. On the examination of this cave there were
found two shirts, two pair of stockings, a piece of
ham, and the part of a bottle of wine.

Some vain attempts were made to take this notorious offender into custody; among the rest the
huntsman of a gentleman of the neighbourhood
went in search of him with bloodhounds. Turpin
perceiving them, and recollecting that king Charles

II. evaded his pursuers under covert of the friendly branches of the oak, he mounted one of those
trees, under which the hounds passed, to his inex-
pressible terror ; so that he determined to make a
retreat into Yorkshire.

Going first to Long Sutton, in Lincolnshire, he
stole some horses, for which he was taken into
custody, but he escaped from the constable as he
was conducting him before a magistrate, and
hastened to Welton, in Yorkshire, where he went
by the name of John Palmer, and assumed the
character of a gentleman.

He now frequently went into Lincolnshire,
where he stole horses, which he brought into
Yorkshire, and either sold or exchanged them.

He often accompanied the neighbouring gentlemen on their parties of hunting and shooting ;
and one evening on a return from an expedition
of the latter kind, he wantonly shot a cock belonging to his landlord. On this, Mr. Hall, a
neighbour said You have done wrong in shooting
your landlord's cock ; to which Turpin replied,
that if he would stay till he reloaded his gun, he
would shoot him also.

Irritated by this insult, Mr. Hall informed the
landlord of what had passed ; and application being made to some magistrates, a warrant was
granted for the apprehension of the offender, who
being taken into custody, and carried before a
bench of justices, then assembled at the quarter-
sessions, at Beverley, they demanded security for
his good behaviour, which he being unable or unwilling to give, he was committed to Bridewell.

On enquiry, it appeared that he made frequent

journeys into Lincolnshire, and on his return always abounded in money. and was likewise in possession of several horses; so that it was conjectured that he was a horse-stealer and highwayman.

On this the magistrates went to him on the following day, and demanded who he was, where he had lived, and what was his employment? He replied in substance that about two years ago he had lived at Long Sutton, in Lincolnshire, and was by trade a butcher, but that having contracted several debts for sheep that proved rotten, he was obliged to abscond, and come to live in Yorkshire.

The magistrates not being satisfied with this tale, commissioned the clerk of the peace to write into Lincolnshire, to make the necessary inquiries respecting this supposed John Palmer. The letter was carried by a special messenger who brought an answer from a magistrate in the neighbourhood, importing that John Palmer was well known, though he had never carried on trade there: that he had been accused of sheep-stealing, for which he had been in custody, but had made his escape from the peace officers, and that there were several informations lodged against him for horse-stealing.

Hereupon the magistrates thought it prudent to remove him to York Castle, where he had not been more than a month. when two persons from Lincolnshire came and claimed a mare and foal, and likewise a horse, which he had stolen in that county.

After he had been about four months in prison,

he wrote the following letter to his brother in Essex :—

York, Feb. 6, 1739.

" Dear Brother,
    I am sorry to acquaint you that I am now under confinement in York Castle, for horse-stealing. If I could procure an evidence from London to give me a character, that would go a great way towards my being acquitted. I had not been long in this country before my being apprehended, so that it would pass off the readier. For Heaven's sake, dear brother, do not neglect me; you will know what I mean, when I say,
                    I am yours,
                        JOHN PALMER.

This letter being returned, unopened, to the Post office in Essex, because the brother would not pay the postage of it, was accidentally seen by Mr. Smith, a schoolmaster, who having taught Turpin to write, immediately knew his hand, on which he carried the letter to a magistrate, who broke it open ; by which it was discovered that the supposed John Palmer was the real Richard Turpin.

Hereupon the magistrates of Essex dispatched Mr. Smith to York, who immediately selected him from all the other prisoners in the castle. This Mr. Smith, and another gentleman, afterwards proved his identity on his trial.

On a rumour that the noted Turpin was a prisoner in York castle, persons flocked from all parts of the country to take a view of him, and debates ran very high whether he was the real person or not. Amongst others who visited him was a young fellow who pretended to know the famous Turpin, and having regarded him a considerable time with looks of great attention, he told the keeper he would bet him half a guinea that he was not Turpin, on which the prisoner, whispering to the keeper, said, Lay him the wager, I'll go you halves.

When this notorious malefactor was brought to trial, he was convicted on two indictments, and received sentence of death.

After conviction he wrote to his father, imploring him to intercede with a gentleman and lady of rank to make interest that his sentence might be remitted; and that he might be transported. The father did what was in his power; but the notoriety of his character was such, that no person would exert themselves in his favour.

This man lived in the most gay and thoughtless manner after conviction, regardless of all considerations of futurity, and affecting to make a jest of the dreadful fate that awaited him.

Not many days before his execution, he purchased a new fustian frock and a pair of pumps, in order to wear them at the time of his death: and, on the day before he hired five poor men, at ten shillings each, to follow the cart as mourners: and he gave hatbands and gloves to several other persons; he also left a ring, and some other articles to a married woman in Lincolnshire, with whom he had been acquainted.

On the morning of his death he was put into a

eart, and being followed by his mourners, as above-mentioned, he was drawn along to the place of execution, in his way he bowed to the spectators with an air of the most astonishing indifference and intrepidity.

When he came to the fatal tree, he ascended the ladder; when, his right leg trembling, he stamped it down with an air of unassumed courage, as if he was ashamed to be observed to discover any signs of fear. Having conversed with the executioner about half an hour, he threw himself off the ladder and expired in a few minutes.

The spectators of the execution seemed to be much affected at the fate of this man, who was distinguished by the comeliness of his appearance. The corpse was brought to the Blue Boar, in Castle gate, York, when it was interred in the church yard of St. George's parish, with an inscription on the coffin, with the initials of his name, and his age. The grave was remarkably deep, and the people who acted as mourners took such measures as they thought would secure the body; yet about three o'clock on the following morning, some people were observed in the church yard, who carried it off; and the populace having an intimation whither it was conveyed, found it in a garden belonging to one of the surgeons of the city.

Hereupon they took the body, laid it on a board, and having carried it through the streets, in a kind of triumphal manner, they then filled the coffin with unslacked lime, and buried it in the grave where it had been before deposited.

JOHN HAWKINS,

*Executed at Tyburn, on the 21st of May, 1772,
for Highway Robbery.*

JOHN HAWKINS was the son of a poor farmer at Staines, who not being able to afford to educate him properly, he went into the service of a gentleman which he soon quitted, and lived as a waiter at the Red Lion at Brentford; but leaving this place, he again engaged as a gentleman's servant. Having been at length in different families, he became butler to Sir Denis Drury, and was distinguished as a servant of very creditable appearance. His person was uncommonly graceful, and he was remarkably vain of it. He used to frequent gambling tables two or three nights in a week, a practice which led to that ruin which finally befel him. About this time, Sir Denis had been robbed of a considerable quantity of plate: and as Hawkin's mode of life was very expensive, it was suspected that he was the thief: for which reason he was discharged without the advantage of a good character. Being thus destitute of the means of subsistence, he had recourse to the highway, and his first expedition was to Hounslow Heath, where he took eleven pounds from the passengers in a coach: but such was his attachment to gaming, that he repaired directly to London, and lost it all. He continued to rob alone for some time, and then engaged with other highwaymen; but the same fate still attended him;

he lost by gaming what he obtained by so much
risk, and was frequently so reduced as to dine at
an eating house, and sneak off without paying his
reckoning.

Several of his old companions having met their
deserts at the gallows, he became acquainted with
one Wilson, a youth of good education, who had
been articled to a solicitor in chancery, but had
neglected his business through an attachment to
the gaming table.   These associates having committed several robberies in conjunction, were tried
for one of them, but acquitted for want of evidence.   After which Wilson went down to his
mother, who lived at Whitby, in Yorkshire, and
continued with her for about a year, and then
coming to London, lived with a gentleman of the
law: but having lost his money in gaming, renewed his acquaintance with Hawkins, who was
now concerned with a new gang of villains; one
of whom, however, being apprehended, impeached
the rest, which soon dispersed the gang, but not
till some of them had made their exit at Tyburn;
on which Hawkins was obliged to conceal himself
for a considerable time; but at length he ventured to rob a gentleman on Finchley Common, and
shot one of his servants too, who died on the
spot.   His next attack was on the Earl of Bur-
lington and Lord Bruce, in Richmond Lane, from
whom he took about twenty pounds, two gold
watches, and a sapphire ring.   For this ring, a
reward of one hundred pounds was offered to Jonathan Wild; but Hawkins sailed to Holland
with it, and there sold it for forty pounds.

On his return to England he joined his compa-

nions, of whom Wilson was one, and robbed Sir
David Dalrymple of about three pounds, a snuff-
box, and a pocket-book, for which last Sir David
offered sixty pounds reward to Wild; but Hawkins's gang having no connection with that villain,
who did not even know their persons, they sent
the book by a porter to Sir David, without expense. They next stopped Mr. Hyde of Hackney,
in his coach, and robbed him of ten pounds and
his watch, but missed three hundreds pounds,
which the gentleman had in his possession. After
this they stopped the Earl of Westmoreland's
coach in Lincoln's Inn Fields, and robbed him of
a sum of money, though there were three footmen behind the carriage. The footmen called the
watch, but the robbers firing a pistol over their
heads, the guardians of the night decamped.

Hawkins had now resolved to carry the booty
obtained in several late robberies to Holland;
but Jonathan Wild having heard of the connection, caused some of the gang to be apprehended;
on which the rest went into the country to hide
themselves. On this occasion Hawkins and Wilson went to Oxford, and paying a visit to the
Bodleian library, the former wantonly defaced
some pictures in the gallery; and one hundred
pounds reward was offered to discover the offender: when a poor tailor having been taken up on
suspicion, narrowly escaped being whipped, merely
because he was of whiggish principles.

Hawkins and his friends returned to London,
the latter coming of age at that time, succeeded
to a little estate his father had left him, which he
sold for three hundred and fifty pounds, a small

part of which he lent to his companions, to buy horses, and soon dissipated the rest at the gaming table.

The associates now stopped two gentlemen in a chariot on the Hampstead Road who both fired at once, by which three slugs were lodged in Hawkin's shoulder, and the highwaymen got to London with some difficulty. On Hawkins' recovery, they attempted to stop a gentleman's coach in Hyde Park; but the coachman driving hastily, Wilson fired, and wounding himself in the hand, found it difficult to scale the Park wall, to effect his escape. This circumstance occasioned some serious thoughts in his mind, in consequence of which he set out for his mother's house in Yorkshire, where he was kindly received, and determined never to return to his former practices.

While he was engaged in his mother's business, and planning schemes for domestic happiness, he was sent for to a public house, where he found his old acquaintance, Hawkins, in company with one George Simpson, another associate, who was a native of Putney, in Surry. His father was a wine merchant, but being reduced in circumstances removed to Lincolnshire. Young Simpson kept a public house at Lincoln, and acted as sheriff's officer, but quitting the country, he came to London, and was butler to Lord Castlemain; after which he lived in several other creditable places, till he became acquainted with Hawkins. Wilson was shocked at seeing them, and asked what could induce them to take such a journey. Hereupon Hawkins swore violently, said Wilson was impeached, would be taken into custody in a few days. This induced him to go to London with them ; but on his arrival, he found that the story of the impeachment was false.

When in London, they formed connections with other thieves, and committed several robberies, for which some of the gang were executed. They frequented a public house, at London Wall, the master of which kept a livery-stable, so that they rode out at all hours, and robbed the stages, as they were coming into the town. They took not only money, but portmanteaus, &c., and divided the booty with Carter, the master of the livery-stable. Thus they continued their depredations on the public, till one of their associates, named Child, was executed at Aylesbury, and hung in chains, for robbing the mail. This incensed them to such a degree, that they determined to avenge the insult by committing a similar crime. Having mentioned their design in the presence of Carter, the stable keeper, he advised them to stop the mail from Harwich ; but this they declined, because the changing of the wind must render the time of its arrival uncertain. At length it was determined to rob the Bristol mail, and they set out on an expedition for that purpose. It appeared on the trial, that the boy who carried the mail was overtaken at Slough, by a countryman, who carried him to Langley-Broom, when a person rode up to him, and turned back again.

When passing through Colnbrook, they saw the same man again, with two others, who followed them at a small distance, and then pulling their wigs over their foreheads, and holding handkerchiefs in their mouths, came up with them and commanded the post-boy and the countryman to come down a lane, where they ordered them to quit their horses, and then Hawkins, and Simpson, and Wilson, tied them back to back, and fastened them to a tree in a wet ditch, so that they were obliged to stand in the water. This being done, they took such papers as they liked out of the Bath and Bristol bags, and hid the rest in a hedge.

They now crossed the Thames, and riding a little way into Surry, put up their horses at an inn in Bermondsey street. It was now about six o'clock in the morning. when they parted, and went different ways to a public house, in the Minories, where they proposed to divide their ill gotten treasure. The landlord being well acquainted with their persons, and knowing the profession of his guests, shewed them into a private room, and supplied them with pen and ink. Having equally divided the bank notes, they threw the letters into the fire, and then went to their lodgings, in Green Arbour Court, in the Old Bailey.

A few days after this, information was given at the Post-Office, that suspicious people frequented the house of Carter, the stable keeper, at London-Wall; accordingly some persons were sent thither to make the necessary discoveries. Wilson happening to be there at the time, suspected their business, on which he abruptly retired, slipped through some bye alleys, and got into the Moorgate coffee house, which he had occasionally used for nearly two years before, on account of its being frequented by reputable company, and therefore less liable to be searched for suspicious people. He had not been long in the house before a quaker mentioned the search that was making in the neighbourhood, for the men who had robbed the mail. This shocked him so, that he instantly paid his reckoning, and going out at the back door, went to Bedlam, where the melancholy sight of the objects arround him, induced him to draw a comparison between their situation and his own ; and he concluded that he was far more unhappy through the weight of his guilt, than those poor wretches whom it had pleased God to deprive of their intellects.

Having reflected that it would not be safe for him to stay long in London, he resolved to go to Newcastle by sea, and he was confirmed in this resolution, upon being told by a person who wished his safety, that he and his companions were the parties suspected of having robbed the mail. This friend likewise advised him to go to the Post Office, surrender, and turn evidence ; hinting, that if he did not, it was probable Simpson would ; as he had asked some questions which seemed to intimate such a design. Wilson neglected this advice, but held his resolution of going to Newcastle, and with that intention he quitted Bedlam ; but by Moorgate coffee house he met the men he had seen at Carter's. They turned and followed him ; yet, unperceived by them, he entered the coffee house, while they went under the arch of the gate, and if he had returned by the door he had entered, he would have again escaped them ; but going out of the fore door of the house, they

took him into custody, and conducted him to the
post office.   On his first examination he refused
to make any confession ; and on the following day
he seemed equally determined to conceal the
truth, till two circumstances induced him to re-
veal it.   In the first place, the postmaster general
promised that he should be admitted an evidence
if he would discover his accomplices ; and one of
the clerks calling him aside, shewed him a letter
without any name to it, of which the following is
a copy :

    Sir,
I am one of those persons who robbed the
mails, which I am sorry for ; and to make amends
I will secure my two companions as soon as may
be.   He whose handwriting this shall appear to
be. will, I hope, be entitled to the reward and his
pardon.

As Wilson knew this letter to be of Simpson's
handwriting, he thought himself justified in making a full discovery, which he accordingly did, in
consequence of which his associates were apprehended at their lodgings in the Old Bailey two
days afterwards.   At first they made an appearance of resistance, and threatened to shoot the
peace officers; but the latter seeing they were
provided with arms, the offenders yielded, and
they were committed to Newgate.
On the trial, Hawkins endeavoured to prove that
he was in London at the time that the mail was
robbed ; and one Fuller, of Bedfordbury, swore

that he lodged at his house on that night. To ascertain this, Fuller produced a receipt for thirty shillings, which he said Hawkins then paid him for horse-hire. The judge desiring to look at that receipt, observed, that the body of it was written with an ink of a different colour from that of the name at the bottom ; on which he ordered the note to be handed to the jury; and remarked that Fuller's testimony deserved no kind of credit. After examining some other witnesses, the judge then proceeded to sum up the evidence, in which he was interrupted by the following singular occurrence, as stated by the short hand writer :

My ink, as it happened, was very bad, being thick at bottom, and thin and waterish at top; so that according as I dipped my pen, the writing appeared very pale or pretty black. Now, just as the court was remarking on the difference of the ink in Fuller's receipt, a gentleman who stood by me, perceiving something of the same kind in my writing, desired to look upon my notes for a minute. As I was not aware of any ill consequence, I let him take the book out of my hand ; when presently shewing it to his friend, See here, (said he,) what difference there is in the colour of the same ink ! His friend took it, and shewed it to another. Uneasy at this I spoke to them to return me my book. They begged my pardon, and said I should have it in a minute, but this answer was no sooner given. than a curiosity suddenly entered one of the jurymen, who sat just by, and he too begged a sight of the book; which, notwithstanding

my importunity, was immediately handed to him.
He viewed it, and gave it to the next, and so it
passed from one to the other, till the judge perceiving them very busy, called to them—Gentlemen, what are you doing?   What book is that?
They told him it was the writer's book, and they
were observing how the same ink appeared pale
in one place and black in another.   You ought
not, gentlemen, says he, to take notice of any
thing, but what is produced in evidence.   And
then turning to me, demanded what I meant by
shewing that to the jury.   I answered, that I
could not fix upon the persons, for the gentlemen
near me were all strangers to me, and I was far
from imagining I should have any such occasion
for taking particular notice of them.—His lordship then re-assumed the charge to the Jury,
which, being ended, they withdrew to consider
of their verdict.

After staying out about an hour, the jury returned into court without agreeing on a verdict,
saying they could not be convinced that Fuller's
receipt was not genuine, merely on account of the
different colours of the ink.   Hereupon the court
intimated how many witnesses had sworn that
Hawkins was absent from London: to contradict
all of whom there was only the evidence of Fuller,
which was at least rendered doubtful by the ink
appearing of two colours ; and it was submitted
whether Fuller's testimony ought to be held of
equal validity with that of the opposing parties.
Hereupon the jury went out of the court, and, on
their return, gave a verdict of Guilty against both

the prisoners.   At the place of execution Hawkins addressed the surrounding multitude, acknowledging his sins, professing to die in charity with all mankind, and begging the prayers of those who were witnesses of his melancholy departure. He died with great difficulty ; but Simpson was out of his pain almost without a struggle.

THE END.

INDEX.